Taming

RAPTOR

ROYAL BASTARDS MC

EST 2019

KRISTINE ALLEN

I'm Adrien Krow, but they call me Raptor.

Ten years ago, Sage was too damn young for my darkness, so I put up a wall. It worked—until the day it didn't. Being with her wasn't supposed to rock my world, but it sure as hell did.

The last thing I planned to do was move back to Texas and the secrets I left behind.

But all debts must be paid, and I owed a big one.

Now I'm the President of the Dallas, Texas chapter, and I'm haunted by the woman I left behind. I tell myself I'm better off alone, and I'm almost convinced. But then she shows up on the back of my brother's goddamn bike with trouble nipping at her heels.

If that isn't enough to piss me off, her trouble catches up, leaving both her and my chapter in the sights of a contract killer. I'm not taking either situation lying down. I'm stealing her from my brother, and I'm eliminating the threat against us.

Because Sage and the Dallas chapter are mine—and no one touches what's mine.

Royal Bastards MC Facebook Group
www.facebook.com/groups/royalbastardsmc

Website
www.royalbastardsmc.com

ROYAL BASTARDS CODE

PROTECT: The club and your brothers come before anything else and must be protected at all costs. CLUB is FAMILY.

RESPECT: Earn it & Give it. Respect club law. Respect the patch. Respect your brothers. Disrespect a member and there will be hell to pay.

HONOR: Being patched in is an honor, not a right. Your colors are sacred, not to be left alone, and NEVER let them touch the ground.

OL' LADIES: Never disrespect a member's or brother's ol' lady. PERIOD.

CHURCH is MANDATORY.

LOYALTY: Takes precedence over all, including well-being.

HONESTY: Never LIE, CHEAT, or STEAL from another member or the club.

TERRITORY: You are to respect your brothers' property and follow their Chapter's club rules.

TRUST: Years to earn it… seconds to lose it.

NEVER RIDE OFF: Brothers do not abandon their family.

To Christie—this one's for you. Not only for coming up with Cookie's real name for me, but for being an awesome reader and someone I like to consider my friend!

!!IMPORTANT—PLEASE READ!!
Attention Readers:

Consider this your "T" Warning! This story might be darker than you're used to from me. Yes, Raptor is a lot kinkier than I realized, but not in a bad way, so there's that, but there's more. I've touched on some emotional issues in the past that may have been uncomfortable for some and painful for others. If you know Cookie from my past RBMC books, you have to know she has a story. What you might not have figured out is that it's a pretty fucked-up one. In her story there may be some extremely sensitive situations and memories that could be the big "T" for some. It happens during the second part of chapter seventeen, if you need to skip it—and I will understand—but she wants her story told. Please know and understand that **you were warned**. A lot of it is implied, but if you know—you know.

If you choose to read the book in its entirety, I thank you from the bottom of my heart. Also know that this **is** a romance, and it will have an HEA. MUAH!

Taming

RAPTOR

ROYAL BASTARDS MC

PROLOGUE

I held my young son close to my chest. No, I never planned on being a dad two times over by the time I was twenty-one, but there I was. Scared shitless and preparing to leave for my first deployment.

"You don't need to do this," Falina spat with fire in her gaze.

"Yes, I do. Jesus, Falina, I signed a contract. My brothers are deploying, and I need to be there for them." As if he sensed my irritation, Samuel fussed and wiggled.

"Bullshit. Your family could get you out of it, if you would just ask, Adrien," she shot back with a scowl as she rested a hand on her very pregnant stomach.

Falina was my high-school sweetheart, and we had impulsively gotten married once we graduated, the week after she turned eighteen. When she got pregnant shortly after, I did what a lot of kids do when they're desperate—I joined the Army. In my mind, it made sense. I would have a guaranteed paycheck, benefits, a roof over our heads, and I would be making my own way in the world.

I never expected to feel the pride I would experience as a soldier.

My family didn't understand my need to be independent. My dad had been pissed because he would've helped us, but there were always conditions. I had no desire to become a surgeon and live off of the Krow name. Maybe it would've been easier, but it didn't feel right. That was likely because I was more like my grandfather. He had been born into money, but instead of living an indulgent lifestyle, he invested his money and tripled its worth. Like him, I wanted make a name for myself from my own accomplishments.

"I'm not doing that. I'm a man of my word, and I took an oath when I joined."

Falina plucked our now fussing son from my arms with a snort. He reached for me as he cried, "Daddy!"

"Fat lot of good it will do you if you're dead," she snapped.

"Don't," I pleaded as I cupped her cheek with my hand. She refused to look at me and jerked away from my touch. Samuel cried because at two, he had no idea what was going on.

Sighing in frustration, I dropped my head to kiss her, but at the last second, she turned away. My lips landed on her temple. Things had been strained since I joined the Army. She didn't understand my need to be independent any more than my parents did. She hated leaving her family, she hated post housing, she hated me being in the field, and she hated the fact that there was a war going on and I was soon to be a part of it.

Sometimes I was pretty sure she hated me.

"Just go," she said with her jaw ticking angrily.

My grandfather died of a heart attack when I was in AIT and my father told me the only way I'd inherit anything was if I came home for good. He was furious when I told him I didn't give a shit about the money. Falina didn't like my decision either. In her opinion, it was my rightful place, and I was being stubborn. I disagreed. My cousins could have it all.

Hurt etched on my face, I released her to pick up my heavy duffel. "I'll call when I can, and I'll email you and write."

"Boy, that will be a big help when I'm trying to deal with a toddler and a newborn on my own. I can't believe you expect me to stay here by myself, taking care of your children, while you go off to play G.I. Joe." She sneered and rolled her eyes.

"Last I checked, they are *our* children. Whether we were here or home, you would still be their mother and would need to take care of them—unless you want to go to work." It was an argument we'd had a million times.

"But if we were at home, I'd at least have help, Adrien!"

"This is our home, but if you want, I can arrange for you to go back to your family during my deployment. I told you that already." She went home all the time anyway. Not that we could afford it, but her parents paid for her to travel.

"And will you be getting out after you get back?"

"Uh, no. Like I said, I have a contract." I was fast losing my patience.

"Well, don't expect me to be here when you get back, then."

A horn honked out front.

"It's okay. I'll have leave after I get home. I can fly back to Texas, pick you, Samuel, and the baby up, and then we can drive back. We'll figure everything out. Now, I have to get going—that's my ride." Specialist Murphy was a friend of mine from basic training. He ended up stationed at Fort Lewis with me but in a different brigade. Murphy offered to pick me, Gibson, and MacKenzie up and take us to the company so Falina wouldn't have to take Samuel out in the rain.

Except MacKenzie had declined. He was from over in Seattle, so his parents were here to see him off. It would only be Gibson

3

and me hitching a ride. It did hurt a little that my parents didn't fly in to see me off, but I wasn't surprised.

I kissed my son on his head, and with one last regretful glance at Falina, I left.

On that deployment, I met Venom—Decker Pruitt. Though he was barely four years older than me, he was a sergeant, and it was his third rotation. We bonded when we found out I was from Texas, and he was stationed there. The first mortar attack terrified me when it hit during my time off. I was coming out of the MWR—Morale, Welfare and Recreation—tent as all hell broke loose. He went running past me, shouting out instructions that I scrambled to obey. When I started to freak out, he turned back and gripped my head in his hands.

"Calm the fuck down," he ordered in his no nonsense way. Amazingly, I did—it was weird.

That was the first time I wondered if there was something different about him. I carried my own secret that I was forbidden to reveal, so I didn't ask the questions that floated around in my head.

Toward the end of our rotation, I was assigned to a supply convoy. On our way back to the FOB—Forward Operating Base—something seemed off. Cautiously, I sent my inner hawk free and used my remote sight to check things out. About two clicks out from our location was a group of insurgents preparing for an ambush. Heart hammering, I tried to tell my TC, the truck commander, that I thought something was wrong. The problem was, I couldn't tell him exactly what I saw or how I knew. Which was why he blew me off and didn't send it up the chain.

The small-arms ambush resulted in me getting shot in the

arm, shattering my humerus. Venom, or Sergeant Pruitt as he was to me then, was the first one to visit me in the infirmary. I'd been lucky it was relatively minor, but it also meant that I was being sent home. In my impulsive decision to join the military, I never once considered how I'd handle an injury.

It could bring up questions I couldn't answer without creating a shitstorm of epic proportions. Though I hated to do it, I would need to contact my father ASAP.

"I need to ask you something," Decker quietly murmured as he glanced around, eyes darting nervously. Satisfied that the soldiers in the beds surrounding mine were either sedated or occupied, he returned his attention to me.

"Um, okay?"

"When I first stopped by, you were pretty sedated."

"I still am," I joked as I lifted my good arm that held the IV tubing connected to it.

His sober stare sent a chill skating up my arms and down my spine.

"You were babbling shit about seeing the ambush coming but no one would listen."

"Like you said, I was high as fuck on pain meds." I tried to play it off because I was afraid of what I might've said.

"Yeah, you were. And if I hadn't seen your eyes, I might've left it at that."

"M-my eyes?" My heart rate spiked, and the alarm went off on the portable monitor I was hooked up to. Fear of what I might've inadvertently revealed had me in near panic.

That was when he firmly gripped my good hand. His eyes seemed to ripple, and the color shifted. I froze and my heart lurched. Except as quickly as my anxiety had exploded, it fizzled out, leaving a peaceful calm in its wake.

"You feel that?" He nodded at our hands.

"You holding my hand?" My voice seemed foreign to my own ears.

The answer to his question seemed to flit around in the deep recesses of my mind. Almost within reach but never close enough to grasp.

"The change in your mood," he clarified. His eyes kept changing colors—like a kaleidoscope.

"What did you do?"

"Nothing that will hurt you. But let's say I think we have something in common."

"You're an empath," I deduced when I finally recognized the calming effect he'd had on me.

"And you have remote sight?" he asked, answering my observation with a question.

For a moment, I simply blinked at him. In those silent moments, a bond was formed that neither of us had expected. For some strange reason, I trusted him—but not with everything.

I gave him a single nod that eased the stern look from his face.

"We'll keep in touch, Krow," he promised with an easy grin. "Leave it to you to land a million-dollar wound during your first trip to Afghanistan."

"What-the-fuck-ever," I grumbled. I had mixed feelings about being sent home. My excitement to see my wife and kids warred with my loyalty to my battle buddies. Though we only had a few months left, I hated that I was leaving them behind.

He sobered. "Trust me when I tell you that you should be thankful. You could be going home in a body bag."

Too many of our friends had already taken their final trip home in those, and the thought put things into perspective for me. "You're right."

"I'm always right," he teased, lightening the mood again. "Enjoy your kids. Kiss that new baby boy for me."

"I sure will." My youngest son had been born while I was gone. I hated that I missed his birth and so many of his and Samuel's firsts.

We had parted ways, and I was Evac'ed, first to Landstuhl for the initial surgery, then back to the states. Though I shouldn't have been, I was shocked when my father walked into my room at Walter Reed Army Medical Center after I woke up from the second surgery. The nurse was documenting on the computer when he introduced himself as my surgeon.

The moment she left, he closed the door and rounded on me.

"Do you know how lucky you were that I was able to get into that OR with your cousins? I called in a shitload of favors to get proper credentials to access a government system." My father's harsh whisper hit me with guilt so heavy, it was suffocating me. I'd jeopardized my entire family, and I damn well knew it.

There was a reason the majority of the people in my family became general practitioners and surgeons. Others became OR techs, nurses, or whatever were the needs of the kettle—our clan. It protected our secrets.

"I'm sorry, Dad." And I was—debilitatingly so.

"You need to come home—it's time," he insisted as he jerked the fake hospital badge from his scrubs.

"Dad," I started.

"No. Adrien, it's past time. Your family is there." My father was pacing in agitation.

"I'm a grown-ass man. You can't dictate what I can and can't do," I snapped.

"Well, the fact that your cousins and I had to do a mock surgery in a goddamn military hospital to protect our secrets says otherwise. This was a stupid move on your part." He stopped to stare out the window as he ran a hand through his graying hair.

"I needed to do this. For me. For my sons. You knew I never wanted to be a surgeon."

He spun to face me. Anger and resignation warred in his golden eyes, darkening them to near obsidian. "You didn't have to be a surgeon! You could've been any number of things that benefit our community. You could've led the watch."

"What if I didn't want that? Initially, I signed on the dotted line to provide for my wife and pending child—without relying on my family's money. It was about being a man and standing on my own two feet. Then I realized I wanted to make a difference to the country—to the world."

"Adrien." He sighed. "You're only one man."

"But it has to start somewhere, right? If no one stands up for those that live in tyranny and are held under the thumb of a dictatorship, then how can we ever think anything will change? If we all expect 'someone else' to step up to protect our country, but no one does, what's to stop that evil from bleeding over and happening here? Then where will our people be?"

"I understand that, but you are my only son." The crack in his voice hurt, and I had to glance away. The loss of my brother would forever be etched into my soul. I'd looked up to him. He was the one set to follow in our father's footsteps. It was never supposed to be me.

"If I promise you that I won't let anyone find out our secret, would you let me live my life?"

His eyes were hard, and a muscle jumped in his jaw when his gaze clashed with mine. Finally, he gave a curt nod and walked to the door. With his skilled fingers curled around the handle, he paused and looked over his shoulder. "I don't think I can survive if you die, Adrien."

"I won't."

It was a promise we both knew I couldn't guarantee, but I

8

would do everything in my power to stay safe. Once my time in the Army was done, I'd make everyone happy and move home with my family.

After I was discharged from Walter Reed, they flew me back to Ft. Lewis. Falina and the boys were in Texas with her family, so I planned to use some of my leave to drive down there with my truck and pick them up. That way they didn't need to travel back to Washington alone.

Except when I walked through my front door, my footsteps echoed in the empty house. Disbelief made me check the house room by room. The only thing left behind were my clothes in the closet—and me. Everything I had in the dresser was tossed into a single square box sitting in the middle of the bedroom floor.

With a scowl, I pulled out my phone and called Falina. My blood was boiling.

"I'm sorry, but the number you have called has been disconnected or is no longer in service."

"What the fuck?" I had talked to her as I was being discharged from Walter Reed and again before I got on the plane that would bring me back to Fort Lewis. Though she had seemed distant, I suspected nothing. Now her phone was disconnected?

Though I was stunned, the greatest shock of all was what I found when I got to Texas.

PART I

ONE

Raptor

"THE LITTLE THINGS GIVE YOU AWAY"—LINKIN PARK

Five years later....

Beer rained down over my head and onto my cut amidst whooping shouts and cheers. Every patched member hugged me and welcomed me to the club.

"Congrats, bro. I knew you could do it. You're going to be one helluva brother and member of the club," Venom said to me with a huge grin. It was because of him that I was being patched in today.

We'd kept in touch after that first deployment and our friendship grew. When he PCS'd from Fort Hood to Fort Riley, I kept hoping to get stationed with him. I'd been over the moon when my Branch Manager told me I was heading to Kansas— especially since I hated Washington with a passion by then. Decker and I deployed together two more times after that.

We'd been best friends ever since. After he'd gotten out of the Army, he had returned to his home of record—Iowa. Once my contract was up, I went to visit, and he asked what I thought about moving to Iowa. The rest was history.

After a year of busting my ass and the chapter busting my balls, it was finally my patch party.

"Thanks. That means a lot." Prospecting for the Royal Bastards hadn't been a walk in the park, but I'd been determined to get patched. If there was one thing I learned, it was that *this* was family. Every single one of them had my back, which was more than I could say about my blood family.

My family and Falina's betrayal still sat bitter in my throat. I closed the door on that part of my life and was doing my best to leave it all behind.

The light scent of some fruity flowery shit wrapped around me, teasing at my nose. I glanced around, looking for the source. A leggy bombshell with white-blonde hair and tits to die for was laughing at something Nico said. He was the young kid we had saved that night in the alley after I thought he was fucking with the bikes. My heart seemed to drop into slow motion before it shot forward at light speed when she appeared to sense my stare. Those brilliant blue eyes locked with mine, and she boldly scanned me from head to toe.

Nico realized she wasn't paying attention to him and scanned the area. A mixture of frustration and relief swept over his features. I wondered what was up with that, but I didn't really care. I only had eyes for her. I raised my beer to her with a cocked brow.

Her heated gaze raked over me, and a sultry smile lifted one corner of her mouth. She bit her lower lip, and I had an instant boner.

"Dude, she's practically jailbait." Venom nudged me, pulling me out of the trance she had me in.

"Huh?"

He chuckled. "She showed up with Blade and told Hawk she was nineteen, but I'm pretty sure I heard him say he found out she's only seventeen. Since you looked like you were going to eat her alive, I figured I better give you a heads-up. Besides, I think your tongue was dragging the ground."

"What-the-fuck-ever," I grumbled. Except he wasn't wrong. It had taken all of three seconds for me to have visions of her tied spread-eagle on my bed with my face between her legs. And that was the mildest of my thoughts. "She's with Blade?"

Blade and I prospected together. Though he was quite a bit younger than me, we'd become pretty good friends.

"You do what you want, but I'm just saying, she's under eighteen, and I think you'd break her."

I snorted. But that reality check had my visions crashing and burning. Even if she'd been eighteen, I don't think she had the experience and maturity to handle my preferences. After Falina's bullshit, I was a fucking mess. Going through her betrayal was brutal—it changed me. I didn't trust women much, and I always had to be in control—because then they couldn't fuck with my emotions or fuck me over.

Later, I went around the building to take a piss. I'd just tucked my dick back into my pants when I sensed eyes on me. I whipped around to see the blonde leaning a shoulder against the exterior of the clubhouse with a smirk.

"Nice package you've got there," she practically purred as her gaze dropped to my crotch and my rapidly growing erection.

"What are you doing?" I asked her as I crossed my arms over my chest and looked down my nose at her. Fuck, she had banging curves, but no way was I giving her any indication of how much she affected me. At least not any more than my dick already was.

She pushed off the building and moved closer to me with seductive grace—a characteristic a girl her age shouldn't have. I held my ground refusing to allow the little minx to intimidate me, despite wanting to slam her against the wall and drive my cock into her. When she was a foot away, she reached up and trailed a rounded fingertip over the ink on my forearm.

I glared at her, and a rumble started in my chest. Dark lashes lifted as she tilted her chin and coyly looked up at me.

Despite the fact that she looked older than her age, I had to remind myself she was still a kid. At twenty-five, I didn't need high school bullshit drama, and I sure as hell didn't need to be locked up for fucking with a minor. That would not only get my ass in trouble with the law, it could also get me center-punched or worse. The chapter was strict when it came to messing with underage girls.

"Look—" I paused, not knowing her name, and gave her a meaningful brow lift.

"Cookie," she supplied, and I snorted.

"Right. Cookie." I rolled my eyes and shook my head. "You're a pretty girl, but you're not even eighteen."

"I'm nineteen," she argued, but I gave her a knowing stare. She huffed and couldn't maintain eye contact.

"You're a kid," I continued, but she interrupted.

"I haven't been a *kid* for a long fucking time," she snapped with a sneer. Her eyes were so blue, I was practically drowning in their depths, but I had to pull myself out of the lust-induced haze she created in me. Repeatedly, I reminded myself she was seventeen, and I shouldn't be having these types of thoughts about her—no matter how those tits of hers demanded to fill my hands.

I bit back a groan when she raked her nails over my denim-clad dick. Before I realized what I was doing, my hand shot out, and her pale strands were wrapped around my fist. A little gasp escaped those full lips. I used my other hand to grip her throat, using my thumb and forefinger to tilt her head to where I needed it. My lips crashed to hers, and I did something I knew I'd regret.

I tasted her.

Devoured her.

Finally, sanity prevailed as my conscience screamed at me to stop. With a regretful groan, I ripped my mouth away. Her chest rapidly rose and fell as her dazed and heavy-lidded gaze remained locked on mine.

Disgusted at my lack of control, I released her like she was on fire. Then to cover my slip, I snarled, "Go back to your boy, Nico."

Then I stormed away from the temptress in the shadows.

Though an irrational flare of anger burned through me at the thought of the pretty little thing fucking Nico, I knew I had to mark her as off-limits.

Because Venom was right—I'd break her in two.

But that didn't stop me from fantasizing about her more than was healthy.

TWO

Raptor

"ENOUGH"—ASHES TO NEW

Ten years later....

The sky opened up right as I parked in front of the clubhouse. I ran inside but still got drenched. Once inside, I shook some of the rain from my hair. Then I ran a hand through it, trying to fluff it dry.

It was perfectly sunny earlier today, except it sure as hell wasn't now. Welcome to Iowa weather. Then again, it was early fall, which was unpredictable. The nights were already getting cool.

"You cut your hair again?" Venom asked me with a look that told me he thought I was nuts.

I shrugged and joined them by the pool table. "Sort of."

"He's going through a midlife crisis," teased Ghost as he lined up and took his shot. The balls clicked and he sunk two stripes.

"Fuck you," I muttered. Venom snickered and went to the bar.

"I think he looks sexy as fuck," Voodoo teased with a smirk and a wink before he made stupid kissy lips at me.

As I rolled my eyes, I flipped him off. Then the hairs on my arms stood up, and a thrill skated down my spine, straight to my dick.

"If you asked me, he absolutely looks sexy as fuck," Cookie crooned as she trailed a fingernail down my arm. It didn't matter how far away from me she was at any given time, I sensed her. This time, I prayed she would keep walking, but of course she had to fuck with me. I think she took perverse pleasure in pushing my buttons.

"Don't," I practically growled.

Her eyes narrowed and her jaw ticked. Then she gave me the same sultry smile she'd given me ten years ago—and damn near every day since. Then she flipped that goddamn platinum blonde hair over her shoulder before she stepped into my personal space. She wet her lower lip and pulled it between her teeth.

Every move she made sent my restraint into a tailspin. I gave no outward sign that she was getting to me.

Voodoo and Ghost wandered over to the bar to get a beer, leaving me and Cookie alone by the pool table. They were used to Cookie's games with me and ignored us.

I suddenly had vivid visions of tossing her up onto the green felt, spreading her legs, and burying my face between her long, lean legs.

"Why won't you fuck me, Raptor?" she whispered in my ear as she cupped my rock-hard cock over my jeans and squeezed. "Is it because I'm a *whore?*"

She said the last with a snide tone and rage erupted in my

chest. And with that, my unaffected facade cracked. I grasped her silky locks in an unrelenting grip and pulled her head back until her neck arched and her eyelids lowered slightly as she stared at me. Those parted ruby-red lips taunted me.

"Never call yourself that," I ground out. My jaw clenched angrily, and I couldn't breathe fast enough to get the necessary oxygen to my lungs.

"Then tell me why," she demanded in a choked voice.

Bringing my mouth to her ear, I said in a quiet but deadly tone, "Because I don't. Fucking. Share."

"So it *is* because I've fucked your brothers, then," she taunted. The sultry scent of her perfume drifted up and left me damn near light-headed.

A humorless laugh left my lips. "No. It's because you couldn't handle me. And if I was to put my cock in your pretty little cunt, it would be the only one that you'd be fucking."

"You think you can satisfy me?" she asked, boldly pushing me and not even flinching when I wrapped her hair tighter around my fist.

"I know I can."

"Prove it," she taunted on a breathy whisper.

With that softly worded dare, the self-control I'd exercised for years crumbled, and the wall I'd erected shattered. I bit down on the exposed slope of her shoulder and reveled in the sexy little whimper she made. My brothers were likely watching, but I didn't give two shits that they were witnessing my downfall.

It seemed like I'd stayed away from her for-fucking-ever. It didn't matter that all she had to do was breeze by me, and I had an instant hard-on, I remained strong. I always held myself back—until today. And I hadn't been lying to her—I didn't share. Did I hate seeing her go off with one or more of my brothers each night, knowing they were going to fuck her? You're goddamn right I did, but I kept my mouth shut. Truthfully, I did it out of self-preservation. Something about her scared the shit out of me.

It wasn't only the eight-year age difference, because now that didn't really matter. Ten years ago, when she was barely seventeen and I was twenty-five, I was ashamed of the things I wanted to do to her. I'd been fresh out of the Army, newly patched, and jaded as a motherfucker. I'd forced myself to stay away and marked her off-limits for her own good. Now that I knew I was lying to myself—it was for my own good.

Cookie was no whore. I hated society's need to label shit like that. It pissed me off that a man could fuck anything with a pulse, and no one cared, but let a woman do the same and they wanted to label her a slut, easy, a whore, a tramp—it was all bullshit. There was nothing wrong with a woman who liked sex. So, as far as I was concerned, she was free to ride anyone's cock she wanted to, but I didn't have to like it.

Except that was going to stop tonight.

Because I was finally going to give in to my baser urges and fuck the living hell out of her.

She relaxed, and her head fell back, giving me better access. I took immediate advantage. Using my teeth, I moved up the graceful column of her neck.

Then I lifted my head and stared her in the eye. My heart raced a hundred miles a minute, and my lungs could barely keep up. It took a couple of deep breaths to get that shit under control.

"If we do this, I have stipulations." I had to make sure she understood and agreed to what I needed.

"Of course, you do."

"If I do anything you don't like, I need to know," I quietly explained, ignoring her smart-ass comment.

"You mean, like a safeword?"

"Exactly like that," I clarified. The instant peaking of her

21

nipples through the sexy shirt she was wearing didn't escape my notice.

"Giraffe. Anything else?"

"You fuck me when I want, where I want, and how I want. If you agree to that, I promise you that you will never be left unsatisfied."

"I'll reserve my answer until after you show me what you've got," she loftily shot back. Her blue eyes flashed. "Words are cheap, Raptor."

"I never make a promise I can't keep."

Without another word, I grabbed her hand and practically dragged her behind me to my room I used when I stayed at the clubhouse. I ignored the gaping mouths and bugged eyes of my brothers as we passed them.

I paused long enough to throw the door open and then kick it shut behind us.

"You like to play with fire," I growled. I grabbed her by the throat and pulled her body flush with my painfully hard cock and spoke against her lush lips. "The problem with playing with fire, is you eventually get burned."

"Then torch me," the little vixen dared me.

With no care for how her clothes were supposed to come off, I shoved the off-the shoulder shirt down to her waist, trapping her arms in it. The strapless bra went to the floor with a practiced flick of my fingers.

"Jesus fucking Christ," I groaned as I cupped one of her firm, pert tits. It wasn't like I hadn't ever seen them, but this was different. Before she took over the hiring and firing of the dancers at Royal Heaven, she danced full-time. Now she only filled in when we were short-staffed or had a call-in, but I'd watched her lithe body undulate and work the pole enough times to know every inch of her body was that of a goddess.

When I fell to my knees to suck her rose-pink nipple into my mouth, I clutched her shirt in the back to keep her arms immobile. The thought of her at my mercy damn near had me blowing my load in my jeans—something I hadn't done since I was a teenager.

She tasted like salt and sunshine from being outside enjoying the beautiful day before the rain hit.

With little mewling, needy sounds, she tried to get her arms free. I released her tit from my mouth and looked up at her. "No."

One word and she knew exactly what I was saying, because she immediately stilled. Those bright blue eyes stared at me with lust burning in their depths. Now that she knew to stay still, I released my grip on the back of her shirt. Maintaining eye contact, I returned to my worship of her breasts. I cupped one, and while I pinched the puckered tip, I carefully bit the other.

Her gasp and the ragged breaths she took along with the way she tried to push them closer told me she liked it. Releasing her nipple from my teeth, I circled it with my tongue before I gently suckled it. Once I'd given them both equal attention, I moved on.

She was a work of art—something precious to be appreciated and savored. I used my hands and mouth to work my way down her soft, tanned torso. When I reached the button of her tiny denim shorts, I held her firm ass in my hands and used my teeth to unfasten them. Then I slowly dragged the zipper down, moved my hands, and they fell from her curved hips to hit the floor. While I did that, I stroked up and down her smooth legs. With each upstroke, I let my fingers get closer to the minuscule scrap of fabric between her legs. To call them underwear would be a gross misrepresentation.

"Raptor," she begged in a needy whimper.

I bit her clit through the thin silk, and she gasped.

"Adrien," I corrected. If I was going to break all my rules and let my cock slide between those luscious, lean legs, then she was going to scream my real name.

"Adrien," she whispered on a sigh as I slowly tugged her shirt down over her hips. She stood there in nothing but that sorry excuse for panties, and it was a heavenly sight. The only thing that would make it better....

After I licked along the lacy edge, I hooked my fingers in the thin elastic sides. With a quick jerk, they ripped apart and fell useless at her feet.

There, that's perfect.

"Goddamn, your pussy smells divine," I growled before darting my tongue in for a taste. That was my undoing—because a single lick only whetted my appetite. I sucked on her clit, then became frustrated because the position didn't allow me to do what I wanted.

"On the bed," I demanded. She was quick to obey but slow to get there because she kicked off her sandals and swung that sexy ass in my face with each sultry step. Then when she slowly climbed on the bed, she made sure that I got a full view of her glistening pink pussy.

Motherfucker.

The wicked little enchantress settled on her back, but made a show of arching her back as she scooted further up on the pillow. Then she cupped those perfectly rounded tits and played with them as she boldly stared me in the eye.

I hung my damp cut on the back of the desk chair and kicked off my boots. The only time I released her lusty gaze was when I ripped my shirt over my head. Then I decided two could play at her game, and I took my time unbuckling my belt and unfastening my jeans.

Her tongue wetting her lips was the first tell that I was getting to her. The way her thighs opened invitingly was the second.

"See something you like?" I rumbled when my pants hit my thighs and I stroked my hard length.

"You know I do," she replied in a husky tone that was her third tell.

As I continued sliding my hand from my root to tip and back, I made a decision so out of character that it stunned me, but it didn't stop me. "Do you always have the guys use condoms, and are you protected?"

She scoffed. "Of course, do I look stupid?"

"I want you bare," I admitted. Insanely, my heart stopped beating while I waited for her answer.

I watched her breathing get faster and she pinched her nipples—hard. Then her ass wiggled slightly against the bedding. She hesitated at first. Then she asked, "Are you clean?"

"Yes." I knew I was, because I'd gotten tested after I ended a long-term friends-with-benefits arrangement when unexpectedly she told me she was getting married, even though I'd never gone unwrapped with her. I already knew Cookie was clean. All the dancers at Royal Heaven were routinely tested.

"Then, yes."

"Put your arms up."

She did as she was told, and my cock bobbed in excitement. I approached the bed and trailed my fingertips from her ankle up to her hip. Then I reached down to grab the soft restraint and lifted it. The chain it was attached to clinked as it ran over the rail of the bed.

"Hold this." I placed the padded cuff in her hand and her fingers curled obediently around it. I loved that she not only trusted me, but she also immediately did as she was told without question.

Making my way around the bed, I repeated my actions. Once she had both wrist cuffs clutched tightly, I climbed up between her thighs. She was fucking gorgeous. Platinum hair in disarray on my pillow, arms spread like an offering, she was beautiful. But with her tits rising and falling with each breath and her legs parted, she was stunning.

Reverently, I slid my splayed hands up the lengths of her legs. When I reached the apex, she sucked in a breath and watched me as I studied her. With a light touch, I teased the sensitive area at the top of her thigh where it connected to her pelvis. Though I would've loved to see her actually chained to my bed, I liked to work women up to what I wanted.

"If you let go, I'll put the restraints on you. Understand?"

She nodded.

Satisfaction lifted the corner of my mouth. "Good."

Then I leaned down and kissed the inside of her knee before I worked my way north. When her lust-swollen pussy was close enough that I could touch it with my nose, I moved to the other side. By the time I was done, she was trembling with need. Only then did I lick through her wet center and over her clit.

A needy whine told me she liked that.

"Fuck, you taste like you were made for me," I murmured as I kissed her pussy lips, then I delved into her with gusto. Like a man starving, I devoured every inch of her delectable and needy pussy. Intermittently, I speared my tongue inside to fuck her like my cock would soon enough. Through it all, she whimpered and gasped. When I sucked on her clit again, she groaned and lifted her hips in encouragement. Except she couldn't handle it for long. Eventually, she fought to pull the overly stimulated and sensitive nub away from me. I bit it and pushed her thighs wide as I held them down.

"Raptor!"

I bit it again, then growled my correction. "Adrien."

"Adrien," she cried. It pleased me to hear her say my name. I hated it when women called me Raptor in bed. Never liked it. If a woman was gonna scream my name, she was gonna scream the right one.

"Good girl," I praised before I went back to work. I slid two fingers into her throbbing cunt, pleased at how tight she was. Alternating between flicking the tip of my tongue over it and sucking on it, I kept at her clit while raking my fingers over her G-spot until her breathing went ragged and she thrashed beneath me. Then I pushed her over the edge until I could feel her pulsing around my fingers, and the sweet but tangy taste of her cum hit my tongue. I removed my hand and fucking lapped that shit up.

There was no way to describe the way a woman tasted. They were all different, yet there were some that were downright addictive. Cookie was that for me, just as I'd always known she would be.

Once her spasms tapered off, I slid up her body to kiss her. I wanted her to taste herself. When she sucked on my tongue, my eyes nearly crossed. I broke free and nibbled along her jaw.

"Let go," I ordered, and like the good girl she was, the chains instantly slid down to the floor to land with a loud rattling clunk.

Then I rolled onto my back, bringing her with me. Her pale tresses curtained around us as she rested over me with our lips a breath from touching.

"Fuck me," I demanded.

Her lips curved into a satisfied grin.

THREE

Sage ("Cookie")

"YOU DON'T OWN ME"—SAYGRACE (FEAT. G-EAZY)

His dark eyes practically glowed as he stared intently at me. The amber flecks licked through them like flames.

Doing as he said, I settled over his hips and slid his length through my wet slit without taking him into my body. The only signs that I was getting to him were the slight tensing of his jaw and his fingers digging into my hips.

"Let's see what you're made of, Raptor. Show me how you're going to ruin me for other men," I said, impertinently pushing him, knowing I was poking the bear.

He practically growled in irritation. "I told you, if my cock is in you, don't call me Raptor. Any other time, yes, but not when we're in bed. Now let's see what *you've* got."

I smirked. If there were two things I was really goddamn good at, it was dancing and fucking. And I loved to do both. With a tilt of my hips as I lifted and moved forward, I caught the tip of his hard cock and worked it in inch by inch. His nostrils flared, and he thrust his hips up, driving in to the hilt. Though I tried to appear unaffected by his efforts, I gasped. Never one to compare dicks, I loved them all—well, to a point. But Raptor—Adrien—was a blessed man and stretched me in the very best way.

Seductively, I began to ride him, reveling in the way his thick shaft dragged against the walls of my pussy. Each time I rose, I tightened my walls around his thick length. I'd always had a feeling that he'd be amazing inside me, but I hadn't counted on the tingles that started the second he sheathed that beautiful cock inside me. The moment he circled my clit with his thumb, it intensified to something akin to the hum you could hear on a power line as electricity surged through it.

"You like the feel of my cock fucking you?" he asked as he drove up so hard that I gasped. He hit something that sent a ripple of sensation that practically short-circuited my brain.

"Yes," I hissed as I rode the building waves of pleasure.

Suddenly, he wrapped his fingers around my throat as he pulled me toward him and squeezed lightly. He drove deep and held my ass tightly in place with his other hand.

"Then tell me this is the only cock that will be in this tight, wet cunt until I tell you I'm done with you," he demanded. His eyes flashed, and the golden-brown flecks seemed to shift.

"No," I gasped, forcing his hand—insanely wanting to see how far he would take this.

His thick tattooed fingers tightened, and I could only bring in shallow breaths. Still, I remained silent, stubbornly refusing to give him what he wanted. His eyes darkened, and his cock pulsed.

"Tell. Me," he ground out through clenched teeth. Black dots swam before my eyes.

"No," I mouthed.

The hand that had gripped my ass in a bruising hold smacked my flesh lightly before he shifted so his thumb returned to my clit. But it didn't stay there long before he slid his splayed hand up my stomach and over my ribs to hold my tit. My sheath tightened around him, and the corner of his mouth hooked up in a wicked grin. Then he pinched my nipple hard and tightened his hold on my throat until I couldn't breathe at all.

Call me crazy, but I never thought a man could make me come without so much as moving. Perfect dick buried to the base, I exploded around him. Unable to draw in the oxygen I needed, my vision began to dim. He raised his torso from the bed, skimming my jaw with his lips and teeth.

"You're mine now," he whispered in my ear. "Whether you like it or not. So, tell me whose goddamn fucking pussy this is."

"Yours," I gasped when he let up on the pressure around my neck, and pure sweet oxygen rushed into my lungs as he thrust up. The euphoria hit me as my blood rushed to my head. It was what he'd been waiting for—my surrender. We both knew it.

In one smooth motion, he rolled us over. Hand still around my throat, but now looser, he gently stroked over my pounding pulse. He dropped to one elbow and nipped the slope of my shoulder, sending a shiver of need racing along my skin. Then he slid that hand under my head and gripped my hair at the same time as he withdrew and plunged back into my needy core.

"Wrap your leg around me," he commanded, and I instantly complied. The second I did, he fucked me like a goddamn sex machine.

I don't know if it was his angle, his force, or his magical goddamn dick, but whatever he hit made my eyes roll. An odd but heavenly sensation hit me like a gale force wind, and everything went a little numb before pleasure exploded through every cell of my being.

My pussy, traitorous bitch that she was, came again as he slammed into me, our skin loudly slapping with the force. Every move he made was calculated to bring me compliantly to my knees. Despite how goddamn good he made me feel, I really believed I could maintain the upper hand. I thought I was made of stronger stuff.

For him, I was weak.

"Oh fuck, I'm going to come again," I burst out in shocked surprise as the familiar pressure built. My body tensed, no longer able to meet his animalistic motions. Lost in the pending release, I couldn't focus. Like a savage beast, he drove me toward the edge with each stroke of his talented body. When the dam burst, I screamed, and my vision went white as the almost violent contractions of my pussy gripped his amazing cock. Through it all, he continued to fuck me as I cried out his name on repeat.

"Fuuuuuck!" I barely heard him groan out in a strained curse. If I thought my orgasm had been mind-blowing, the pulsing of his cock told me his was just as powerful.

"Yessss," I rasped as his release brought on yet another of my own.

But he wasn't done.

After he came, he proceeded to taste every square inch of my body until I was seeing stars. By the time he was done, he was hard again, and I was trembling with need. He flipped me over and rammed that thick cock into my primed and ready pussy as he shoved my chest into the bed.

The first smack echoed through the roof, and the sharp sting on my asscheek startled the hell out of me. I tensed up—everywhere.

"Fucking hell," he gasped, and I loved that I'd made him do that. It wasn't long before he took back control. His hand made contact with my burning flesh as he alternated sides. With each impact, my pussy tightened up, then gushed.

"You love that, don't you," he demanded between grunts and the steady slam of his hips against my ass.

"Yes," I breathlessly replied with my hands braced on the headboard slats to keep my head from banging into it.

"Tell me again… whose pretty little cunt is this?" he asked as he rammed his blessed cock in my greedy pussy like a goddamn jackhammer.

"Yours," I immediately replied—because it was the truth. And the dirtier he spoke, the more turned on I got.

"Who else can put their cock in here?"

By then my brain was half scrambled, and his words barely registered. He took that for a refusal to answer, and he jerked his hard length out, leaving me empty and aching. He swatted my ass again, and I yelped in surprise.

"Answer me. I asked you who else's cock can use your pussy?" he barked as he teased me with his thumb.

"No one's," I whined, then I ground out, "Now please put that thick, beautiful cock back in *your* cunt and fuck me like you promised."

His chuckle was deep and dark as he teasingly prodded the tip of his shaft against my opening until I whimpered. Then he drove it home, and I saw fucking stars. When he slipped his thumb into my ass, I figured out why he'd been dipping it in my dripping wet slit.

And that was when I lost my ever-loving mind.

"Yes, oh God, holy shit, yessss," I babbled as I wiggled my hips in an attempt to get him to move.

"Baby, I'm going to fuck your tight cunt, your beautiful mouth, and right here," he promised as he slowly slid his thumb in and out of my tight, puckered hole. "And then I'm going to do it again, and again, and again. Because this"—thrust—"is"—thrust—"mine!"

For hours, he owned every inch of my body and made sure I

knew it. By the time I passed out from exhaustion, I was terrified he owned more than that.

Unsurprisingly, I woke up alone, my body aching like I'd competed in a decathlon.

Though I hated to admit it, I was pretty sure I couldn't handle more than him. He was possibly as wild as I was. He was also a complete anomaly in my book—a unicorn among men.

A man that actually left me happily satiated.

For the moment.

Arching my back, I stretched and winced at the pull in my muscles. Then I climbed out of his bed and searched for my clothing. When I found the ripped triangle of silk that used to be my underwear, I smirked and set them on his pillow. Foregoing the bra, I dressed and, sans panties, padded down the hall.

To get to the room I used, I had to enter the common area and go up the stairs. Since it was a Monday morning, I figured the brothers would be at work or busy. What I didn't expect was to find most of them chilling around the common area in the AC. They all stopped, and their conversations came to an abrupt halt as they stared at me with my sandals in hand and wearing the same clothes as yesterday. Some with wide eyes, others with jaws hanging, a few with both.

"Good morning, boys," I called out as I took my time walking to the base of the steps. I knew damn well I looked well-fucked, and I didn't care. Never had before and didn't now. With a sway to my hips, I climbed the stairs. My foot touched the landing, and I heard the voice that had my body on alert.

"Don't you guys have shit to do?" Raptor grumbled. I glanced downstairs in time to see Venom hide his silent laughter behind Raptor's back. The rest of the guys still gaped at their VP. None of them were paying any attention to me.

Raptor's scowl hit me, and I crossed my arms, pushing my

braless tits up as I cocked a hip. The furrow between his brows deepened when he realized I didn't have a bra on. My nipples reacted to his gaze, and I wanted to tell them to knock it off.

I half expected him to tell me to put a bra on or go to my room, but I should've known better. That wasn't how he operated. He was dominant but not controlling. And as long as I was his plaything, no one touched me. He had gotten me to agree that I wouldn't fuck anyone else, and he was the type who expected people to stay true to their word.

And I would.

Until he eventually bored me—which was why I'd never committed to one man. They tended to wear out their appeal.

He surprised me though. Like a wild animal, he stalked toward the lower landing, then stormed up until we were eye to eye. His tawny eyes reminded me of tiny kaleidoscopes. With flecks of deep chocolate brown, golden topaz, and a hint of soft green, they flickered and shifted—ever-changing. At the moment, they were more gold than anything else, and my chest squeezed at how beautifully rugged the man was.

For several heartbeats we stood there, eyes locked. I lifted a single brow, daring him to say something. Then he wrapped his inked hand around the back of my neck and pulled me close. The second his lips crashed into mine, I gasped, giving him the opening he needed. His hot tongue swept in and slid along mine—enticing it to an erotic duel.

When he broke free, I was panting, and my heart was pounding. Hot breath fanning across my ear, he whispered, "I fucking love your tits."

Then he pinched one of the overly sensitive nubs, causing me to groan. It was a very public announcement that he was fucking me. And that wasn't like him.

"I have work to do. Be waiting for me tonight."

He didn't remind me that I wasn't supposed to fuck anyone else, because he'd already made that clear. And no one questioned him—no one except me, that was.

"I'll think about it." I smirked before I spun out of his hold and sauntered to my room with an extra sway to my hips.

I damn sure would be there, but he didn't need to know that.

FOUR

Raptor

"HELP"—PAPA ROACH

"What's up with that?" Venom asked when I returned to the first floor of the clubhouse and stomped to the exit. My answering grunt made the fucker chuckle as he followed me out the clubhouse door.

I snagged my helmet from my handlebars and jerked it onto my head. Venom did the same.

"Don't fucking start," I grumbled.

He burst out laughing. "You're so fucked. Do you know how long she's wanted a piece of you?"

"It's just fucking. No different than any other woman I've been with. I don't do relationships with all the dating and flowers bullshit. I fuck. Just because I like to have an exclusive partner doesn't make it a relationship—unless being fuck buddies equals a relationship." I stared stoically at him as he continued to find great humor in my goddamn sex life. When he started his bike, I started mine.

"I didn't say that it was. I just think it's fucking hilarious watching you with her. Christ, you've avoided her bed for damn near ten years or maybe more. Every one of the brothers knows that too. Then you practically pissed on her in there—right in front of them. I'm not sure which was more priceless—their expressions or your situation," he explained loudly enough to be heard over our engines. With a shake of his head and a shit-eating grin, he put his bike in gear and twisted the throttle.

I followed him out of the lot, and we hit the road. We were meeting with the President of the Demented Sons MC about half-way in Fort Dodge. Venom and Snow had grown up together and had been friends most of their lives. It was a personal visit, and Venom had asked if I wanted to ride along. As soon as he said he was going to Ja-Mar's, I was on board. They had the best fucking burgers I'd ever had.

A little over an hour later, we were pulling into town and parked outside of the old drive-in style restaurant. Snow and a couple of his guys were already here, so we parked beside them and headed inside.

Snow lifted a hand to signal us from the corner table they were at, and we made our way over. I recognized the two with him as Reaper and Soap. When we got close, they stood up.

"Good to see you, brother," Snow told Venom as they embraced. With a solid back slap, they parted. "How's Margaret?"

"Ornery as ever," Venom snorted, drawing a laugh out of his friend. Once they'd said their hellos, everyone in the group greeted each other, then we took a seat. The waitress came over as soon as we did, which told me she'd been waiting for us to wrap up our greetings.

"Hey, gentlemen. What can I get you to drink?" She had blonde hair and pale blue eyes, but that's about all I noticed.

"I'll take a water, darlin'," I replied when she got to me. My light Texas drawl slipped out, and she giggled. Confused, I glanced up at her. That's when I realized she was a pretty girl, but the way she wet her lip as she gave me a coy wink did nothing for me.

Reaper nudged me when she walked off. "I think she likes you."

I scoffed. "Man, whatever."

"He's not interested because he's hooking up with Cookie," Venom told them with a shit-eating grin.

"No fucking way," Reaper replied.

"Oh shit, really?" Snow added.

"What?" I snapped. For some unknown reason, the thought that they too had fucked Cookie in the past pissed me off.

"Easy, bro. I'm just saying that you practically ignored her every time we've been to your clubhouse to party. That chick always gives you such heated stares, I can't believe you never caught fire. I'm surprised you're with her, since you never seemed interested before," Reaper explained with a shrug.

I didn't say anything, and Venom started bullshitting with Snow. Thankful for his save, I kept my mouth shut. I'd never been big on airing my dirty laundry. Lost in thought, I tuned them out as I flipped through the menu.

Reaper was right. So was Venom, and I kinda hated it. For years after she came to us, I intentionally ignored her because I firmly believed she was too young for me. She had practically been a kid, and my tastes were a little rough even then. Then as the years went by, I watched her hooking up with my brothers.

I told myself I wasn't pissed off, but in a way, maybe I was. It was like I'd fucked up my chance. If I hadn't pushed her away in the beginning, maybe I would've been enough for her. Well, after she was old enough. Fuck. I shook my head. No sense going there. I liked my life exactly the way it was.

"Venom, I wanted to see you and catch up on life, but we have a favor to ask," Snow revealed as he dropped his voice to deter possible eavesdroppers.

I immediately perked up. We were there after the lunch rush, and the only people were several tables away, but this was obviously important.

All conversation ceased when the waitress came back to take our orders. Once she was gone, Snow glanced at Venom to gauge his reaction.

"Okay," Venom drawled out as his brow furrowed. "You know I'd do anything in my power to help you, but if it involves my club, then I need to take it to the table."

Snow nodded his understanding. "You called to check on me, so I know you already know about our clubhouse being attacked several weeks ago. Hacker was a cunt hair away from figuring out who it was, but then shit locked down tighter than Fort Knox. It was like they knew what we were doing and were one step ahead of us. We have a few leads but not much to go on. We wanted to take you up on your initial offer to see if Facet could find out anything more. We'll pay for the information, then depending on who it is, we might be paying you to take care of the situation." Snow stroked his salt-and-pepper beard.

Soap was silent, but I noticed his jaw clench as he fisted his hand that rested on the table.

Intrigued, I watched the three of them like a hawk—no pun intended. Reaper's fingers strummed the table in an obvious show of irritation. Soap was about ready to crack a tooth, and Snow's initial good mood was doused.

"Brother, I already told you we would help. The minute that happened, we voted to lend a hand, but you declined, and

I respected that. However, if you've hit a dead end, we have no problem digging into it."

Snow scratched his jaw in contemplative silence and appeared torn.

"Luke, you have always been there for me. You bailed me and Loralei out without question when shit hit the fan for her. Clubs set aside, you're not just my best friend, you're also my brother, as far as I'm concerned. We can handle the situation for you regardless of who it turns out to be. This is what we do. Can you send Facet what you have so far?" Venom asked.

"I'll do one better. After the weird way every lead went cold, Hacker didn't want to send anything over the net. I guess there's an encrypted link on there for Facet to follow. He said if Facet was as good as he thought he was, he'd figure it out." Snow inconspicuously slid a thumb drive across the table as he reached for a napkin.

With a snort, Venom rested his hand over it, then grinned and acted like they were talking about riding weather. There was a bit of friendly competition between Facet and the DSMC's computer geek, Hacker. Honestly, they were both smarter than all of us put together. The difference was, when Hacker and the DSMC needed really dirty work done, they paid us. They had slightly more moral fiber than we did—which was okay. We were happy to pick up that fiber and wrap it around a fucker's neck.

From the corner of my eye, I saw the waitress approach with our food.

"Can I get you boys anything else?" she asked after she had distributed our plates.

"No, thank you." Venom grinned and the girl blushed.

I'd have bet my last two dollars that she would stick around and flirt, but she must've been too overwhelmed by the amount of testosterone at the table. I chuckled.

40

When she was checking on the other diners, Venom carefully pocketed the thumb drive.

"I'll get this to Facet as soon as we get back," Venom assured Snow.

"Appreciate it, brother." Snow nodded with a flat-lipped stare before he cast a glance at Soap.

Something was off with the big guy. At first, I thought maybe it was the shooting, but it seemed deeper than that.

Snow and Venom bullshitted for the rest of the meal, the rest of us chiming in every so often. By the end of our visit, I was convinced Soap was dealing with some shit—and not dealing with it well.

Venom had to take a piss before we headed out, so I waited for him at the table. I watched as Soap seemed to lose his shit on his president. Snow gave it right back, and Soap quickly came to heel. Reaper stepped between them, and I saw him snap at Soap who then gripped his hair and bent over at the waist. I thought he was gonna puke, but then he righted himself and must've apologized, because Snow gripped him by the shoulders and rested his forehead to Soap's. They spoke briefly.

The handful of times I'd met Soap, I had liked him, but disrespect was something that wasn't tolerated. Which was why I was glad to see that he appeared remorseful of his outburst. I was also very curious and made a mental note to have Facet pull up the details of the shooting for me. Since we didn't end up stepping in, I had forgotten half of what was said in church the day we discussed it.

That also could've been because I was a bit preoccupied with a certain sexy blonde dancer, and I hadn't been sure how to process that. Instead, I ignored it, boxing it up and shoving it into the deepest, darkest corner of my mind. The same place all my secrets and regrets lingered.

"What's going on out there?" Venom asked as he grabbed his sunglasses from the table.

"No clue."

"Hmm. Well, we better get on the road."

We made our way through the dining room and out the door. When we got to the bikes the three men were talking quietly. I read Reaper's lips when he spoke to Soap. He asked him, "Are you sure that's what you want to do?"

Soap nodded and dropped his gaze to the asphalt. Snow and Reaper shot each other looks of resignation.

"Hey, Venom!" Snow called out. "Do you have a minute to talk to Soap?"

My president and I shot glances at each other before Venom nodded.

Soap approached, and Venom rested his ass sideways on his bike. Arms crossed and shades on, he wasn't the most approachable guy. He waited for Soap to get close.

"Venom. Raptor," he greeted.

"What can I do for you, son?"

"I want to pay you to do a job," he announced. Again, Venom and I shot quick glances at each other.

"And that job is?" Venom prompted.

Soap took a deep breath and released it. His Adam's apple bobbed as he swallowed hard. "The guys who shot our clubhouse up… I want to pay you to find them."

My brows drew down as I frowned. "Dude, we're gonna look into it. I promise," I reassured him.

"I need you to more than look into it. I know it's a long shot, but I know you guys are damn good at what you do." He paused and dug in his pocket.

On alert, though I knew these guys and wasn't too worried

about them going psycho on us, I tilted my head a bit and watched each move he made.

"I need you to find out who shot these." He held out his hand, and in his palm were several spent bullets. I only recognized the dried blood in the creased spots of the metal pieces because I'd seen it before. My gaze narrowed, and I watched his every move closely.

"Okay, and if by chance we find them?" Venom prompted as he stared at Soap with a narrowed gaze.

"Then I want to be the one to take them out." The hard set of Soap's jaw matched his flintlike gaze. By then, I was pretty sure he had lost his mind.

"We don't exactly work like that," Venom cautiously replied.

"Venom… I need to," he argued, and the pain in his eyes was nearly palpable.

"This is personal to you—not so much your club," Venom observed.

"They attacked my club." He clenched his fists and lifted his chin defiantly. Soap was generally a pretty nice guy and a bit of a jokester, despite his looks. The fact that he was damn near as big as me and possibly rivaled me in tattoos probably scared little old ladies.

Venom cocked a brow.

Jaw set, he practically trembled, his muscles were so tense. "They killed my girl."

Well, fuck.

Venom promised him we would consider his request and told us we would discuss it with our chapter.

"Bro, we can't find whoever killed his girl and hand them

over to him. He's not equipped to deal with that. And I'm not just talking about the mess that could be made and the dead body or *bodies* to dispose of—I'm talking about the psychological ramifications. He's a teddy bear. The guy is one of the biggest jokesters I've ever met, well, next to Squirrel maybe. Okay, Blade's a little funny, but he's also a little nuts. Jesus, we're all a little off our rockers. The difference between us and him is that we know it and we've been living this life a helluva lot longer than he could even think about," I rattled on as I paced and ran a hand though my hair.

"Raptor."

"They aren't a club like ours. I mean, yeah—I know they've done some shit, but there's a difference between doing some shit and *doing some shit*." I kept pacing. I liked Soap, but even I had to admit the guy was nothing like the Soap I remembered.

"Raptor."

"Jesus, do you think Snow and Reaper really knew what he was going to ask us?"

"Raptor!"

I stopped, my hand falling from the top of my head where it was practically pulling my hair out, and stared at my president and best friend.

"Did you get a real hard look at Soap today?" Venom asked from his seat at his desk. He patiently waited for my answer.

The thing was, I wasn't a rash kind of guy—usually. I paid attention. I thought things through. For the most part. Cookie… I hadn't thought that through, and now I was in a place I didn't understand.

"Yeah, I did," I finally replied with a sigh.

"He's likely as fucked in the head as we are at this point. When we got back, I talked to Snow while you were checking on shit over at the farm. Adrien, she died in his arms. Covered in her blood, too late to do a damn thing, he held her helplessly." Venom gave me a pained stare.

He'd called me Adrien, and that meant he was in his emotions. Which didn't happen often unless it had to do with Loralei. Shit had happened with her last Christmas, and I know he beat himself up over it for a long while. He ran a lot of coulda, shoulda, wouldas though his head. Most men would react the same. I didn't have an ol' lady, but Cookie popped into my head.

The thought of her dying in my arms did something really fucking awful to me. Fury boiled in my blood, and rage drove each ragged breath. Fuck, yeah… I could imagine the shit he was feeling, and it had to be worse for him because he loved her. At that thought, I steeled my spine. Fuck no, I didn't love Cookie. I didn't love anyone but my brothers and my mother—and I hadn't talked to her in months because the last time we spoke, we argued about me going home.

"Raptor."

That time he just sounded tired. I glanced his way to see him stand up and set his bottle of whiskey and the two shot glasses to the side. "Yeah?"

"I'm going home to my ol' lady. I want to kiss my baby girl and watch her sleep for a minute before I fuck my ol' lady. Then I'm going to hold her like there's no tomorrow because we never know when we might end up like Soap. Go find Cookie." He patted my back and gave my shoulder a squeeze as he walked past me, flipped off the light in the office, and moved with a purpose down the hall.

I glanced at the clock. It was still early. I wondered if Cookie would be waiting for me like I told her to. And like that, I was horny as a motherfucker. All thoughts of emotional bullshit went out the window because all I could think about was losing myself between her firm thighs. No, that's not true. I was also thinking about the look on her face as she shattered with my dick shoved balls deep in her tight pussy.

With that thought, I followed Venom's footsteps, but instead of turning to leave, I went straight to the room I used when I stayed at the clubhouse—the room she better be waiting in. Actually, I kind of hoped she wasn't because the thought of leaving red handprints on her ass had me adjusting my junk as I reached the door.

Swinging it open, I held my breath.

It all came out in a rush when I found her sitting on her feet in the middle of my bed. Hands resting lightly on her thighs, tits perky and crying for my mouth to engulf the puckered pink nipples, and bright blue eyes staring at me with fire burning in their depths.

"I've been waiting for you," she murmured, then smirked. "Sir."

Holy fucking shit.

I slowly closed the door.

FIVE

Sage ("Cookie")

"LOVE BITES (SO DO I)"—HALESTORM

Mid-February

We'd been hooking up almost every day for the past five months. Color me shocked when true to his word, we remained exclusive. Not that I expected less from him, because I'd heard that he liked to have a regular partner, just not a relationship-type one.

It was me I was surprised by. I'd never been one who was happy with one guy. Maybe it was my upbringing, or maybe I was just fucked in the head—maybe both.

"Why do you have to go? You're the VP," I grumbled as I watched Raptor pack. Pouting, I was lying on my stomach on his bed with my head propped on my hand and my feet kicking leisurely in the air. After our last round of mind-blowing sex, I was still lazing around naked.

"Because I'm going," he muttered as he shoved some socks into the bag followed by a few T-shirts.

Mentally, I chastised myself because I knew he hated being questioned, and he didn't discuss club business with me. He wasn't a pillow-talk kinda guy.

"I'm going to miss you," I softly murmured. There was an unfamiliar ache in my chest at the thought of not seeing him for a week or more.

"Don't," he warned, darting his golden-flecked gaze to mine.

"What?"

"Don't make this more than it is. I told you in the beginning what I expected. You agreed."

"Yeah, I know I did, but that doesn't mean I won't miss that cock," I replied with a smirk, trying to cover up my slip. He couldn't know that I'd come to need him. Raptor was the kind that would end this without thinking twice if he thought I was getting attached or if he thought I was developing feelings.

He zipped the small bag, tossed it onto the desk where it landed with a thud, and then he started toward me. The man was pure sex, and he didn't walk—he gracefully stalked. All lean muscle and tattoos, he was gorgeous to look at—but what he could do to my body was mind-blowing.

When he reached the bed, he smacked my bare ass with a naughty grin, and I clenched my thighs together. "Then maybe I need to give you something to hold you over until I get back."

That would never happen, but I'd take what I could get.

"Mmm, I thought you'd never ask," I purred with a smug smile.

"Minx." He glanced at his watch. "We have about seven hours before I have to get on the road."

Though I wouldn't, I was dying to ask him why he was really

going. I'd overheard the guys whispering, and everyone knew that he never went on Texas runs. There was some kind of bad blood with him and his family, from what I'd pieced together over the years. I also gathered there was an ex-wife and kids. No one talked about the story behind that, but I knew he never saw his kids.

Worry clutched my chest, making it difficult to breathe. It squeezed painfully at the thought that he might still have feelings for her. What if he was going down there to get back with her? What if he'd been talking to her the entire time we'd been together? Did I miss the signs?

The clink of his buckle pulled me out of my head in time to see him slide it out of his belt loops. He looped it around my hands, and my heart hammered. Deep down, I knew he'd never hurt me, but the feeling of being restrained sent adrenaline racing through my veins. Maybe that was what made the sex so fucking good.

Who was I kidding? Yeah, it might amplify the rush, but Raptor was simply that good.

The man had always been my kryptonite. I'd wanted him the second I'd laid eyes on him as a young but jaded seventeen-year-old, except he refused to sleep with me. Part of that rejection could've been that in the beginning, I was a feisty young girl who showed up with Blade—who'd been a prospect at the time. I'd brazenly made my way through many of the brothers, high on the power it gave me. For years, everyone believed Blade and I were an on-again, off-again thing. They'd have been surprised if they knew he and I hadn't actually fucked when we were alone together.

They'd be more surprised if they knew the whole of our story and what Blade was to me.

The leather around my wrists was pulled tight, but not so much that it hurt me. He then quickly fastened the leather to the center of the headboard.

"Damn, that was quick. Were you a Boy Scout?" I teased.

He snorted. "Not hardly."

"Are you ever going to let me tie you up?" I asked, but the question ended in a squeal when he pulled my peaked nipple into his hot mouth. He sucked hard before releasing it with a pop and moving over to do the same to the other.

"Hell no," he murmured around my flesh. His breath fanning my damp skin made me shiver. Then he looked up and caught my gaze as he circled the puckered bud with the tip of his tongue.

He pushed himself up and leaned across me to open the drawer of his nightstand. When he righted himself, he set a small black box between my tits, and my heart clenched then took off like a bullet.

"I bought you a gift."

For a moment, I simply stared at the unassuming box. Torn between being ecstatic that he'd bought me a present and afraid that my hopeful soul was going to be disappointed, I swallowed the lump in my throat. He hadn't gotten me a thing for Christmas, so this was highly unusual.

"Are you going to open it?" he asked with a wide-eyed inno-cent expression as he settled next to me with his head resting on one hand and the other tracing invisible patterns over my torso. The brat knew I couldn't without disobeying and freeing my hands. This was also a touchy situation because he'd been quick to tell me this wasn't more than sex, yet he bought me a gift.

Afraid my trembling hands would give me away, I clenched them tightly then relaxed, wiggling my fingers before I clutched the belt that held me to the bed.

"Ahhh, yes. You're a little immobilized, aren't you?" The cocky fucker smirked. "Okay, I'll open it for you."

He continued to trail one finger up the sensitive skin on the back of my arm. A shiver sent tiny goosebumps in its wake as he made his way back to the box. He teased the edge of one breast as he slowly worked his way over to lift the lid.

The sparkle of clear stones caught my eye, and I raised my head to see better. I immediately knew exactly what they were, and I chuckled. Disappointment warred with excitement. The silly girl in me wished it was an actual gift of sentiment, though the woman in me knew that was stupid thinking.

"Nipple clamps?"

"Not just nipple clamps," he drawled and lifted a brow. When he took the first one out, the bedside lamp caught the facets, sending a sprinkling of light over my chest. As he lowered it, the dangling gems teased my skin much as his hands had before. By then, my chest rapidly rose and fell with each stuttering breath.

"Diamonds to adorn my good girl—are you my good girl, Sage?"

My breath caught at his use of my real name. No one called me that here—except Finley, but that was rare. To hear it leave Raptor's lips did something fluttery inside to me. I had no idea he even knew it, let alone would've thought of me as anything other than Cookie.

Slowly, he clipped one to my left nipple. The sensation was similar to when he squeezed them—until he nudged the small slider up. I gasped and closed my eyes.

He tugged lightly on the draped jewelry. "I asked you a question?"

"Yes!"

Sensuously soft, he whispered, "Yes, what?"

I didn't mistake his light words: the demand was there. The question was, how much did I want to push him.

"Yes, sir, I'm your good girl," I rasped out as he teased and tugged until I couldn't see straight.

"Have you ever used them?"

"Yes," I replied in a rush.

"Are you okay with them?"

"Yessss," I groaned as he placed the other one. I loved that he ensured I agreed when he added something new. Once he knew it was a go, he pushed both sliders until there was the slightest pain, but not so much that I didn't enjoy the hell out of it.

"That's not all," he whispered against my skin.

As I lay there with my eyes closed, I could hear his breathing, the pounding of my heart, and muted sounds from the other club members out in the common area. At the sound of further rustling, I peeked to see him lifting the velvet padding from the box. He pulled out another sparkling piece.

With a wicked grin, he moved lower, raining kisses periodically as he went. My breath caught when he swiped his tongue teasingly through my greedy and wet pussy. I literally quit breathing when he exposed my clit, flicked it a few times, then applied the clamp to it.

"Breathe," he softly drew out, and I let out a massive lungful full of air in a whoosh.

"Holy fucking shit."

"Still good?"

"Fuck yes. So good. So, so, so good." I squirmed a bit and tried to reach for him, only to be reminded I was bound to the bed with the soft leather of his belt. I grunted in frustration.

His chuckle teased over my clit before he wiggled it with a fingertip. I hissed and bucked my hips. When his tongue dipped into my aching, wet slit, I groaned. Then he slowly moved the dangling pieces back and forth to tickle my pussy lips, and I cursed under my breath.

"I need you," I panted as I wrapped my fingers around the leather above my bound hands.

"What do you say?" he crooned as if I was a child asking for an ice cream.

"Please, Adrien, I need you to fuck me," I practically begged in savage desperation.

"Open your legs farther," he demanded as he got to his knees and gripped the base of his shaft.

"Yes, sir," I purred, knowing he loved it when I called him that, and also because I was happy that I wouldn't be waiting much longer. Which was a good thing, because I ached for him. "Whatever you say, sir."

My response elicited a low growl that rumbled from his chest, and he slowly stroked his cock until the clear bead of liquid at the tip grew and spilled over. I whined at the travesty. When I wetted my lower lip with my tongue, his gaze grew heated, and he caught the precum with his finger and painted my lips with it.

I quickly licked it off. He gripped his cock tighter, and I heard him suck in a sharp breath.

"Is that all I get?" I smirked.

"Are you being a smart-ass?" he asked in a deceptively calm tone as he reached down to slide a finger between my pussy lips that were already slick from my eager anticipation.

"Never," I lied, but he squeezed the clamp and my eyes rolled back.

"What was that?"

"No, sir," I replied in a rush.

"There's my good girl," he crooned, and I swear I gushed over his teasing fingertips.

When he notched the tip of his cock into my drenched opening, I practically whimpered. I lifted my hips to grant him easier access, and he slowly slid in. It was the sweetest torture. My eyes practically crossed, and I moaned at the sensation of his hot, smooth skin sliding through my slippery sheath. There was definitely something to be said about going bare.

Once he was fully seated, he hooked his hands under my knees and pushed them toward my chest. The way it changed the angle made me gasp, and my back arched from the bed, it was that damn good. When he started moving, it was slow and sensuous. I practically quit breathing. The combination of his cock and the jewelry was putting me in sensory overload—and it was fucking amazing.

After teasing me for the first few moments, he drove hard and deep, his weight braced on his arms that now flanked my own raised arms. Thighs pressed to my chest, shins against his, I took everything he gave. My heart stopped at the amazing feel of him thrusting hard and deep in my pussy. If it was possible to die from incredible sex, he was going to put me in my grave.

"Fuck, you feel good," he grunted as he snapped his hips faster. He shifted one hand to anchor my ass. With each brutal thrust, he pulled me against him for maximum impact. My flesh would be bruised from his grip, but I didn't care.

The combination of his words and what he was doing to my body was driving me crazy. With the clit clamp magnifying each sensation as he plunged into me, I was already on the verge of losing control. Except I watched him from beneath hooded eyes because he was a magnificent sight.

Hard muscles flexed with each movement, and the bedside lamp cast enough light to cause his inked skin to glisten with a thin sheen of sweat. His dark hair was a sexy mess, and I was dying to grip it tight, but with my hands bound, that wasn't happening. Instead, I held the belt tightly, sure I was leaving nail impressions in the leather.

"Jesus fucking Christ, you're gonna make me come already," he ground out, and his darkening gaze locked on mine. His rhythm faltered, and I could feel his thick cock swell slightly as it pulsed a couple of times.

"God, yes, fuck me, Adrien," I begged as I moved my hips with his—I was so close.

At the sound of his name, his eyes seemed to flicker as if a fire had been lit in their depths. The golden flecks shimmered as he rasped, "What do you want me to do?"

"Fuck my pussy, Adrien. Fuck it hard," I demanded through gritted teeth.

With a growl, he complied, and I gasped. He practically threw my legs over his shoulders and then put everything he had into each drive of his hips. My eyes rolled and my breath came in a choppy staccato as my nerve endings popped and brain short-circuited. His fingers dug into my thighs, and he filled the room with the echo of our damp skin slapping.

"Whose tight cunt is this?" he growled out as he continued to forcefully drive in and out. Wet, dark hair hung down, nearly obscuring one dark, glittering eye as he practically stared into my soul.

Desperate for release, I didn't hesitate for a second. "Yours."

"Fuck yes. This is *my* goddamn pussy. You wanted something to remember me by while I'm gone, so I'm going to fill it with so much cum, it will be leaking out of you for days." His words were punctuated by the primal desperation in his thrusts.

"Yes!" I choked out as the first flutter hit my core, and my stomach rippled as I trembled in anticipation. Between the dangling gems on the nipple clamps tickling my skin with each bounce of my tits and how deep he was going, I shattered. The pressure that had been building finally exploded, and ecstasy was mine for a few sweet moments.

"Goddamn, you just…. Oh fuck…. Motherfucking fuck," he rambled before he gave one last thrust, and I forced my eyes open when they wanted to close. He gave one last groaned "Fuuuuuuck", and I could feel him explode.

He was absolutely beautiful. Muscles tensed, he held himself deep as his cock pulsed in time with the powerful contractions of my pussy walls around it. His bearded jaw rested on his chest, and he drew in a huge stuttering breath. With the last few spasms of his shaft, a shudder moved through him, and he released my legs to lean forward. Breathing heavily, he went down onto his elbows on either side of my ribs and dropped his head to slowly circle my aching nipples with the tip of his tongue.

I was not expecting the aftershocks of my orgasm to hit so violently when he released the overly sensitive nubs from the metal clamps. "Holy shit!" I shouted and jerked as my pussy throbbed with more pleasure than I thought possible.

It was like flying. Or like riding along on the waves of bliss. As I drifted back to consciousness, it was to find him pressing soft kisses along the side of my neck. Pausing over my pulse, he slowly swiped his tongue over it as if he was tasting each beat of my heart.

When he nuzzled his face into the crook of my neck and inhaled deeply, there was a tug at my wrists, and the belt fell free. A hiss escaped me when I lowered my arms and the blood rushed back to my extremities. He lifted his head and saw the redness around my wrists. Gently, he wrapped his large hand around my forearm. Slowly, he brought it to his lips.

As he soothed it with his kisses, he glanced up at me.

"It's fine," I assured him before I combed my fingers through his hair.

"You're sure?"

"Yes. I would tell you if it wasn't."

"Good, because this isn't about hurting you."

"I know."

He nipped my jaw playfully, then fell off me to cuddle against my side. Like I weighed nothing, he rolled me and tugged me to fit in his big spoon. Never in a million years would I have guessed that Adrien "Raptor" Krow would be a snuggler. Though I loved it, he shouldn't be so sweet and playful. It muddled the lines in my mind.

The calm that washed over me as I lay protected by his large, sculpted body should've been my next clue that this arrangement had not gone as planned.

Deep in my heart, I knew I was well and truly screwed, and I had to face the truth—I had developed feelings for him.

Planning to enjoy every second before he left, I intended to stay awake until he had to go. Except I was lulled into a peaceful sleep by the feel of his steady breathing and the comforting weight of his arm wrapped protectively around my waist.

When I woke with a start, it was to find myself sitting up, heart racing, and alone in the bed. The silence seemed oppressive as I glanced around Raptor's room. His cut and bag were gone. The emptiness in my chest was suffocating.

With a deep sigh, I crawled out of bed, wincing at the ache between my legs but having zero regret. I dressed in my pale pink satin nightgown, pinned my hair up in a messy cascade of waves, and shrugged on the matching robe. I slipped my feet into feathered house shoes and sighed as I gave the mussed bed one last longing glance. When I saw the twinkling gems of the jewelry on the night-stand, the smile that curved my lips was one of wicked delight.

That was when I noticed the second box. This one was much bigger than the one he gave me last night. Feeling torn between cautious and excited, I lifted the smooth matte black cover to find what I was certain were three glass butt plugs. I may not have any experience using them before, but I wasn't an idiot. I'd seen them before, but nothing like these. They were graduated and appeared to be hand blown with varied shades of pink twisted through them. There was a small envelope taped in the lid that I carefully removed.

I slid the thick card out. Raptor had penned a noted to me in bold, slanted writing.

Sage,

While I'm gone, follow the instructions located under your gifts. Be ready when I get back.

-A

I blew out the breath I hadn't realized I was holding, then tucked the card back into the box and closed the lid. A quick glance at the dusty old alarm clock on the nightstand told me it was still early. Maybe I hadn't missed him yet. I set the box down. Quietly, I let myself out and made my way to the common area. Disappointment drooped my shoulders when he wasn't there.

"He's gone. Left about an hour ago," Blade said from his place at the bar.

He was drinking, and I arched a brow at the glass.

"It's not day drinking if you haven't gone to bed yet," he replied to my unspoken question before lifting the glass to his lips. He set it down and turned his barstool to face me. "Besides, it's mostly water now."

"Mmm" was my noncommittal reply before I took the glass and emptied it in one swallow.

"You sure you know what you're doing?"

Unprepared for it, I practically gagged at the taste of pure Patron. Mostly water, my ass. I knew better than to believe him, but I didn't dare show him that the burn from the tequila might've set my throat on fire.

"If it's good enough for your breakfast, it's good enough for mine." I shrugged and gave him a wink.

"That's not what I'm talking about, and you damn well know it."

I sighed, stood on the brass foot rail, and reached over the bar to snag the bottle I knew he'd been drinking from. Not in the mood for a lecture, I filled the glass halfway and downed it too, trying not to cough. Then I replaced some for him and slid the glass in front of him.

"I'm a big girl, Blade. Now, don't let me stop you from your breakfast of champions," I teased as I got up off of the stool.

Quick as a snake striking, he grabbed my arm. Startled and a little taken aback, I glanced down at his inked fingers wrapped around my arm with the pale silky fabric peeking between them. "I know you, Sage. And I know you've been half in love with him since the first night you saw him. He's not that guy—he's never going to give you what you want from him."

I scoffed but I didn't have a quick-witted answer. Somewhere in the clubhouse, a toilet flushed, and there were muted voices as those who stayed the night in the clubhouse came to life. "You're wrong, Blade. I don't believe in love."

"I think that's a lie, but I don't expect you to admit it. I'm just worried about you. If you get hurt, there's not a damn thing I can do about it without going against one of my brothers."

The frown that marred his forehead made me feel guilty. I smoothed it with my fingertips. "Don't worry. There aren't any feelings in play here, and I'm not like some of the club girls that are chasing a patch. I'm just a stripper, right? I know my place," I replied with a self-deprecating smirk. What I didn't add was that the reality of my position did bother me.

Because I was a big, fat liar.

There were so many feelings in play that I was drowning in them.

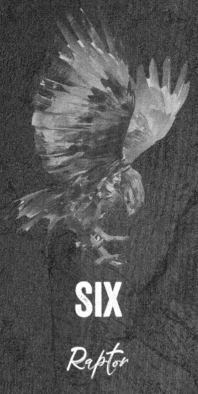

SIX

Raptor

"HOLD ON TO MEMORIES"—DISTURBED

I'd made the trip to Texas with Voodoo and Phoenix for partially selfish reasons. I sure as hell hadn't planned on it, but the timing was coincidentally perfect. It would mean I wouldn't need to make the trip alone. The morning before, my mom had called to tell me my grandfather had died.

While Voodoo focused on his ritual to see what he could gather about the chick we came down to investigate, I had rolled a joint and decided to take a few hours to myself. If I was going to follow through with my plan, I was gonna need it. Phoenix decided to grab a drink.

I'd seen the perfect spot when we'd gone out to eat after arriving and getting checked into our hotel. If there had been a way to the roof of the hotel, I might've tried that. Since there wasn't, I walked down the road and into the small park. Inside, my inner hawk was trembling with excitement, while I remained unmoved. It had been years—more than I could count—since he'd stretched his wings. Trying to prepare myself for what was to come, I skirted the playground equipment, keeping to the shadows the best I could.

"Fuck," I whispered as I closed my eyes, searching for strength and inner peace. When that didn't work, I dug in my pocket for the joint I'd stuffed in there. My hands trembled when I tried to get the lighter to produce a fucking flame. Finally, I got it lit and took a hit. Then another—and maybe a few more.

Once I was as calm as I was gonna get without passing out, I pinched off the lit end and ensured I was still alone. Satisfied it was safe, I slipped into the deep shadows of the small, wooded border that separated the little oasis from the rest of the hustle and bustle. During the day, it probably wasn't much for privacy, but it worked for me in the dark.

Quickly, I undressed and neatly folded my jeans, socks, and boots, then I placed them under a bush and covered them with old leaves. I rolled my shirt and boxer briefs tightly around my phone and secured them with an elastic hair tie I'd never gotten away from carrying with me. The cool night air sent a shiver clean through to my soul as my hawk practically trembled in anticipation. Knowing it wouldn't do to get caught in a park with my dick swinging, I crouched.

The excruciating pain stole my breath, and I dropped my head. Muscles tensed, I could not only feel but *hear* the bones shifting and resetting in their new pattern. The tattoos on my body seemed to bleed, and every surface of my skin darkened before I was covered in the sleek brown and white feathers of my red-tailed hawk.

Headlights flashed, and my gaze darted to the police cruiser I hadn't seen pull up. It must've been when I was transitioning. Awkwardly, I flew up to a tree branch, banging into a few smaller ones as I did, and sat still as the beams of their flashlights scanned the tree line.

Full of haughty disdain, my hawk chastised me. *Stop fighting me.*

Goddamn, give me a break. It's been a while.

Well, whose fault is that?

Shut up.

As I sat unmoving, I glanced down and saw my rolled T-shirt peeking out from under the bush.

Shit.

"You see anything?" one of the officers asked the other.

"Nope. Sure as fuck smell that weed, though."

Their light beams scanned the area once more, and then the other one hit the button for the radio on his shoulder. His booted toe rested against the end of my rolled black T-shirt, and I held my breath.

"No sign of anyone. Likely it was some kids hiding over along the trees, smoking. They must've cleared out."

When they turned on their heels and made their way back to their cruiser, I could finally drag oxygen into my starved lungs. Of course, I realized how dumb that was because even if they heard me breathe or move, they would've only seen a large hawk perched in the tree. Once I was certain they were gone, I swooped down, grabbed the bundle, and my powerful wings drove me higher.

Sloppy, Adrien.

And I repeat... shut up.

At first, I may have been awkward and unsure, but it wasn't long before I soared above the rooftops and trees. My hawk's contentment hummed through every fiber of our being. Streets bustled with the nightlife crowd. Laughter and the drone of voices rose up to where I flew, but no one paid attention to an oversized bird flying high above them in the night sky. The more I flew, the more relaxed and at peace I was.

After the streetlights became few and far between, I gave in to the hawk side of me. Exhilarated, we dove and climbed. As I coasted for a moment, a gust of wind ruffled my feathers, and I was pushed slightly off course, but I quickly corrected. There was nothing I could compare to the feeling of flying, and it wasn't long before I had to admit that I missed it.

Told you.

Because I was so happy, I didn't put up much of an argument. Basking in the freedom, I wondered why I'd denied myself this feeling for so long. Honestly, I think I was hiding from who I was—a slight case of cutting off my nose to spite my face.

My inner hawk cheered at my revelation.

As if I was on autopilot, I made my way to my destination. Lost in my head, before I knew it, I had passed over the high fence. It surrounded the over four-thousand acres that made up the Triple Kettle Ranch. Though it was far more than a ranch. To the outside world and from above, it appeared to be a fully operational ranch complete with livestock and crops. It was actually a self-sustaining community that my great-great-grandfather had established to keep our clan safe.

It was *home*.

Suddenly, I could sense I wasn't alone. Having been away for so long, I had no idea who might be assigned to the watch.

Several hawks swooped in, and one essentially shouldered me, sending me tumbling for a moment. The watch had found me. It was good to know they were still so disciplined. Another dove at me, but inside my head, I heard one of them shout, "*Malachi! Stop!*"

Immediately the bird changed course. Malachi? Surely that wasn't June Wilmington's youngest.

"*Adrien?*"

The voice sounded familiar, but I couldn't place it. I wracked my brain to determine who it was. It was nearly impossible in the dark—then again, even in daylight I might not recognize everyone after all these years. What I did know was that they were not kin to me, as they didn't have my family's markings.

I could've fucked with them and possibly made it to the house before they caught me, but I decided I'd better not. It had been years since I'd been in hawk form. Despite my time at the gym, as a hawk I likely wasn't in the same shape as before. Unsure of who they were, though they had recognized me, my hawk and I replied, "*Yes.*" Then I started the swooping spiral with them known as a kettle. It was where the ranch had gotten its name. The "Triple" was for my ancestor's three sons.

They flanked me the entire way until I landed with a thud on the wooden porch. "*I'm not going to stand here naked in front of all of you. You have a watch to maintain,*" I admonished the other hawks hovering above the house.

They laughed, and one of them landed in the yard, its sharp gaze on me. "*You've been gone longer than I realized if you're afraid to transition in front of us.*"

It was the same hawk that had called my name. I cocked my head and eyed him quizzically.

The front door flew open. "Adrien!" my mother cried and dropped to her knees by my side. Realizing another hawk was in the yard, she made a shooing motion. "Drago! Go back to your watch!"

My heart ached at the realization that my childhood best friend was right before me, and I hadn't recognized him. Truthfully, I had missed him during my self-imposed exile.

"*I'll see you around,*" he told me before he took off. "*Hector! Wait up!*" he called out as he flew higher.

"Please don't leave," Mom begged. I shook my head. She placed one splayed hand over her chest and the other over her mouth as tears welled in her dark brown eyes. "Come in when you're ready."

The second she cleared the threshold, I transitioned back to my human form, wincing at the agony that shot through me. Gasping, I rested my hands on my knees until it subsided. Once I could move without stabbing pain, I dressed in my clothes and grabbed my phone from the solid but worn wood under my feet.

I went in, and Mom immediately handed me a pair of jeans. "They're your father's. You look to be close in size, though they may be a bit big on you. You look like you've been starving yourself."

Some things never changed. With a chuckle, I pulled the denim over my legs and folded the waistband over so I could keep them up. The second they were situated, my mother flew into my arms.

"I can't tell you how happy I am to see you, Adrien," my mother whispered as she held me close. I pretended I didn't notice the traces of gray that highlighted her usually dark hair. Seeing the little signs that showed my mom had aged was a reminder of how long I'd been gone. I chastised myself for that. She sniffled, and I knew she was crying. My heart ached at the sadness she carried because of me and my prideful decisions.

"I'm sorry I haven't been home sooner." That was the truth. For no other reason than that my mother always believed in me. She loved me unconditionally, without expectations or disappointment in my choices. Closing my eyes against the weakness threatening to flow, I placed a kiss on top of her head. That wasn't completely true. There was another reason for my regret—I wasn't able to see my grandfather before he died. "I'm sorry about Pops."

"Your grandfather was always proud of you, you know," she murmured. That ache behind my lids burned down to my throat. Both because of the loss and because she didn't include my father in that sentiment. The only girl in a family with six sons, Mom had been my grandfather's pride and joy, and he had doted on her, as had my uncles. Losing her father had to have been crippling for her.

"I should've—"

My mother leaned back and stopped me with a finger to my lips. She tilted her head. The sorrow in her tear-filled eyes was damn near debilitating, and I hated myself a little for being part of the cause.

"Do I wish you wouldn't have stayed away so long? Yes. But you know what? It doesn't matter. We can't live our tomorrows carrying the regrets of yesterday. What a miserable existence that would be."

How did I explain to her that it was purely my own hurt and stubbornness that had kept me away? If I came back, I knew there was no chance of avoiding my cousin. There was always the chance I'd run into Falina's bitch ass too. And fuck, even after all these years, if I was to see the boys knowing I had no rights to them—I couldn't even imagine it without my chest caving in.

"You know they aren't together." She spoke as if she could read my mind.

"Don't, Ma," I warned. I didn't want to talk about it because it immediately dredged up old hurt and anger toward my cousin. "It doesn't change what he did."

"You should talk to him. Let him explain," she tried again, but I shot her down.

"There's nothing to explain. I came home from getting my ass shot in combat to find my wife and kids shacked up with Evan. Then I get slapped with a restraining order and formal notice telling me my boys weren't *mine*, so I had no rights to them. What more is there to explain than that?" She winced at my harsh tone, and I sighed. "Ma, what he did was unforgivable."

"But—"

"No. Not now. Not ever. I'm here to see *you*."

She gave me a smile that didn't quite reach her eyes and stepped out of my arms. Then she patted my chest. "It's your lucky day. I made your favorite this morning."

The corner of my mouth lifted in a half-hearted grin. "I thought I smelled apple-cinnamon bread when I came in."

Taking a seat at the kitchen table, I glanced around. The kitchen had been remodeled, but it still was my favorite place to be. "Dad on shift?" I asked when I realized there was no one else in the house.

She nodded. "He'll be sorry he missed you."

I snorted in disbelief.

"Adrien, don't. He misses you too."

"We'll agree to disagree on that," I muttered. Obviously, he hadn't told her what he'd said. When I'd gotten out of the Army and I refused to come back because of the betrayal from my own blood, my father had told me to never come back, because I was dead to him.

We visited for the next hour or so and consumed the rest of the loaf of bread before my phone rang. When I saw that it was Phoenix, I motioned to my mom and held up my phone. "I need to take this. Let me step out front."

A confused and questioning "Okay" was her reply.

I answered before I got outside. "Yeah," I said as the screen door closed, and I paced the front porch.

"Hey, VP. Voodoo said to call you to let you know we need you. We're at the Blue Broomsticks place, meeting with Voodoo's witch."

"I'm on my way." No more needed to be said. The moment he said, "We need you," I was there, because that's what we did. We were loyal and dependable when it came to brothers. No questions asked. It was a loyalty I once thought I shared with my family as well.

When I went back inside, my mother's expression was re-signed. Pretty sure she knew I was leaving. Her next words con-firmed it. "Will I see you again before you go?"

"Yes. I promise."

Her smile was brighter than it had been all night. "Good. Maybe you can bring whoever you're here with," she suggested.

My mother was one of the most understanding and supportive people I knew, but I wasn't sure she was ready to see exactly what my life entailed. If I had to guess, I'd say she had no idea I was in a motorcycle club. On the rare occasions I called her, I never dis-cussed much about myself. I sure as hell wasn't going to tell her I was part of a group of "gifted" men who made it their mission to take out society's trash.

"We'll see" was the best I could give her. Besides, from the look on her face, I think she had the wrong idea. I was definitely not here with a woman. That had me wondering what my mom would think of Cookie if she met her. As quickly as the thought came, I shoved it into a box. That wasn't ever going to happen—for more reasons than one.

The trip back to Sloane's shop hadn't been near long enough to pre-pare me for the clusterfuck of epic proportions that would ensue. Nor was I expecting that I would have to call in favors that would come at a serious cost.

Shit had hit the fan before I even got to the shop. We found ourselves smack-dab in the middle of a feud stemming from events that were centuries old. On top of that, we found out that Voodoo's biological father was more unhinged than we could've imagined.

Knowing we didn't have the manpower to handle the situation

on our own, I knew my only option was to ask my family for help. In general, I hated to ask for favors. It made it worse that those favors would have to come from my family. Regretfully, I made the call.

"Hello?" My father's voice hadn't changed one bit. I hated that I had to blink back tears.

"Dad, it's me Adrien." I paused, needing a moment to get the words out. "I need a favor," I explained, then ground my molars in irritated distaste.

"Adrien." My name came out in an exhale of disbelief. "Anything."

For a moment, I was speechless. My chest ached at his immediate and stunning response. With the way we ended things and after all these years, I never thought that would be his reply. Then I explained what we needed and briefly skimmed over what was going on.

"We're on our way. But I have a condition."

As I knew he would. "What?"

"I want you to come home," he firmly stated. "For good."

The oxygen was ripped from my lungs. It tore me apart as I stood there, lips pressed together, my body angrily twitching. The pain inside when I thought about walking away from my brothers was akin to being shredded apart by my father's talons. Nor could I ask Sage to uproot herself for me when I couldn't promise her a damn thing. But the thought of leaving her nearly brought me to my knees. He had no idea what he was asking of me.

Yet, if I didn't do this, I could lose the people I considered family—and that possibility was worse. Better to not be around them and know they're safe than to stay there after their catastrophic loss—or be dead alongside them.

Squeezing my eyes shut and fighting back the pain my choice was causing, I took a deep breath and slowly let it out. "Okay."

We quickly worked out the details.

"Leaving now, so we'll be there soon," my father assured me before he ended the call.

My world imploded.

Of course, nothing went as smoothly as we'd hoped. Everything had escalated from there—but that was Phoenix's story to tell. Everything with Sloane settled, I now had enough of my own crap to deal with.

It was time to pay the piper.

We were in the chapel of the old Dallas clubhouse, and my debts were being called in.

"Jesus fucking Christ," I muttered, pacing and gripping my hair. "Immediately?"

"Son, we made a deal. We agreed to help you and your friends if you agreed to come home—permanently." Arms crossed, he stared me down like the predator he was. The hawk in me wanted to fight to defend itself.

"I know what we agreed to, but I don't know why. You told me I was dead to you," I spat out. "Remember?"

Sorrow darkened his gaze and his shoulders drooped. It aged him before my eyes. "I was wrong for that. I was angry and hurt. That you would allow that woman you married to come between you and your family like you did made me want to lash out. And that's exactly what I let happen. I would rather have made her leave—I should have made her leave. But I thought they were my grandsons. With all the trouble she's caused…." He trailed off and took a deep breath that he slowly exhaled. Then he squared his shoulders. "Son, I love you, and I've missed you."

Always too damn proud, I gritted my teeth and fought back acknowledgment of his sentiment and the acceptance of his apology. The reminder of the boys I once thought were mine was like salt on a wound I thought was healed. It made me want to turn my back and walk away. However, I had to honor my promises.

"Fine."

Hope and relief lit his eyes—the ones that perfectly matched mine. Another trait of our bloodline. While most of the hawks in the clan had the dark brown eyes like my mother, the Krows all had a curious blend of hazel.

"I'll see you in a month—maybe less," I added. "I have to have time to prepare. But understand this—I agreed to come home to Texas. I did not agree to move onto the ranch or be a member of the kettle."

His jaw tensed but he gave me a curt nod. Though he wasn't happy about that, he knew I was right.

We both walked out of the office. When we reached the common area, my cousins and Drago stood up. Refusing to look him in the eye, I ignored Evan. Drago took a step forward but hesitated. I approached him and held out my hand. With a grin, he shook my hand but quickly pulled me into his embrace.

"Fuck, man, I've missed you." He released me and stepped back but still gripped my shoulder. "Is it true? You're coming home?"

Pressing my lips flat, I nodded.

I was moving back to Texas.

"Fuck yeah!" He whooped.

At least someone was excited about the move.

SEVEN

Raptor

"STAY"—BLACK STONE CHERRY

"Venom, I never wanted this. This right here is my family." I stabbed my finger on the surface next to the glass I was drinking from. "Not the people that took my deceitful ex-wife into the fold and took her side over mine." Elbow resting on the bar top, I massaged my aching head.

"I'm not saying I want you to leave, because you know damn well that isn't true. But I understand. Fuck, I wish we could've gotten down there in time to help you out so you wouldn't have had to bring them in. Then none of this would be an issue." He downed the rest of the whiskey in his glass.

"The worst part is having to walk away from the club. I never saw myself leaving the Royal Bastards. Yet, here I am, having to walk away," I muttered, still pissed about my situation.

"I wouldn't be too sure about that."

My head tilted as I looked at Venom like he'd lost his damn mind. At one time, there had been two chapters in the Dallas/ Fort Worth area. Several of the members laid down their colors because they couldn't stand behind the shit Rancid was doing, and the officers in both chapters were Rancid's little butt monkeys. Both chapters had been shut down when Rancid was finally taken down. So those weren't an option.

"What, go nomad?" The thought never appealed to me. I enjoyed the camaraderie and the feeling of family I got from being in a chapter. This had become my home.

"I mean, if that's what you want, sure." He shrugged. "I was actually thinking maybe you could talk to Nationals and ask about reopening a chapter there."

"And who's gonna be president?" I asked, staring him down because I knew where he was going with this, and he knew damn well I never had the desire to hold that title. He was a few years older than me and more experienced in the club. When he was nominated, I knew he'd make a solid president, and I was damn happy to be his right-hand man. That didn't mean I *ever* envied his position.

His shit-eating grin told me I was right about his idea, and I rolled my eyes.

"You," he drawled out, then chuckled.

"Ugh." I palmed my face, drawing my hands down, distorting my face.

He continued to laugh, then he sobered. "I'm actually serious."

"Venom, bro—"

"No. Hear me out." His eyes shifted from blue to green to gray. "Anytime I needed you to cover down, you kept shit wired tight. The brothers look up to you because you're a damn good leader too. You're just quieter and hate to talk on the phone." He grinned.

"I'm gonna need more whiskey to consider this," I grumbled right as Willow walked behind the bar. She quickly set a bottle of Jameson in front of me with a glass and a wink.

"Where's Cookie?" I asked her. For some reason, the thought of leaving her behind didn't sit well with me. In fact, it made me feel like someone plunged their hand in my chest and ripped me apart. The problem was, it wouldn't be right to ask her to completely uproot her life to go to Dallas so we could keep fucking. It would give her the wrong idea.

"Don't know," Willow replied with a shrug. "She was talking to Blade in the gym earlier."

Tension coiled between my shoulders, and I experienced something that if I didn't know better, I would think was jealousy. That was something I didn't want to examine too closely. I stood, pushing back my barstool with a screech.

"Go find her and lose yourself between her thighs for a while. Then think about what I said."

I gritted my teeth at the casual way he discussed me and Cookie. He made it sound like I was simply fucking a club whore. The sobering thought hit me—I was getting all worked up over something that was supposed to be casual. Somewhere along the lines, I'd gotten attached, and that was a mistake.

Stomping off to find her, I repeatedly reminded myself that this was just sex. In my head I repeated that Cookie was not special. She had fucked my brothers before me, and she would go back to it after I was gone.

Except none of it helped. That last thought had me seeing red. That's when I knew I had fucked up and fucked up bad.

EIGHT

Sage ("Cookie")

"YOU'LL BE FINE"—PALAYE ROYALE

When Raptor returned from the run to Texas with Voodoo and Phoenix, he sought me out. I was in the gym, working off some of my frustration—both sexual and emotional. It had been almost a week, and I hadn't heard a single word from him, so I was a little pissed at us both.

"Focus!" Blade shouted inside my head. It was still a little freaky, though he'd been doing it since we were young.

"I'm trying!" I panted.

I nearly caught Blade on his chest with my foot when I kicked at the pads he let drop as he looked at the door when it slammed open. "Don't look now, but the beast has returned for you, Beauty."

Raptor didn't say a word. He just stormed in, grabbed my hand, shot a glare at Blade, and hauled me to his room.

The door slammed shut so hard, I was sure the walls shook.

Fierce, he sank his fingers into my hair and held my head as he crashed his lips to mine in a desperate, bordering on violent, kiss. He broke free when I was breathless, and he found my earlobe with his teeth before he moved on to my neck. Then he dropped to his knees and bit my pert nipple through my sports bra.

"Adrien," I gasped when he licked my sweaty cleavage. "I need a shower!"

"Why? I love the way you taste—and you're just going to get sweaty again," he replied into my boobs, and I couldn't help but laugh. However, the second he looked up at me, what I saw in his eyes shut it down.

"Take it off," he demanded, his voice cracking slightly and pain in his gaze.

Confused at his behavior, I slowly unzipped the center of the bra. It popped open and fell off my shoulders. Once my breasts were exposed, he growled and jerked my Spanx shorts and panties to my ankles in one fell swoop.

Before I had a chance to step out of them, he'd wrapped his hands around my sides, and he tossed me on the bed. I squealed in surprise, but it quickly morphed to a moan when he shoved my legs open and licked through the wet center of my pussy lips. The man was a muff-diving champion. I'd always loved when a guy ate me out, but I rarely actually came that way. With him, it was a guarantee. He drove his tongue into my sheath, then up to circle my clit. Wild and needy, I grabbed his hair. It didn't stop there, though. He was relentless—biting, licking, and sucking until I arched from the bed and practically convulsed. It was then that I shattered.

A silent scream parted my lips. Finally, my vision cleared, and my limbs trembled as I floated in the post-euphoric bliss.

"Fuck, you taste amazing," he murmured with one last swipe of his gloriously talented tongue. Everything the man did was hot as fuck. When he shamelessly wiped his mouth on the shoulder of his T-shirt and then pushed off the bed, my breath hitched. Mesmerized, I watched him shrug off his cut and hang it over the back of his desk chair. The rest of his clothing scattered as he discarded each item. He made every move sexy as fuck. Once he was standing in nothing but his tattoos, he prowled toward the bed. The second his knees hit the edge, he was on the mattress and crawling up over me until we were eye to eye. "Turn over. Ass in the air."

"Yes, sir," I smartly replied, eliciting a growl from him. In no time at all, I was positioned exactly as he demanded. His inhale was a hiss. With my cheek pressed to the pillow, I could only see so much. But God, could I *feel*. He kneed my legs further apart and circled the glass tip of the plug he'd given me.

"You wore this during your workout?"

"Yes. You told me not to take it out unless I had to—you know."

His rough palms skimmed over my hips before he slid them up my spine and back down my sides. Like he was tracing me in an effort to memorize me, he did that until I impatiently got to my hands and knees to look back at him questioningly. The sharp smack to my asscheek both startled me and made me gush until I was sure I was dripping on the bed.

"What did I tell you?"

With a mock glare, I resumed my position. The soft feeling of silk slipped around my wrist. When I instinctively turned my head to see what he was doing, he smacked my ass again. The silk went around my other wrist before he did something that slowly drew my arms behind my back. Then he must've tied them together, because my hands now rested behind me, secured in place.

My muscles tensed in anticipation—including the ones in my pussy as he teased my slit. Jesus, when he pressed two fingers inside, my eyes crossed. Then he began finger fucking me in a slow sensuous rhythm as he tugged repeatedly on the plug, and I damn near came on the spot.

"Goddamn, you're drenched," he observed, and I could hear that he was pleased. I imagined the satisfied lift at the corner of his mouth.

Before Adrien, I'd never been much into bondage, the whole Dom/sub thing, or the BDSM scene. Not that he had pushed me, nor had he gone too crazy on me, but he definitely pushed my envelope. When he said he wanted to work me up to things, he obviously meant it. From what I'd read—because yes, I read up—he'd been pretty mild so far. The crazy thing was, I'd have probably let him do almost anything to me.

As he continued to play with me, he rubbed the silken length of his cock along my hip. How something hard as steel could feel encased in silk was a mystery, but it was one that I loved.

He momentarily stilled and leaned over to reach for the nightstand drawer. I heard him pull something out and set it on the bed. Then I heard the crinkle of plastic and what sounded like him rolling a condom on. I didn't dare look because he'd told me to keep my head down.

When he began playing with the glass plug again, I moaned.

"Does that hurt?" he whispered.

"N-n-no," I choked. "It's… oh God."

He darkly chuckled as he tugged, twisted gently, and pushed it back in. "That's right. I'm your god—the only fucking god that is going to answer you right now."

"Yesssss." I gasped when he pulled it out and I was left feeling empty. Except not for long. Something cold touched me, and I realized it was whatever lubricant he had on his finger when he started to slowly finger fuck my ass. Then he reached around, and his hard chest rested on my bound arms as he circled my clit with his free hand, and I inhaled a stuttering breath.

"I'm going to fuck this tonight," he murmured against my back as he kept at the agonizingly slow and steady pace. I whimpered. "Would you like that?"

"Please! God yes, Adrien… sir," I pleaded. By then I would've let him do anything to me.

"Good girl," he crooned. When he had me losing my goddamn mind, he rose up and lined his sheathed dick with my puckered hole that up until then had been played with but never fucked. I'd never trusted a man enough for that.

Until him.

"Relax," he urged as he added more lube. Then I could feel the tip of his cock pushing at my opening before he slowly worked past the tight ring as I clutched at air behind my back reaching for him. "Breathe, baby," he softly encouraged when I gasped at the initial burn.

Complying, I found myself relaxing and he worked himself further in. Before I knew it, I could feel his entire length inside me. He groaned, and I let out a final rush of air.

"Motherfucker—that's so fucking good," he praised. "I'm going to move. Are you ready?"

"Mm-hm," was all I could get out. Words were too far away to process.

My face started tingling when he began to slowly move in and out. The feeling was unreal and totally unexpected. At first his movements were shallow, but when I didn't complain, he grew bolder.

"Jesus fucking Christ…. Where's my cock, baby?" he asked as he kept slowly sliding in and out with long even strokes.

"In my ass," I wheezed. He smacked my ass. "Sir!"

"That's right. And what am I doing?"

"Fucking my ass," I whispered, and he spanked the side of my asscheek again.

"What? I can't hear you. What am I doing?" he demanded as he gave a harder thrust. I gasped.

"Fucking my ass! Oh God... sir.... You're fucking my ass!"

"That's right, baby. I'm your god now, and I'm going to fuck this ass because, like your cunt... I own it." He finished the last part in a sinister whisper.

Rubbing the side of my face on my pillow, I nodded repeatedly and filed his recurring term of endearment away for later consideration.

Taking full control, he gripped me in the same place he'd smacked and increased his speed. There was nothing that would've prepared me for that feeling. No amount of damn glass plugs could imitate the feel of his thick shaft driving into a place I never would've thought I'd like to be fucked.

"Holy fuck, your tight little ass is gonna make me come already," he ground out.

"Yes, yes, yes," I chanted in time with each thrust because, insanely, I was on the verge of the craziest orgasm I'd ever experienced. It was absolutely *not* what I expected.

When he suddenly reached around and rubbed my clit, I lost my fucking mind. I screamed as my pussy clenched, and he drove deep and held still. Amazingly, I could feel every pulse of his cock as he grunted and shuddered. I wept and had no earthly idea why.

Both breathing heavily, we simply existed in the cocoon of bliss that wrapped around us in our post-euphoric world.

He finally gripped the end of the condom and withdrew, leaving me whimpering. "Don't move," he whispered.

"Fucking hell, I couldn't move if I wanted to right now," I dazedly mumbled into the pillow. His chuckle followed him as I heard him pad to the bathroom. When I heard the water come on, I presumed he disposed of the condom and was rinsing off.

Ass still in the air and throbbing slightly, I waited. I might've even dozed off. At least I had until I felt his tongue lick my wet slit and pierce into my needy pussy. He did that a few times before he left me, and I whined.

"I want you to suck my cock and make me hard so I can fuck your pretty little pussy this time."

"Okay," I gasped. "But I need a little help," I tacked on as I wiggled my fingers.

The man's strength never ceased to amaze me either. He scooped me up at the waist and gently set me on my feet.

"Get on your knees."

I was a dancer and I was graceful, but I'd never done it with my hands behind my back. Initially, I wobbled so he fisted my hair, using it to help balance me. The slight tug on my scalp felt insanely good.

Once I was on my knees, I looked at his thick, veined, hardening shaft, and my mouth actually watered. Some women might say there was nothing pretty about a dick, but I disagreed. I'd never seen one that was more attractive than Adrien's. Or maybe I was biased. Regardless of why, I gently rubbed one cheek along the side of it and then nudged it up with my nose so I could tease the bottom with my tongue. It grew harder as I licked up until my softly parted lips moved across the head, then I repeated the motion down the other side of his length with my other cheek.

I loved the feel of the soft, smooth skin on mine, but I loved the feel of that same length in my mouth even more. To me, sex not only felt amazing—with the right guy—it made me feel powerful. Though I was the one physically on my knees, by skillfully working my mouth over them, I brought them to their metaphorical knees. Sometimes that was a much more advantageous position.

He sucked in a sharp breath when I ran my tongue from base to tip. I swirled around the head to catch the clear bead of his excitement before I sucked the now firm shaft into my mouth with very little pressure. I was licking and sucking on it as if it was a popsicle. It made him tighten the grip he still had on my hair.

"Suck me. But don't let me come. I want to fill that pretty pussy to overflowing."

My hum in response had him groaning, and I couldn't help the smile of satisfaction that pulled at my busy lips. Ever obedient, my cheeks hollowed as I sucked until he held my head gently and began fucking my face. I started to gag a few times, but he always pulled back quickly when that happened. It wasn't long before he jerked my head back by the hair with a grunt. When I released his now pulsing and bobbing cock, I pressed a soft kiss on the tip before licking the escaping drop.

"Jesus, woman."

He helped me to my feet, but instead of guiding me to the bed, he dropped his head to trail his lips along my heated skin. This was not a wild need to taste me. It was as if he was worshipping me inch by inch. Reverently, he drew his short beard over my hypersensitive flesh. By the time he was done, I was gasping, and my inner thighs were soaked.

"Adrien," I groaned, his name like a plea on my lips.

Then he surprised me. As he continued his sweet, slow torture, he released my hands, the silk ribbon falling at our feet. I thought he meant to switch me to the restraints on the bed. Instead, he laid me back and lifted my legs. I scooted myself up to rest my head on his pillow. He continued his ministrations, moving from my ankles up my legs to my stomach as he settled between my legs, then over my breasts, and finally up to my neck.

When he lined the tip of his cock at my entrance, I drew my brows down in confusion. "No restraints?"

"No," he whispered into my ear as he worked himself in and out until he was fully seated. "I need to feel your hands on my skin."

I was a little shocked. Only a handful of times in the past

months had he let me touch him while we fucked. Then his wording sunk in. He hadn't said he *wanted* to feel my hands, he had said he *needed* to feel it.

Something was wrong.

But when he slid his arms under my body to hook his fingers over my shoulders and pulled back until he nearly left my body, I whimpered. Then he drove hard and deep. That's when all organized thought dissipated. There was nothing but the slick friction where we connected on the deepest level and the sound of our ragged breaths. I reveled in the feel of his firm muscles flexing under my hands as I smoothed them over him everywhere I could reach. I rejoiced in the way my pussy perfectly sheathed him and he filled me as if we'd been made for each other.

The weight of his body over mine wasn't suffocating—it was protective, and I loved it.

"I'm so close," I whispered as the familiar pressure began to build. Between his mouth biting, kissing, and sucking along my neck and shoulders and his cock in my pussy, I was almost cross-eyed.

"Give it to me. Come on my cock," he demanded. Like the well-trained thing it had become, my body readily complied.

My nails scored his shoulders and back as I braced myself for the looming impact. Little swirls of ecstasy teased on the periphery of my consciousness. They came closer and closer until bliss exploded from the core of my being. The pressure unleashed and swept through me in heatwaves of utter ebullience. Unable to pinpoint one single detail, everything was simply a collage of color, flashes of the brightest light, and the deep primitive pulse of my orgasm as I fell apart in his arms.

"Fuck." He buried his face in my neck and his breath tickled my neck. His splayed fingers clutched my shoulders as he gave one last powerful thrust. The throbbing of his release set off the aftershocks of my own.

I think I screamed his name, but it might've been unintelligible babble, for all I knew. As the raging seas of pleasure began to calm, I clung to him—desperate to stay afloat and so afraid I would drown in him.

For a moment we lay there, mute and panting. I turned my head to press my lips to the racing pulse in his neck. When I did, he held me tighter. We lay like that until I was starting to doze off. I whimpered when he suddenly withdrew, but I sighed in contentment when he snuggled into my side. His heavy arm wrapped rested over my waist, pinning me in place.

Lazily, I rolled my head to take him in. His cheek was nestled into my shoulder, and he huffed out a contented breath but didn't otherwise move. Still reeling from the intensity of our coupling, I lay there, wanting to trace the fine lines at the corners of his eyes.

With the way his dark lashes fanned his cheeks and his mouth parted slightly, he appeared boyish in sleep. It was a disguise, though—because beneath those closed lids were the mesmerizing eyes of the predator he was named after. In his chest beat the heart of a wild beast—never to be tamed, always elusive.

Sex with him was like that too. Fierce, crazy, intense—but amazing. He was addictive, and that scared me—because something had changed, and I wasn't sure it was the change I hoped for.

Tonight, I couldn't help but feel he was saying goodbye.

NINE

Raptor

"POISON"—ALICE COOPER

I had no idea what caused it, but I suddenly startled and was instantly awake, sitting up in bed. After a few moments, my heart rate slowed to normal, and I dragged my hands down my face. The bedside light on her side of the bed was still on, so I turned to shut it off.

The soft slope of her hips caught my attention, and I took that time in the wee hours of the morning to drink her in.

Silken blonde hair—in a wild disarray thanks to our earlier activities—beckoned my touch. Unable to stop myself, I gently lifted the ends and sifted them through my fingers.

My dick was immediately in the game, but for once, I ignored it. Just like I ignored the fact that she was sleeping in my bed. That was something I'd never done in the past. In all my relationships, they were out of my bed and out of my room after sex. Sure, I was attentive and kind because I appreciated the power they gave me when they entrusted their body to me—but they never stayed.

I'd always known giving in to her would be dangerous. Hell, there was a reason that for years, I'd used every excuse in the book to keep her away. She was under my skin and in my blood. Because of that, it was likely a blessing in disguise that I would soon be leaving. But motherfucker, the thought of her going back to fucking my brothers after I left sent rage boiling through my veins.

Ignoring the thoughts bombarding me, I traced her silhouette with a featherlight touch. Her skin was so soft, and her curves lured me in. She was the most beautiful woman I'd ever met. Even when she was too young for me, I'd thought she was stunning. Intent to enjoy every moment, I spooned her warm body. Slowly, I ran my parted lips over the smooth slope of her shoulder.

"Mmmm," she hummed and wiggled her ass against my already hard length. In a voice husky with sleep, she murmured, "Is that a banana in your pocket or are you happy to see me?"

Before I could hold it back, I chuckled against the back of her arm. Knowing she was awake, I nipped the tender skin where my lips had come to rest. She rolled to face me, and her hand went straight to my erection.

"Oh, baby, it's definitely not a banana," I assured her.

"Oh my, then I'd say you're quite happy to see me."

With a growl, I kicked the sheet to the foot of the bed. Then I proceeded to act as if I was attacking her with bites to every inch I could reach. The sound of her giggles and the way she felt in my arms had me smiling. As I continued my playful torture, she rolled onto her back, and I quickly took advantage of her position to maneuver my way between her legs. The way her heated skin set mine afire should be illegal.

My forearms framed her head, allowing me to drop mine to brush my lips across hers. She rested her hands gently on my rib cage, and I gave an involuntary shudder. We continued to softly rub our parted lips back and forth against each other's, content to breathe each other in and enjoy the light touch. That damn little voice in the back of my head cackled with glee at my unusual behavior.

For a wild and crazy moment, I considered asking her to go with me. But what could I offer her there? Nothing. She had a life here, though my empty chest ached at the thought of her going on with that life without me. Instead of examining those feelings, I shoved them away. Like I did with all of my feelings.

"I'm very happy to see you," I murmured before nuzzling her nose with mine. Her lips parted, and little puffs of her breathe tickled my cheek as I dragged my mouth lightly along her jaw until I was at her ear. After a nip at the lobe, I whispered, "I need to be inside you."

She tilted her hips in invitation, causing my length to slide through her wet folds.

Fuck, she was going to be the death of me.

All it took was the slightest adjustment of my hips, and the tip of my cock was notched in the slippery opening of her pussy. The way she lifted her legs and wrapped them around my ass told me she wanted more. Instead of giving her what we both wanted, I teased her by only making her shallow little forays into her until she clenched around me, and then I'd pull out. Rarely one to be playful or gentle in bed, I was a bit shocked that it was so natural with her.

"Adrien, stop teasing. I need you," she whimpered and dug her heels into my ass.

Instead of running for my life like I should've done, I impaled her on my hard and desperate cock. It was instant Nirvana.

"Fuck, you feel good," I ground out as I fought to keep the beast inside at bay. It warred with the voice whispering that I could always ask her to leave with me. Except that was foolish thinking. I wasn't an idiot—I'd seen the look in her eyes when she didn't think I knew she was staring at me. I'd felt the difference in her body, her sounds, her touch.

That's why you wanted her hands free tonight, the voice taunted, and I shoved it away.

I couldn't let a woman get in my head like that. Not again. No matter the crazy connection we had. She would want more than I could ever give her. My heart had been destroyed years ago, and there was no salvaging even a piece of it. But I could make her feel good, and I could ruin any future encounters she might have.

Ignoring the voice that told me I was a dumb fuck, I gave her as much of myself as I could. I worshipped at the altar of her body, and when we both eventually shattered, we held each other as if just holding each other could change everything.

But it changed nothing.

The next day, I practically stumbled out of my room after I don't know how many rounds between her legs.

"Hey, VP," a prospect called out from behind the bar where he was drying glasses. "I'm supposed to tell you that Prez wants to talk to you."

I nodded. "Give me a shot of Jameson first."

He immediately complied and set the glass in front of me. I tossed it back, and with a nod, pushed off and made my way back to his office.

Sitting there with his head bowed, he was going over the paperwork in front of him. I chuckled at the reading glasses he wore. He glanced up and shot me a glare. Knowing exactly what I found funny, he whipped the glasses off and stuffed them in his top drawer.

"Don't be embarrassed that you need readers," I teased.

He grunted. "Fuck you. You'll be there soon."

I dropped into the chair in front of his desk and kicked my feet out. "What's up?"

He leaned back and studied me for a moment.

I cocked a brow.

"Jameson called early this morning." Jameson was the national P and was based out of the national chapter in New Orleans.

"Yeah. And?"

"I took the liberty of feeling him out about the chapter in Dallas."

At those words, tension zipped down my spine. I leaned my elbows on my thighs and breathed into my hands. Then I dropped them and met his gaze. Unsure of what I wanted, I didn't know what to say.

"Nationals had church to discuss it, and they think it's a great idea to re-establish our footing in the Dallas area. He also likes the idea of a seasoned chapter fairly close by to guide the new chapter down in Cedar Creek. Rumor has it, they would benefit from our type of guidance." He sat there, quietly watching and reading my tells.

I breathed deep, puffed out my cheeks as I exhaled, and sat back. "Shit."

It was all I could say because I wasn't expecting this so soon.

"You said you need to be down there in about a month or less, and it wasn't like I could drag my feet on this. That's now only a few weeks away. He knows you weren't aware I was asking. He assured me they wouldn't hold it against you if you didn't want it—but he hopes you do."

"I'm not sure I'm cut out to do the job," I admitted as I absently scratched my short beard. I also didn't like the reminder that my time here was coming to an end.

"Bullshit."

"Fuck, this is fast."

"So is your move."

"Touché."

"Look, bro, I hate to lose you, but I'd be a fool not to see your natural leadership ability. The brothers all respect and look up to you. You're steady and capable. In my opinion, you'd be great down there. Hell, if I wasn't able to fulfill my obligations as president, I'd want you in my place."

"I'd be starting at ground zero for club-owned businesses. There's nothing left there."

He tapped his desktop rapidly as he chewed on his lip and tugged the piercing with his teeth. "What if we opened a second location for biological cleaning services? Dallas is a big area. You know damn well they have a need. And Jameson said they had leased out the strip club and the car washes, but they expire in a little over a few months. It would give you time to build up the chapter before you took over, and in the meantime, you'd have the income from the cleaning business."

"Can I think about it for a few days?" I nervously plucked at the frayed spot on the thigh of my worn jeans as my knee bounced.

"Of course, but they have a short window for notification of the tenants. Contract says they have to give them a ninety-day notice that the lease won't be renewed," he replied with a wince.

"Fuck."

"You said you don't want to leave the club. You also said the idea of going nomad didn't appeal to you. I think this is a good solution. Hell, I think it's a great situation. The only thing better would be you staying here," he argued as he thoughtfully stroked his beard.

"Yeah," I hesitantly admitted.

"You still want some time?"

I sighed. "No. I suppose it's not often that a chapter gets dropped into a man's lap."

"You're right about that. And Jameson said they would be offering probationary patches for anyone that you choose. No prospecting for your first five members. Now, a probationary patch can be taken away a lot easier if they fuck up, but I trust you'll choose solid brothers."

We stared each other down for a few minutes before I finally nodded. "Okay."

A grin lit his face, and I couldn't help but reciprocate. "Brother, I hate to see you go, but I think this is an amazing opportunity, and you're going to rock the fuck out of it. Now, what about Cookie?"

My smile fell. "What about her?"

"You taking her with you?"

"No." Without waiting for further comments, I got to my feet and walked out. The entire way through the clubhouse, I didn't acknowledge a single soul. When I burst through the back door into the cold late February air, I fought for composure. Thanks to the ice storm that came through last night, our bikes were grounded in the shop next to the clubhouse.

So, I chose the next best thing. Not giving a fuck about the cold but needing to feel the wind on my face, I dropped my clothes into a lawn chair and shifted into my hawk. Then, spreading my wings, I burst into the air.

As the miles went by with no destination in mind, I tried to chase thoughts of her out of my head. That was about as hopeless as separating myself from my hawk. Because my hawk and I were one and the same.

I'd have to tell her I was leaving soon. Avoiding the topic by fucking nonstop wasn't going to work forever—though I'd enjoy the hell out of it. Eventually she'd hear someone talking.

I wasn't looking forward to that conversation one fucking bit.

And I didn't want to think about why.

TEN

Sage ("Cookie")

"HUMAN NATURE"—POP EVIL

Something was definitely going on. Adrien had been acting strange for over a week. Ever since he came back from Texas, he'd been moody, and unless we were fucking, he had a permanent scowl on his face. Anytime the brothers were talking, they shut up when I walked in.

"Hey, Cookie, I, uh, need to take the night off," Foxy announced from the doorway of my office, drawing my attention from my thoughts and the schedule I was working on.

"Tonight? Right now?" I asked flabbergasted. She would be the second girl to call off tonight.

"Yeah, I, uh, got a phone call that my babysitter is sick. You know how it is," she explained with a nervous laugh at the end.

No, I didn't, and I ignored the pang that thought caused. It was unlikely I ever would have children. Because I'd never want them raised knowing their mother was fucked up, a freaking nympho, and danced part time as a stripper—which it looked like I'd be doing tonight.

Studying her with a narrowed gaze, I asked, "Are you high?"

I didn't give two shits about what the girls did in their free time, but if they were onstage, there was a strict no drugs, no alcohol rule. We didn't need someone falling off the stage and hurting themselves or a customer. Things like that brought publicity to the business and in turn, the club. Then again, she was telling me she wasn't performing. But still—was the entire world off?

"Ms. Cookie, you know I don't do drugs. I'd never risk losing Ricky." That I did know about her, and I felt bad for asking. The thing was, her behavior was suspect, so I had a right to ask. And though she was young, she was a good girl who had ended up in bad circumstances. Poor thing had gotten pregnant in high school, her boyfriend bailed, and her parents kicked out of her home. *That* was something I could commiserate with.

"Okay, fine. Thanks for letting me know," I acknowledged with a wane smile. The minute she was out the door, I dropped my head in my hands. Except rubbing my temples didn't help my headache one damn bit.

"Rough night already?"

I looked up to find Blade standing in the space Foxy had vacated.

"You on tonight?" I asked, leaning back in my chair. The club always had at least one member that was around each night as a deterrent and to step in if some idiot still acted up and the bouncers couldn't handle shit alone.

"Yeah," he replied before he pushed off the doorframe and made his way around the desk. He started to rub my shoulders and I winced. "I passed Foxy as I was coming in. She didn't look ready to get onstage in an hour."

"That would be because she cancelled. On top of Denim, that makes me short two dancers. Porsche can cover a dance, as will Buffy, and I know Ruby will always be open to picking up a slot or two, but I'm still short."

"Can you call anyone else in?"

"I already tried after Denim called in."

"So, I guess that means you're up?"

"Yeah," I said with a sigh. Then he hit the knot of tension. "Mmm, oh God, right there."

He chuckled. "You sound like—"

Blade got no further in his thought before Raptor blasted into my office. He froze when he saw Blade's hands on my shoulders, then his gaze narrowed. His jaw muscle ticked, and his eyes flashed. He might as well have spoken his jealousy aloud because he certainly didn't have a poker face. I also wasn't stupid—I knew damn well he thought I was in my office fucking someone.

The mix of relief and anger in his expression might've been comical if it hadn't cut me to the bone. I'd made a promise to him, and he obviously didn't think much of me if he thought I'd broken it. I fought tears because I. Didn't. Cry.

Blade put his hands up in a passive gesture. "Bro, it's definitely not like that."

"I didn't say anything," Raptor snarled.

Blade chuckled. "You didn't need to." Then with a shit-eating grin on his face, he kept his hands up as he moved around my desk and toward a very angry Raptor. When he stepped past his brother, I was pretty sure Raptor growled at him. Blade cast one last glance my way, complete with a wink, and gave me a wave before he was on his way up front.

"What the fuck was he doing in here?" Raptor grumbled, eyes narrowed, and nostrils flared.

"Alexa play 'You Don't Own Me' by Saygrace." With a sardonic lift of a brow, I crossed my arms and pursed my lips, waiting for the first few notes to play.

Though he tried to maintain his grouchy countenance, he covered his mouth to hide the way the corner of his lips fought to tip up. He finally dropped it and gave in. His long legs ate up the distance between us. He held his hand out in invitation.

Making him sweat it for a minute, I glanced at it, then up to his spellbinding eyes. Finally, unable to refuse his touch, I placed my smaller hand in his. He gently tugged me up until he held me plastered to his body.

"I'm sorry, baby. Seeing another man's hands on you does something to me." His contrite words had me fighting my own smile—and I chose not to address the use of the endearment *again*. I'd be a liar if I said it didn't make my insides gooey. It also confused the shit out of me. One minute he was pushing me away and ensuring I knew what we had was "just fucking," and the next he was calling me "baby" and essentially admitting to the jealousy I already recognized.

"Hmpf. Why did you come by? Blade is assigned here tonight."

"I needed to see you." His hands slipped under my short skirt and cupped my bare ass.

"Is that right? Well, here I am. I don't have much time—I need to get ready."

"Ready for what?" That wicked grin along with the way he rubbed his hard cock against my clit left my thong soaked. The layers of fabric between us might as well be nothing. Hazel eyes darkening, his gaze dropped to my lips.

"I had two dancers call out, so I'm onstage tonight."

Those flashing eyes squinted as he stared. Displeasure rolled off of him in waves.

"Don't. That was never part of our bargain. If you keep getting all jealous like this, you could give a girl the wrong idea." I said it in jest, but that hopeful little part of my spirit that hadn't died waited with bated breath.

"Fine." It was his turn to cock a brow. "But you're gonna bend over this desk, and I'm going to fuck you until you scream. I'm going to come in this pussy so that all those assholes out there will see it and know you've been fucked and fucked well. I want every single one of them to know you're mine."

In truth, maybe I should've been pissed and insulted, but fuck if that didn't turn me on. It was also something I'd agreed to in the beginning—anytime, anywhere.

"Bend over," he whispered as he moved to stand behind me.

Without question, I did as he instructed. Palms flat on the desktop, eyes closed, I waited with trembling legs. The sound of his belt buckle clanking came from behind me before one thick finger tested to see if I was ready. "Goddamn, you're wet already."

The smooth heated skin over his shaft felt amazing as he teasingly rubbed it over my ass cheeks. He pulled the center of my thong to the side and poked at my opening with the head of his thick cock. I gasped when he pushed in halfway. My eyes popped open, and I realized the door was still open.

"Adrien!" I hissed. "The door!"

He leaned over me and whispered, "I hope they all hear. Now, tits on the desk."

Turned on by the borderline exhibitionism, I leaked onto my inner thighs. It clearly didn't escape his notice because he chuckled darkly and drove deep.

"Now hang on," he warned before he made good on his words.

The song ended and the lights went out on the stage. Sweat trickled down my back, and my chest rapidly rose and fell as I rested on my knees, legs spread, head bowed. The whooping and cheering echoed with the last of the song vibrating through my ears.

The second I lifted my gaze, it locked with the heated hazel one of the man who had become entirely too important to me. His smirk told me that he knew exactly what I was doing with the pose at the end of my performance. I'd impulsively added it when I saw him enter the main part of the club a third of the way through my performance.

I got to my feet and bowed, the nipple tassels swinging lightly with my movements. Raptor pushed off the wall and started cutting through the crowd toward the back hall.

As I went behind the curtain, Solomon handed me my red silk robe as I passed Sugar on her way out to the stage. "Thanks, hon," I told him. He smiled and winked.

"You know I got you, babe," he replied. I took no offense to him calling me babe since he called all of the girls that. He was our newest bouncer, and with his bulky size, shaved head, and massive muscles, he cut a formidable figure. The girls loved him because he was so respectful. That he was also the handsomest-as-hell guy didn't hurt—well, a close second to one broody biker, anyway.

By the time I got back to the dressing room, I was already taking my chandelier earrings off. Raptor was waiting at the station I was using for the night. He seemed preoccupied and didn't notice me walk in. For a moment, I stared at him. He sent my heart into a skittering flutter as I watched him chewing on his lip.

"You didn't need to stick around all night," I finally said as I moved his way, heels clicking on the concrete floor of the dressing room.

His heated gaze practically burned me as the corner of his perfect mouth kicked up. "I know."

With a small smile, I shook my head and dropped the earrings on the dressing table. With his silent attention locked on me instead of the other two women sitting topless at their stations where they were getting ready, I was conscious of my every movement.

"You done for the night?"

"Yeah," I replied as I twisted my hair and clipped it up. The waves cascaded down to my shoulders, giving me a Grecian goddess look.

He reached out, grabbing one of my curls and smoothing it between his thumb and fingers. "Need a ride?"

I paused and met his gaze in the mirror. Then I turned in my seat, resting my elbow on the table and propping my chin on my hand. "You offering?"

"I have my bike. Thought maybe we could go for a ride before we went back to the clubhouse."

He picked at his thumbnail and wouldn't look at me as he waited for an answer. Yep, something was definitely wrong. This had all started after his return from Texas. My stomach dropped when I wondered if he was tired of me and preparing me for it—the end.

"Sure," I replied, pasting a falsely bright grin on my face.

"Cool. I'll meet you out back." He leaned over and looked me in the eyes. For half a heartbeat, something passed through his that stole my breath. It was quickly replaced with a blankness that was so unlike him that I swallowed hard and dropped my gaze to his boots. Using two of his fingers, he touched the underside of my chin and tipped my head up to bring my attention back to him. He leaned in and brushed a featherlight kiss over my lips, then he righted himself and walked out of the room.

He left me so confused, my head spun.

Anxious, I quickly took my hair back down, braided it, and changed. Wearing skinny jeans, tall heeled boots, and a bustier top with a short leather jacket, I waved to the girls and left the dressing room.

"Solomon, I'm taking off. Can you help Frankie and Scott close up tonight?"

"Of course, Miss Cookie."

I chuckled. "Thank you. You can call me Sage, you know."

"Sorry, it's habit, since that's how you introduced yourself when you hired me. Have a good night then, Miss Sage," he offered with a jaunty wave and a grin. I blew him a kiss and went out the back door.

The night air was crisp, and I questioned my decision. At least I did until I saw Raptor sitting on his bike, one foot resting up on the floorboard while he messed with his phone. He turned his head my direction when the door closed. The cocky little smirk he gave me had my heart fluttering again.

"Damn. I'm not sure if you look better now or when you were on the stage earlier." He pocketed his phone and handed me a helmet decorated with pink dragonflies. I looked at it curiously. "I borrowed it from Loralei. You two look like you're about the same size."

Relief hit me when he confirmed it wasn't bought for some other chick or a community helmet for all the other women he had ride on his bike.

As if he'd read my mind, he chuckled. "Just so you know, I'm picky about who rides back there."

"I wasn't even thinking about that," I lied.

His dark eyes twinkled in the glow of the parking lot light, but he didn't say anything until I put the helmet on. "Looks good on you."

"I look like a bobblehead doll."

"You look sexy as fuck."

"Aww, you're probably just saying that to get in my pants."

His smile fell into an evil grin as he reached out to cup me between my legs. "No, I get to fuck you whenever I want—because you're my good little girl."

My pussy clenched at his words, and I was sure I'd be soaked by the time we made it back to the clubhouse. I'd never understand how this particular man held so much power over me. He was a craving that was never fulfilled, an itch that was never fully scratched. I seriously believed I might never get enough of him.

"Get on."

When I rested a hand on his shoulder for balance, he reached up and grabbed my wrist. Looking over his shoulder, he murmured, "I felt that, by the way."

Shooting him my own wicked glance, I replied, "Good. Hopefully you'll be feeling a lot more real soon."

His laughter made me feel all gooey inside, and that wasn't me. I wasn't one to experience all the lovey-dovey bullshit, so this was new for me. And truth be told, it was a little frightening because it only helped confirm that I was in deep. If he was preparing to end shit, I was fucked. I snapped the visor down in an effort to put up some kind of barrier. He fastened a neoprene face mask on, covering too much of his handsome face for my liking. With a sigh, I told myself I wouldn't be able to see him during the ride anyway.

The second I was settled behind him, he met my gaze in one of his mirrors. Inhaling, I savored the hint of his cologne mixed with the cold air, exhaust, and leather that crept up under the helmet to tease my senses. He gave me a thumbs-up with a questioning glance, to which I nodded. Once my arms were wrapped around his waist, he stood the bike up, started it, and eased back on the throttle.

As soon as we were off the gravel and had both wheels on the blacktop, he took off. I tightened my arms, and he reached down to give me a comforting pat. The cold air made me tunnel my hands under his cut for warmth. When he dropped his hand and reached back to stroke my calf, I moaned, thankful he couldn't hear me. Everything about the ride was setting off alarm bells—I was heading down the path of no return at high speed and with no brakes.

He took the long way around to get back to the clubhouse, and I simply enjoyed the ride and being close to him. Once we were back, he parked in the smaller building where they all left their bikes in the winter months. It was now mid-March, but the weather was so unpredictable.

"Enjoy the ride?" he asked once we were both off the bike. His voice was raspy, and I noticed his nose was pink despite the face mask he'd worn.

He sucked in a hissing breath when I cradled his face with my cold hands. Reflexively, he gripped my wrists so tightly, it made me wince. He immediately eased his hold. "Sorry, baby—you just startled me is all."

Bringing my wrists to his mouth in turn, he kissed my wildly racing pulse. A squeak of surprise passed my lips when he grabbed my ass and hauled me up. I wrapped my legs tightly around his waist as he ate up the ground with his long stride. We passed Phoenix's truck with his trailer on the back, but at the time, I was too preoccupied with the heated kisses I was receiving to notice.

That night we didn't sleep. He pulled out all the stops. First, he used two spreader bars and fastened them so my arms were in the air and hooked to the ceiling, and my feet were spread wide. Slowly, he circled me, trailing an erotic path over my skin with his hands until I was trembling with need. When he stopped behind me, I heard drawers being opened.

I jumped when he reached around me from behind. His dark chuckle had giddy anticipation firing off butterflies in my stomach. The way he cupped my tits should've been my clue, but when he clipped the nipple clamps on, I sucked in a startled breath.

Next came the slippery satin of the cloth he used to cover my eyes. Unable to see, my other senses took over trying to track his movements and prepare for what was next.

"Adrien," I whispered when he gathered my hair and laid it over my shoulder. His touch was so light that it tickled and teased with each movement. That was nothing compared to when he held the weight of my tits in his hands and tugged on the clamps while he kissed my shoulders with his heated lips and nipped all the areas he knew drove me crazy.

"Fuck, you're beautiful," he whispered against the skin left damp by his mouth.

I shivered, and my head fell forward, but it shot up again when he pulled out the next item. The familiar feel of the butter-soft leather strands trailing my flesh made me sigh, as I knew what was coming.

It was with equal parts excitement and dread that I pleaded, "Adrien, please—I need you."

"Shh, my good girl has to wait patiently. Are you not my good girl?"

As I squeezed my eyes tightly closed behind the mask, I whimpered. The soft strands landed on my ass, and my muscles tightened at the mild sting.

"Or have you been bad? Is that it? Do you need to be punished for your impatience?"

A cry came unbidden from deep in my chest when the flogger hit my already sensitive breasts. He taunted and teased as he whipped my ass until, despite the mild level of the flogger, the globes of my ass burned. My hips greedily drove forward as I sought the friction of his hand when he dipped his fingers in my slit.

"That's my girl," he crooned before he dropped to his knees and held my hips in his capable hands. Soft kisses rained on my stomach and slowly lower. So slowly that I was crying with the need to feel him—any part of him—against my wet pussy lips and aching clit.

He spent what felt like hours playing with me—bringing me to the precipice before backing off and starting over. By the time he let me come, I was a screaming, shuddering mess.

"Fucking beautiful," he murmured against my inner thigh.

Then he lifted the mask, unfastened the cuffs attached to the bars, and gently carried me to the bed. Tenderly, he smoothed my skin with my favorite lotion. Reverently, he kissed the areas he'd spent the most time on with the flogger, periodically dropping kisses on my heated body.

With his massive form pressed to mine, he leaned over me to place a soft and sultry kiss to my lips. I threaded my fingers through his thick hair and cradled his head as I took as much as I gave.

Where before he played, building my body up for the explosion, this time he was full of passion. It was intense and deep. As the kiss deepened, he drew my hands to the side of my head where he laced his fingers with mine. When he entered my body, we locked together and held on for dear life—it was like the world settled and balanced. Though I knew it was unlikely, I would almost think he was making love to me.

When he finally tensed and came inside me, I arched up as I shattered and cried out his name.

The first wisps of morning light shone through the blinds when we finally collapsed onto the mussed bed. I was boneless, lying on the wrinkled sheet with him curved around me—his arm heavy and protective over my chest.

I must've dozed off, because the sound of a zipper startled me awake. It took less than a blink for me to realize I was cold and very much alone in the bed. A rustle made me sit up, and my eyes fell on him as he stuffed something into one of his saddlebag inserts and zipped it closed.

"You have a run?" I was confused because he hadn't mentioned leaving. He may not ever tell me details of club business, but he usually told me when he was going out of town.

"No." His voice was soft and low. I swore I heard a hint of regret in that single word. Ignoring my nudity, I scrambled out of the bed.

"Raptor? What's going on?" I asked as I approached him, bare feet padding on the cool concrete floor.

My heart froze in my chest when he caught me by the upper arms and stopped me before I could get up against him. His cut was folded on the desk next to the bags. I noticed the short threads that formed the shape of his bottom rocker that was no longer sewn on.

"Raptor?" Panic began to claw at my throat. I struggled to free myself, but he was much too strong.

"I'm leaving." He wouldn't make eye contact.

"Leaving?" I shouted in shock. "What do you mean *leaving?* Like, you have a cross-country run?"

That time, when I fought to get free, he released me and didn't make an attempt to help me when, off balance, I stumbled.

Hands clenched in fists at his sides, he swallowed hard, and his dark gaze finally locked on mine. He lifted his chin slightly. "No, Cookie. I'm leaving for good."

I paused. He never called me Cookie in here anymore.

"What?" I was flabbergasted. This had to be a horrible dream. Why wouldn't he have said something to me sooner? I had no time to pack. Then I froze, running over what he said. He called me Cookie.

He had no intention of taking me with him.

My brows pulled in and my lower lip trembled. "You're leaving me behind."

It wasn't a question; it was a statement of understanding. He rubbed his inked hand over his mouth uncomfortably. I was sure

I was crumbling from the inside out and any moment I would fall to pieces.

"Look, it's best that this happened now. It was fun while it lasted. Right? Just think… you can go back to all the other cocks you enjoyed before me. It's not like you'll be lonely."

Each bitter word was a knife to my soul. Inflicting pain. Drawing blood. Reminding me that he had warned me—I was the one that ignored that warning when what we had seemed like so much more.

Didn't he know that he was the only one I wanted now? Clutching my chest, trying to hold the pieces of my heart together by sheer will, I staggered. I would've gone with him.

He grabbed his sunglasses and covered up the eyes I'd grown to love, especially when they were on me. Then he took his cut and walked out of the room and my life.

PART II

ELEVEN

Raptor

"TUESDAY'S GONE"—METALLICA

Two Months later….

Sweat ran down my back as I powered the chainsaw through the tough cedar trunk. I hated cedars. They fucked with my sinuses, but they also spread like crazy. With the Dallas property sitting empty for so many years, they'd gone wild.

I'd talked with Nationals, and we were set to close on the land over the winter. It would give me time to get things rolling.

Over the years, I'd saved up quite a bit. I wanted to purchase an acre of the RBMC land to build a house on it. That had sparked an idea that had quickly taken root in my mind.

Initially, the idea to build cabins on the acreage was a way to keep everyone close. We'd had a few run-ins with a local motorcycle club that was trying to establish a foothold in the area. It was time to show them that this was our territory. To do that, we'd need a safe place to land.

The more I thought about it, the more I liked the idea of a housing area for us back behind the clubhouse. To create our own neighborhood—much like the Ankeny chapter had done by slowly taking over the neighborhood they lived in. Except in this instance, we would be starting it exclusively for us.

There would be several smaller cabins for visiting brothers and their families—kind of like those tiny homes everyone was so fond of nowadays. Then I had plans to add on to the clubhouse to allow for a bigger common area and more rooms. Those would be designated for single members, visitors, and long-term club girls. They would also be open to widows who needed a place to stay, because unfortunately shit happened. I prayed we wouldn't need them for that, but I wanted it to be an option.

It would take time, but I was happy for the work that kept my mind off of Sage. With each day that passed, my regret grew.

"Jesus, it's hot as fuck today, and it's only ten in the morning," Tigger grumbled. He'd been a nomad while he was working the oil fields and had agreed to join me when the announcement went out that we were reopening Dallas.

Torque rested the tip of his lopper on the ground and pulled off his ball cap. He wiped the sweat from his face and settled the hat back on his head. He'd been with one of our central Texas support clubs and was friends with Gator. Phoenix had met him once when he'd had a job down here. Phoenix and Gator vouched for him—which was good enough for me—for a probationary patch. Time would tell if he could hang with the big dogs.

"Quit grumblin'. You're sounding like a whiny little bitch," One Short shot back. He and Gator had both come back after laying down their colors under the old regime that supported Rancid.

They refused to support the way the chapter was going, but they did shit the right way, so they weren't out bad. Gator had also been friends with Torque for years, going back to when they grew up down by Houston.

"Fuck you. I didn't stop working, I was just making a statement," Tigger snapped.

"For fuck's sake. Both of you shut it," Phoenix growled.

"It's easy for you to talk. You could live in a fucking oven and be fine with it," One Short mumbled as he wiped sweat off his forehead. He was a good guy and a solid brother but had his cantankerous moments for sure.

"Look, it's only gonna get hotter, so best we get what we can before lunchtime. We're all hot, and we're all sweating our asses off. We're wasting time bickering," I reasoned. They made faces but kept their mouths shut and went back to work.

"And that's why you're a good president, Raptor," Gator quietly said after he walked back from the truck with several bottles of water. He handed one to me, then called out, "Heads up."

Torque, One Short, Tigger, and Phoenix each caught one. We dropped our chainsaws, axes, and loppers as we all chugged the cold water. I dumped the last little bit of it on my head. Then I shoved my hair out of my face and looked at how much we'd accomplish in a few short hours. After crumpling the bottle and recapping it, I tossed it into the bed of the truck.

Losing steam, I resumed my task by dragging the felled cedar to the trailer and then heaved it up onto it. "Hey! Let's go dump the trailer and call it a day."

I didn't need to tell them twice. They all grabbed up the last of the smaller trees they were cutting down and tossed them on top of the heap. Once the tools and equipment were in the bed, I closed the tailgate.

"Shotgun!" both Phoenix and Torque called out.

One Short flipped them off. "Y'all are dicks."

"But we're the only dicks you love, right? Or do you swing that way? If you do, it's all cool, but just wanted to get it straight," Phoenix teased.

Gator and I shook our heads and got in the front seats, me behind the wheel.

"Hell no, I'm not into dicks…. Well, I like my own just fine, and so do the ladies." He grinned as he stroked his salt-and-pepper beard. Tigger, Torque, and Phoenix groaned.

"Get your asses in the truck unless you want to stay out here to work some more!" I called out as I hit the ignition button. The truck roared to life, and they all scrambled into the backseat, One Short sandwiched in the middle.

Tigger hopped on the utility quad to follow us.

"This is bullshit. I have fucking cleavage, for fuck's sake!" One Short bitched and everyone chuckled. Well, everyone but him—he sat there scowling.

We drove to the back of the property and unloaded the trailer into the pit we'd dug. Once we were out of the burn ban, we'd torch all the trees and brush in the hole. Once it was full, we could cover it up if we needed to.

I grabbed the bottom of my T-shirt and wiped my face. "Let's go back to the clubhouse and have some lunch."

"And a cold beer," added Gator.

"Amen," One Short chimed in.

That evening we decided to take a ride into Dallas—just to show our presence. Sloane and Niara had gone down to Austin to hang out with their friend, Sutton. She had landed herself an NHL player and worked in the ER with another player's wife and one of the members of the Demented Sons chapter down that way. That meant Phoenix was rolling solo.

I'd never met Styx, or any of the other guys, but Snow had assured me they were stand-up guys, and if I ever needed a hand, I should reach out to them.

We made several stops at a couple of restaurants and a few bars. In one establishment, we were given a wide berth, but for the most part, people were curious but not hostile.

The entire night, we slowly made our way back to the compound. Our last stop was a little bar not far from the land the clubhouse sat on.

"Wanna give me a ride?"

Beer inches from my mouth, I paused and glanced down at the hand touching my cut. Then I finished the drink I'd started to take as I stared into the brown eyes of the chick asking the question. Never breaking eye contact, I set my bottle down and turned my bar stool in her direction. She had squeezed her way in between me and Phoenix, and he cocked a brow at me over her shoulder. I ignored him.

"Sweetheart, no one rides on my bike but me," I told her. I wasn't a dick about it, but I really didn't want her or any other woman behind me. There was only one… nope. Not going there.

She bit her bottom lip and dragged it through her teeth as she gazed up at me. Her coyness really didn't do dick shit for me. Neither did the rack she had on display. Speaking of dicks, mine, which usually had a mind of its own, didn't so much as stir. Sweet Jesus, I was officially broken.

"Hey, sugar, I can take you for a spin," One Short said from the stool at the end.

For a moment she looked disappointed, but she quickly changed her mind when she saw him pull out his wad of cash to throw a twenty on the bar. She gave me a little smile and a finger wave before she strutted over to One Short with her ass swaying provocatively. Part of my brain screamed at me to call her back, but I really had no interest.

When One Short palmed her ass, pulling her short skirt up until it was practically hanging out, Gator and Torque leaned back and ogled her. I shook my head. Phoenix snickered.

"You know, no one would blame you if you fucked her. Or any chick, for that matter," Phoenix murmured from my right.

"You know I don't do one-night stands." Ignoring his dropped-jaw stare, I snatched my bottle and downed the remainder. Then I held it aloft and motioned with it to the bartender. With a smile, she finished mixing the drinks she was working on and set them in front of the two guys at the opposite side of the bar.

Then she snagged another bottle from the cooler, popped the top, and set it in front of me. I handed her enough cash for the beer and a generous tip. The corner of her mouth lifted, and she rested on her elbows on the bar. "I've never seen you in here before."

"Nope."

"You new around here, or just passing through?"

Taking in her blonde hair piled up in a crazy-ass bun, soft green eyes lined in coal black, and facial piercings, I tried to determine if she was hitting on me. If so, I was gonna shoot her down too. In a way she reminded me of Sage, but not enough to want to fuck her. She cocked her head and arched a pierced brow as she blew a slow bubble in her gum. Then she caught it between her blood-red lips and popped it.

Remaining silent, I took a slow drink. Then I set the bottle down and leaned toward her. "Not new, but we're definitely back." I didn't plan to elaborate.

"I'm not sure why, but I like you. Maybe because you and your boys haven't stirred up any trouble in my bar tonight. I'm Fallon, by the way." She smirked before blowing another bubble. The front entrance opened, and all of us glanced over to see who it was. I liked this place because the way the bar was situated, we could sit on one side of the U and see the door.

Which was perfect for times like this.

Several guys in cuts walked in and stared right at us. We stared back.

"Fuck," I heard the bartender mutter. She pushed off the bar and stuck her tip in the chest pocket of her bib-overall shorts.

"They trouble?" I asked her, not taking my attention from them for a second. They still hadn't moved, but I could see them talking amongst themselves. Then one broke off and left.

"Always," she muttered as she rounded the bar, told a skinny guy with a dark goatee to hold down the fort, and stomped over to them. For a second I thought she was going to kick the guy standing in the center with her black red-laced Doc Martens. Standing arms akimbo, she confronted them. I stood up, and my brothers did the same. The girl was a trip, and I'd be damned if she was gonna get fucked with while we were there.

These dickwads may not know it yet, but this was our area again.

The guy in the middle with shaggy hair scowled as they appeared to have cross words. He cut his eyes at me, and I lifted my chin.

It was impossible to hear what was being said over the jukebox, but anger poured off of him. He jabbed a finger in our direction, and I'd had enough. While I may not trust women relationship-wise, I wasn't going to watch a guy treat one like shit.

"Uh-oh," Phoenix drawled out, but he quickly had my back.

"Is there a problem?" I asked, sensing the rest of my brothers closing in. They stopped once they flanked me. We were outnumbered, but I wasn't worried about that. I'd had worse odds.

"Yeah. You're in our bar," the tall dude with shaggy brown hair snapped. Lazily checking out his cut, I noticed the "SAA" tab. The club he belonged to was on there too. I'd never heard of them, and I didn't see a diamond thirteen on it either.

"This is *not* your bar," Fallon ground out through gritted teeth.

Adrenaline had already kicked in as I opened and closed my fists. His eyes narrowed as he glanced at them. Then he returned his attention to Fallon.

"It was my grandfather's bar too," he practically growled. The muscle in his jaw jumped as he clenched his teeth.

"Yeah? Well then maybe you should've stepped up to the plate when he died." Fallon's angrily whispered words were like physical lashes to the guy if the way he flinched was an indicator.

I silently tried to figure out the dynamics of the situation as I stood there, coiled for attack. I didn't want to trash Fallon's bar, but I also didn't want her to get hurt.

One of the other guys finally opened his mouth. "So these assholes come back, and you kick us out?" The dude had shifty eyes and a twitch. If I had to guess, I'd say he was high or tweaking like a motherfucker.

"Shut up, Benny." Fallon pointed at him but kept her gaze locked on the SAA.

Benny lunged for Fallon as he snarled, "You bitch!"

Everyone sprang into action as one. My fists hit his chest with a bruising thump at the same time that the SAA whipped his arm out over Benny's abdomen to hold him back. They were suddenly at each other's throats.

"That's my fucking sister!" he shouted in Benny's face.

Well, damn. This little prick is her brother. I wondered why Fallon was running the bar and he wasn't.

"Mav!" she cried out as she grabbed his elbow of the arm he'd drawn back to punch Benny. "Not in the bar, please!"

Towering over all of them, I took the power position. "Outside. Now."

The rest of their chapter members glanced at each other nervously. Pussies. I had to give it to them, though—they did as they were told, but if that had been us, we wouldn't have been ordered around. Once we were all outside, most of them scattered. I heard bikes start up behind the building, then gravel flew as they tore out of the lot.

Fallon rushed outside, but I held my hand up, gesturing her to stay back. Torque gently grabbed her arm to keep her safely out of the way. Thankfully, she didn't fight him.

"One Short, go back in and watch the door. No one comes out without you warning us."

"No problem, boss man," One Short replied as he went back inside.

"Jesus. What a bunch of worthless fucks," Torque muttered.

Tigger silently watched everything, missing nothing.

Benny didn't know when to shut his mouth, though. He lunged at Mav and double-fisted him in the chest—much like I'd done to him, but with less effect.

"You're supposed to have your brother's back! Me and you against the world, remember? That's been our bar since before we got patched!"

"Enough!" Mav finally roared. This was their fight, so I stayed out of it, unless they involved Fallon again. "It was *never* the club's bar. We hung out there—it was our bar as we grew up, sure. But shit like this always starts with somebody in the chapter everywhere we go. Now, not only are we divided, but we have these fuckers to deal with too."

"Hey, now," I warned.

Benny turned on me.

"Who the fuck are you? If you wouldn't have been in there, none of this would've happened. This is *our* town!" Benny spat.

I took on a stance that would allow me to drill the little asshole if he said one more fucking word.

"Shut the fuck up, Benny." Mav ran a hand through his disheveled hair as his eyes darted to me. At least one of them had some sense. Benny gritted his teeth.

Tired of the little fuck's mouth, I stepped closer. "Do you see this patch right here?" I tapped my 1 percent diamond. "This says we outrank you and your motherfucking club. I will end you. Do you hear me?" Though my words were calm, my tone was deadly.

His eyes wild, Benny wouldn't stop. "Fuck. You. When the Demon Runners hear that you guys are here, they are going to annihilate you."

I cast a glance at Gator and found him watching Benny with a narrow-eyed gaze.

"Benny, for Christ's sake, that's enough. Do you not see that we're pretty well outnumbered? The brotherhood that you were so quick to preach fucking bailed on us. They left us to fend for ourselves, and your dumb ass is going to get us killed," Mav practically snarled at his "brother."

When Mav turned to me, he put his back to Benny. Everything happened so fast from there as we all jumped into motion. Benny sucker punched Mav in the back of the head, bringing him to his knees.

Fallon, who had previously been quiet next to Torque, cried out and lunged for her brother. Benny drew back to hit Mav again, and he elbowed her in the face, causing her to stumble. Torque caught Fallon and immediately passed her off to Gator, then drilled Benny in the jaw. He dropped to the ground like a sack of potatoes, then groaned as he held his face and rolled around a bit.

Mav recovered and went after Torque.

The click of the hammer on Tigger's revolver echoed through the small parking lot. As he held it up to Mav's temple. "I think that's enough. Don't let misplaced loyalty lead you down a path you can't return from."

Phoenix had drawn on Benny.

"You okay, sweetheart?" I called out without taking my eyes off Benny and Mav.

"I'm fine," Fallon grumbled.

"Get your asses out of here," I ordered. Benny scurried off like the little rat he was. Mav stood tall, and I narrowed my gaze at him. His jaw worked and he glanced briefly at the ground, then at me before landing his gaze on his sister.

"I'm sorry, sis. I tried to talk them out of coming here. They weren't having it. But if you think we're trouble, we got nothing on these guys." He motioned at me and my brothers. Then his attention was back on me. "You might want to watch your backs. The Demon Runners are ruthless. That's all I'm gonna say."

"Well, guess what?" I leaned in closer to him, then whispered, "We're worse."

TWELVE

Sage ("Cookie")

"BITCH"—MEREDITH BROOKS

The past two and a half months since Raptor left had been miserable. I'd cried every night until I was sick to my stomach. I'd tried to go back to the way my life was before Raptor, but I wasn't having a lot of success.

"Sage, why don't you call him? I gave you his new number," Blade muttered as I sat at the end of the bar, eating a heaping plate of nachos. Willow and I ended up having to dance again on short notice, so I hadn't had time to have dinner. By the time we got back to the clubhouse, I was exhausted and famished.

Porsche had flaked on us and left town without notice. Nilla did the same. Then Denim had quit showing up for work. I had to let her go, even though I hated to. She was a good dancer, but she had called in sick for the past two weeks, and when I offered to have Angel come by to check on her, she hung up on me. Her apartment was vacated the next day. I had no clue where she went.

"And if he had wanted to talk to me, he would've given it to me himself."

Blade was silent at my retort. He knew I was right. "For some stupid reason he's being stubborn," he finally said.

I threw the chip in my hand onto the plate and spun to face him. "Stop. He's probably quite happy and reconciled with his ex. The last thing he wants is me reaching out to him."

Pissed, I hopped off the stool, leaving Blade and my food behind. Trying to make a statement to Blade, I wrapped my arms around Sabre and settled my chin on his shoulder. He stiffened, and I assumed he didn't know it was me.

"Hey, handsome. I thought for sure you'd come see me at some point during all the BS this week. Surely, you're not babysitting twenty-four hours a day," I murmured into his ear. He'd been assigned to watch over the young woman that Venom had taken on because she had amnesia.

"Yeah, I, uh, probably won't be by to see you, Cookie," he apologized as he winced. Voodoo snorted next to him and sipped his beer. I gave them both a calculating glance. Something was definitely up with them.

Soleil, the amnesia girl, slammed her empty bottle down next to Sabre, and he jumped. Curious, I watched everything unfold.

"Sorry. Didn't mean to startle you," Soleil said sarcastically with a sneer, then told the prospect behind the bar that she needed three more beers and a few waters. She seemed to ignore Sabre after that. She collected the bottles and sauntered back to the ol' ladies. Sabre watched her with puppy dog eyes and practically pouted as she passed out the drinks and sat back down. Everything clicked into place.

"Ohhh, it's like that," I observed with a chuckle as I took my arms off of him and claimed the stool next to him. It was actually a relief because I wasn't in the mood. "Buffy isn't going to like that," I teased.

Buffy was one of our dancers that he hooked up with on occasion. She would've given her left tit to be an ol' lady, but that wasn't going to happen.

It had nothing to do with her being one of the dancers and a club girl, but it *was* because she was a manipulative bitch. I wasn't stupid and neither were the guys. They kept her around because she was a damn good dancer who pulled in a lot of customers, which meant money for the club.

"Tough shit," he muttered.

I pursed my lips as I studied him. *We shall see.*

Squirrel came up behind us and looped an arm around me, then nuzzled into my neck. I reached back and scraped my nails slowly through his tousled dark hair, but nothing was the same as it used to be. My interest in any of the guys was nil. I hadn't slept with anyone since Raptor left, but Blade came into my room enough that I think everyone assumed I had moved on to him. Little did they know.

"What's like that?" Squirrel asked as he teasingly bit my ear.

"Sabre here got bit by the lovebug. Another one bites the dust," I explained and chuckled, though I wanted to pull away from his attention.

"Yeah, because—" Squirrel began.

Sabre glared at him, and he snapped his mouth closed. I may be a lot of things, but I was no fucking idiot. I cocked a brow and gave him a questioning smirk, daring him to deny it. Little did he know, his actions gave him away.

"Does she know you're pining for her?" I softly asked as if he had already confided in me.

"Drop it," he snapped.

My eyes went wide at the uncharacteristic response. And that cemented it. He was head over heels for her. Looked like they were going to have a lot to work through.

"Suit yourself," I whispered with a shrug and led Squirrel off toward my room. The entire way, my skin prickled uncomfortably where he touched me. I paused with my hand on my doorknob.

"Everything okay?" he quietly asked.

After pasting a fake-as-fuck smile on, I turned to face him. "It's just been a long-ass week. Raincheck?"

He cocked his head, and it was my turn to be studied. Then he broke the silence. "Is it true? You and Blade? I'm only curious because prior to Raptor, you were a helluva lot of fun. Since he left, you've been spending a lot of time exclusively with Blade. I'm not gonna poach if you're with him."

"Um, yeah, well, sort of," I falsely concurred before apologizing. "I'm sorry, honey. It's nothing personal."

Squirrel shook his head with a smirk. He was cute as hell, and secretly a sweetheart, but he wasn't dumb. "Did I really just get the 'it's not you, it's me' line?"

We both chuckled. He kissed my forehead before he told me, "It's all good, babe. If shit goes south with Blade, you let me know."

I kissed him on the cheek. "Thanks, Squirrel."

I let myself into my room, and as I leaned against the closed door, I cried into my hands.

"What a fucking shit show," I muttered as I got dressed to go out onstage. After Honey, who was supposed to be the third dancer of the night, didn't show up, I had to pull something out of my ass. Again.

"I can move my set up and go out now to buy you a little time," Willow offered.

"It's fine, hon." I quickly dusted some body glitter over the swell of my tits, then jerked the tiny half shirt on. Thanks to all the feelings I'd been eating lately, the buttons practically screamed. "Christ."

"Girl, you know you look hot," Willow kindly offered. The girl was too damn sweet for her own good, and she had no business dancing, but she was amazing at it. She usually waitressed, but she filled in as needed on the stage. Tonight was one of those nights.

"I look fucking fat, but thanks for the words of encouragement." I kissed her cheek and rushed out onto the stage. Twix came off stage right as I got there. Sweat glistened on her skin and she shot me an encouraging smile. I had time to shove my robe into Solomon's hand before I burst through the opening in the curtains.

The intro of "Schoolgirls" by Straight Wicked started and the stage lights came on. This was an old favorite of mine, and thankfully the routine was easy enough that I could do it without rehearsing.

About halfway through my performance, I got closer to the edge of the stage as I crawled toward the VIP table situated there. That's where the businessmen that were in town for the weekend and weren't on the wifey's leash usually sat. They always tipped big and wrote it off as a business expense to hide it from their wives and girlfriends.

When I rose to my knees and slowly unbuttoned the tight white top, the big guy sitting in the center watched me. I'd seen him there before. Pasty-white, pockmarked skin topped by thinning brown hair could have described any number of men, but the birthmark on his jaw was rather unique. He steadily watched my every move while I danced in front of their table. The thick-lipped smile he gave me was creepy as fuck, but I wouldn't be doing any private dances, so I wrote his interest off. By the time I was down to my thong and pasties, I'd essentially forgotten about him.

I wrapped up the song and exited the stage. Edgar would gather up my costume and tips and disperse the money evenly amongst the other girls. I didn't need it. Solomon handed me my robe and took Willow's. He'd been assigned backstage tonight and was expected to be prepared to go out there if anyone tried to get up onstage with the girls. Edgar was on the floor to cover that angle. One of the RBMC members or prospects worked the floor along with Edgar—or Roger on the weekends. They rotated positions nightly. Because of them, we rarely had problems at Royal Heaven, and for that I was always thankful.

"Thanks, Solomon," I said with a breathless smile as I stepped from backstage into the back hall. Because I wasn't expecting anyone to be there, I slammed straight into a broad chest and almost gagged on the heavy cologne.

"Sorry," I wheezed and moved to go around him, but he caught my arms in a bruising grip and grinned. Startled, I looked up and saw it was the creepy guy from the table.

"Mr. Horacio would like a word with you," he informed me in an oil-smooth tone.

I glanced over my shoulder to call for Solomon, but the door had closed behind me. An uneasy feeling washed over me when I tried to break his hold and found he was unmovable.

Trying another tactic, I smiled. "I'm sorry, but I don't know a Mr. Horacio. Also, this is an employees-only hall, so you shouldn't be back here—and I don't do private dances. If he speaks to Frankie or Scott at the bar, they can see who else is available."

Obviously, that wasn't what he wanted to hear, because he leaned his face until his nose practically touched mine. "I don't think you hear real well. Let me repeat myself this one time. Mr.

Horacio wants to see you. Now." He let go of one arm so I could walk beside him.

To get to the private rooms, we'd have to go to the end of the hall nearest the bar, then enter a side door where I'd be visible. We would also need a keycard to get in there, and guests only got one of those if they had paid a hefty sum—in advance. Some of the girls made extra money doing whatever they were willing to do in there, with a cut going to Royal Heaven. At one time I had been one of those girls, so I understood. That was a long time ago, though.

"Look, I don't know who you think you are, but—" He spun faster than I would've ever guessed someone his size could move. He had me against the wall by my neck. Using my nails, I clawed at his meaty fingers, but they didn't budge. Darting my gaze around to look for the camera angles, I realized we were likely in the one dead zone we had—the one that Facet was supposed to fix next week.

Just fucking great.

"When we enter that hall, you smile for the cameras. If I think for one second you're trying to be slick, I'll snap your fucking neck. Got it?"

Wide-eyed with fear and unable to breathe, I nodded.

"Good," he crooned as he patted my cheek twice. "Let's go."

He pulled a card out of his pocket and scanned the reader. The mechanical clicks signaled that the locks had been disengaged. *Shit.*

As we passed the first camera, I stared at it as long as I dared, hoping either Scott or Frankie would see me.

We reached the fourth room, and Meathead pushed me inside, then stood with his arms crossed. A darkly beautiful man sat on the couch with his arms spread over the back. As pretty as he was to look at, his eyes seemed dead.

"Mr. Walters, you may leave," the man instructed. Mr. Meathead-Walters didn't like that very much. When he started to protest, the man I assumed was this Mr. Horacio shot him a narrow-eyed glare, and Meathead instantly became contrite. With a reluctant nod, he stepped out into the hall and closed the door. "I apologize for my associate's crude treatment. That's unacceptable, and I can assure you he will be dealt with."

"Okay, but what makes you any better? I don't give private performances—of any kind. Yet here I am. Against my will."

"I think we got off on the wrong foot." He gave me a smile that didn't come close to reaching his cold gaze. He motioned to the small riser before him. "My name is George Horacio. If you'll have a seat, I have a business proposition for you."

"Look, I already told you—"

"Sit!" he snapped.

Startled, I dropped to my ass where he indicated.

He straightened his tie and shook off the burst of aggression. "Now as I was saying… I've recently opened a gentlemen's club, and I'm looking for talent that meets my expectation levels. I was here several weeks ago and had the pleasure of watching your performance. I understand you also do much of the day-to-day management of both the dancers and the facility. I'm prepared to make you a generous offer to work for me."

Was this guy for real? Did he not know who owned Royal Heaven? And how the hell did he know what I did besides dance for Royal Heaven?

"Well, I'm flattered, but I must respectfully decline." Arms crossed, I stared him down.

"Dear me," he mocked as he pressed a splayed hand to his chest. Then he dryly drawled, "Maybe I wasn't clear. I'll expect you to be at this address at the time written on the back. If you don't show up? Then you won't like what happens. I don't like being disobeyed, and I always get what I want. Oh, and for now, let's keep this agreement between us. Things never work out well for people who run their mouths. Understand?" He held out a business card.

I looked at it but didn't touch it.

One dark sculpted brow lifted, and he smirked. "I like your feistiness. You might become my new favorite, my pet."

When he stood to his full height, he stuck the card in my robe pocket. He brushed the back of his hand intentionally across my nipple before he trailed the backs of his fingers from my cleavage and up my neck where he then gently brushed them against the spot that his asshole "associate" had grabbed. Using the side of his index finger, he lifted my chin to stare me down. Boldly, I met his gaze. Finally, he stepped back, straightened his tie again, and smoothed his tailored jacket. Without another word, he left.

The second the door closed, my adrenaline tanked, and I began to tremble. What the actual fuck just happened? Now that I was alone, none of it seemed real. Except a glance in the mirrored wall showed bruises already forming on my neck. With a shaking hand, I reached into my pocket to find that there was indeed a card in there, so I hadn't imagined that either.

Unsure if I could manage walking in my heels, I kicked them off. Then I bent over to place my head against my knees. The door burst open, and I shrieked. Blade dropped to a crouch in front of me and held my head to make me look him in the eye. His bright blue eyes were full of worry as he searched mine.

Blade was a good-looking guy, and he'd always protected me. There were times over the years that I wished I could look at him as more than a brother, but there was no way.

"What the hell are you doing in here? Facet called me and said he saw you going through the door with some guy. We all know you don't do that anymore. What the fuck, Sage?"

"I-I-I...." It was all I could get out because my numb lips refused to move right, and my tongue seemed frozen in place.

His nostrils flared and his jaw clenched as he stared at my neck.

"Did he do that?" The question wasn't asked by my friend. The man asking me that question was the cold-blooded killer that had saved me years ago.

Afraid he would go after them and get hurt, I desperately clutched his cut. Eyes wild, I shook my head.

"Shh," he said, realizing I was going through mild shock.

He wrapped his thick arms around me, and I clung to him. It was impossible to stop from wishing it were a different set of tattooed arms that held me. Except I knew damn well that was never going to happen again, and I burst into tears.

"So, you're saying this guy expects you to be at this address on Wednesday night?" Venom asked me as he tapped the edge of the card on the table in an agitated staccato. His brows drew together as he thoughtfully stroked his beard and waited for my reply.

Blade had contacted the chapter once I was able to tell him what happened. He helped me get dressed because my entire body was still shaking. I was a tough cookie, that's where I'd gotten my nickname from—not from what one might think. Things didn't usually fuck with my head. Lately, I was *all* kinds of fucked in the head. I knew my problem was that I hadn't been myself since Raptor left.

Slowly, I was falling apart—crumbling at my very foundation.

"Yes," I evenly replied, thanks to the shot of whiskey Blade had poured down my throat when we got back. It didn't hurt that when he went into the chapel to inform everyone what was going on, I had a few more.

"She's not going," Blade immediately insisted. "I'll go, and George Horacio and his goon will end up as fish bait in the lake after I'm done playing with them."

Venom cocked a brow at him. Even I knew he was out of line for his outburst.

"We only have a few days before she needs to be there. Facet, I want everything you can give us on this George Horacio," Venom instructed, but Facet was ahead of him.

"Already on it." Facet clicked a few buttons, and the little box by his computer lit up. Then his screen was projected onto the wall—or what I assumed was his screen, as I could see the cursor moving along with random weird symbols and letters that were being typed on the black background at lightning-fast speed. Suddenly a life-sized image of George Horacio was there. My hands shook so bad from simply looking at that image that I had to clasp them together.

"Damn, Facet. I'm surprised you're actually going away from killing trees every five minutes," Ghost teased. I was confused as I had no clue what they were talking about. Facet glared at him and flipped him off.

"This is running straight through a direct connection from my laptop to the projector. No Bluetooth streaming or chances for someone to intercept a signal. I digress…. George is a self-made millionaire with clear connections to the cartel," Facet explained.

Blade and I stiffened. After that, I didn't hear the rest through the whooshing in my ears.

"Cookie?" Hawk asked, and I jumped because I hadn't noticed him approach. I blinked several times. "Hey, baby girl, are you still with us?"

Another blink and I nodded.

"Cookie, we're not letting you go over there, and we're not going to let anything happen to you. We're going to look into it, and we're going to double up on security at the club. You'll be watched and kept safe. You're one of ours," Venom announced, and the rest of the brothers nodded.

Venom's words meant a lot, and I had to blink again, but that time it was to get rid of the tears. In truth, I was barely above the club whores. Though they never treated me like that. Maybe because I'd never chased a patch. A man was the last thing I wanted—for more than sex, anyway.

Until Raptor… but that didn't matter anymore.

"Okay," I whispered, feeling suddenly dizzy and nauseous.

I got to my feet and flattened my hand to the wall as I attempted to flee the room before I embarrassed myself. Thankfully, my room was closer than the community bathrooms, and I stumbled in. No way I was making it further. I grabbed my trash can by the door, held my hair back, and proceeded to lose my lunch.

A touch to my back mid hurl had me trying to push whoever it was away.

"It's me," Blade murmured near my ear. He took my hair from my unsteady hand and attempted to soothe me the way he used to when we were kids. The way we'd come full circle drew a sob from the depths of my soul. He pulled me into his broad chest and held me. For years, I believed I had full control of my life. It took one tattooed, broody man to yank those beliefs out from under me.

Now I couldn't touch him, but he still had a death grip on me. So much so that sometimes I couldn't breathe for it. "I think you were right," I whispered with my head bowed and my eyes closed.

"About what?" he murmured as he gently stroked my hair away from my face.

Unable to hold back any longer, I burst into tears—and hated myself for my weakness. He pulled me into his embrace, my cheek to his chest.

With my ear against him, his heartbeat strong and steady, he comforted me. I clutched his cut. "I wish it had been you," I choked out.

"Huh?" He paused with one hand palming my head.

Flattening my hands over his chest, I pushed back to look him in the eye. "You said I've been in love with Raptor for years. You were right. But I wish it could've been you because now I love a man that doesn't want me—one who walked away without looking back."

His lids fell as he sighed, and guilt hit me. It was a dumb thing to say. Because I knew damn well he didn't see me like that either, and now I'd made things awkward.

"I didn't mean it like that, Finley. I'm sorry, that wasn't fair of me to say. You're my best friend and the only person who's truly been there for me. I only meant life would've been easier if we both saw the other differently. There will never be enough thanks in the world for everything you've done for me—but thank you." I gave him a pouting smile and cupped his cheek, smoothing his beard. "You're going to make some girl a really good ol' man."

He huffed a laugh. "You of all people should know that's not true. Every single one of my brothers are fucked up in their own ways, but none of them hold a candle to the twisted, dark recesses of *my* mind. No woman wants to deal with that shit."

"You'd be surprised. What about Eliska? What's up with that?" I searched his gaze to ensure he was being honest.

"Not a damn thing." His reply held a tight finality, so I decided to drop it—for now.

Suddenly exhausted after being up all night, I stood up and held my hand out to help Blade up. Once on his feet, he softly brushed his thumb under my eye and gave me a crooked grin. "You look like you could use a nap."

After a deep inhale, I let it out in a big whoosh and nodded. "I think that's the best idea you've had in a while."

He tucked me in like he'd done when I was a young girl. By the time the door clicked shut, I was already drifting off.

True to their word, the guys went to check out George Horacio's place—The Diamond Palace. I stayed back at the clubhouse and didn't make an appearance. That might've been the wrong choice because I was being fucked with, and I was pretty sure it was them. Phone calls in the middle of the night with whispered threats, feeling like I was being watched, then feeling as if I was being followed.

When Blade told me their undercover assignment had been productive, I wasn't expecting what they discovered. I was shocked to learn that several of my girls who had quit, were working there. It was worse than that, though. To hear that they were obviously using drugs broke my heart. We had no idea if all of the girls were working there, since the guys had only been there that one night.

Their hypothesis was that George Horacio was trying to run Royal Heaven out of business by crippling us from the inside out. All but a handful of our dancers had either quit or disappeared. The latest no show was Fiona. Except her defection had been different as I'd discovered when she called me that night to tell me someone had slashed all four of her tires.

"Cookie, I'm scared. Who would do that?"

"I have no idea, doll. You need a ride?" I was so desperate for dancers at that point, I would've bought her a new fucking car if it got her to come into work. I didn't want to have to dance that night—I wasn't feeling good, and I was beat.

"Please? I can't afford to miss my shift. Especially now that I have four new tires to pay for," she groaned. She didn't live too far from the club, but far enough that I didn't want her to have to walk. I could've called her a Lyft, but I was afraid she might flake on me and back out of coming in.

I was already grabbing my keys. "I'm on my way. See you in a few. Watch for me."

"Thank you so much, Cookie. You're a lifesaver." She ended the call, and I shoved my cell phone in my back pocket.

"Roger! I'm running to pick up Fiona." After the bullshit with George and his asshole lackey, we now had someone sitting in the back hall.

"Wait! Let me walk you out!" He rushed over and followed me out the back door.

"Roger, I'm good—my car is right here." I laughed, but he scowled. I'd parked by the backdoor because I had to unload the case of bottled water I'd bought, and I wasn't feeling up to carrying it across the back lot.

"I was told no one goes out without an escort—that includes you."

"Well, I'm safely in my car," I teased as I climbed in. I made a production of locking my doors, and he shook his head at me, the corner of his mouth lifting. As I backed out, he went inside, and I raced over to Fiona's apartment complex.

Within five minutes, I pulled in next to her car and winced at the four flats. I glanced up at the second floor of the side her apartment door would be on, but she wasn't coming out yet. Impatient, I thrummed my fingers on the center console.

Using my hands-free button, I called her. It rang several times, then went to voicemail. "Come on," I muttered and called again. Several attempts yielded the same result.

"Fuck." Irritated, I put the car in Park and shut it off. Grumbling the whole way, I rushed up the stairs. When I reached her door, I went to knock twice, but after the first one, her door popped open a crack.

"Fiona!" I called into the small apartment as I pushed the door open further.

What I saw had me hyperventilating. Most people would've called the cops—not me, despite how panicked I was. The way I grew up and lived, you didn't call the cops. Instead, I called Blade. Nervous, and unsure if someone was still in the apartment, I stepped out onto the landing but pulled the door most of the way closed with the edge of my forearm. No one needed to see that.

"What's up, babe?" he asked without a hello.

"You guys need to get over to Fiona's. Like, now. And bring the Mystery Machine." That was what I called their biological cleanup van. That alone told him it was bad.

"On my way. Let me grab Ghost and Squirrel. Are you alone?"

"Yes."

"Goddammit, Sage. Get your ass back to your car and lock the fucking doors. Do not hang up. Understand?" he demanded as I heard him moving around.

"Y-y-yes," I stuttered, already moving. The reality of what I'd seen was sinking in, and my adrenaline was in overdrive. As I hurried down the stairs, I stumbled and gripped the banister for support. When I hit the landing, I saw a man standing under a tree across the road. He was wearing a dark shirt and jeans. If his eyes hadn't been so intent on me, I might not have noticed what looked like splatters on his arms and neck.

I stopped short and stared. Then the corners of his mouth lifted, and he gestured like he was tipping a hat to me.

With a hand that was covered in something dark.

"Cookie!" Blade snapped, causing me to blink and the man to casually turn and walk away.

"I think he was across the street," I whispered.

"Get. In. Your. Fucking. Car!" he shouted as I heard boots running on hard footing, then slamming doors and squealing tires. It pulled me out of my paralysis, and I ran to my car and practically ripped the door off the hinges before I dove in and hit the lock button.

Hyperaware, I sat there glancing from my rear view to the side mirrors. With each shaky breath I took, I expected the man to be at my window. Every little sound had me jumping.

I'd never in my life forget what I saw in that apartment.

Fiona had been sitting on the couch with her throat cut open and blood everywhere. A paper was stabbed to her chest. In words written in blood, it said, "**NO ONE TELLS ME NO, COOKIE.**"

THIRTEEN

Raptor

"HOPELESS"—BREAKING BENJAMIN

The visit with my mother had left me melancholy. It brought back memories of carefree times as a child on the ranch. On the heels of those memories were the ones of my young love with Falina. I had questioned my inability to see her for what she was—a power-hungry gold digger who was only after our position in the clan and the money my family had amassed. Was I blind to what I thought was love? Had I been an idiot? Too rebellious? Likely, all of the above.

Being at the ranch was also another reminder that I would never see my grandfather again. That hurt every time I thought about it. I wasted so many years being stubborn. If only I'd gone home sooner.

All in all, my morning had left me agitated and in need of a good fuck to clear my head. Unfortunately, I hadn't had time to so much as jack my dick, let alone fuck. Then there was the fact that I couldn't get Sage out of my goddamn head.

At every turn, I remembered the way she tasted… the soft but intoxicating scent of her perfume… the way she felt in my arms.

Tonight was the first night we'd all been able to chill at the clubhouse. Phoenix and Gator were playing a game of pool while Phoenix's ol' lady, Sloane, was sitting at one of the tables with her friend, Niara. They were polishing off their third bottle of wine and giggling like little girls.

That sound reminded me of the sexy husky laugh I'd taken for granted and now missed. If I was honest, I'd been off and unsettled since arriving in Texas. Not even setting my hawk free to fly to his heart's content helped. It was making me a cantankerous asshole.

One Short and Torque were arguing about the comparisons between a Camaro and a Challenger as Rooster and Banshee laughed at them. "You two are both idiots because nuthin' beats a Harley," Rooster inserted into their argument.

He and Banshee were from our Roanoke, VA chapter. Rooster had actually helped saved Phoenix's old lady back when he was a prospect—definitely some fucked-up shit. But now he's fully patched, thanks in part to his actions.

They had arrived last night from Virginia because Rooster used to have family here. He was back to get the estate settled, and Banshee had ridden along. Torque's son was with his grandmother, so we had no kiddos for the night.

I'd been happy to have Torque join us. His dad had passed away, and his mom moved back to Dallas where she grew up. Torque had been with one of our support clubs down by Austin and had planned to go nomad to be near his mom, since there were no chapters of his club up here. Gator recommended him when he found out I was reopening the Dallas chapter. Torque had been stoked.

One Short and Gator had been two of the members who had left when things had gone downhill years ago. They were happy to come back, and I was damn lucky to have them.

We were working on a few probationaries that Torque introduced us to. One was his cousin's boyfriend, the other two were guys he'd worked with in the oil fields years ago. So far, they seemed like strong possibilities, but I had Facet looking into their backgrounds first. I needed to find a tech guru. Not that it was necessary, but it came in handy. Supposedly one of the oil field guys was crazy smart with computers, but we would have to see.

Staring at my phone, I pulled up the number I'd saved though I shouldn't have. Then I typed out a text.

Me: I think about you more than I should. Every morning when I wake up, I want to get in my truck and drive up there, pack your shit, and bring you down here

"Too much after all this time." I backspaced and tried again.

Me: Just wanted to check on you

"Stupid," I muttered and deleted that one too.

Me: I miss you

"You about ready for another one, handsome?" Lola—the one club girl we had—asked. She had arrived with Gator, and I told her if there was no drama, she could stay. She'd been keeping the single brothers happy, so I didn't have an issue with her.

"I'm still good. Thanks." I closed the texting app without sending the message and put my phone in my pocket.

The door to the clubhouse slammed, and the room went silent. Whiskey halfway to my mouth, I quickly turned on my barstool to see who it was. My brows shot to my hairline when I saw the young kid glaring around the room. Phoenix stood casually with his hands resting on top of his pool cue, but I knew his sharp gaze was glued on the ballsy kid.

"Can we help you, son?" Gator asked as he pulled his cigarette from his lips and stubbed it out. He set his pool cue down and crossed his arms. Though the kid was tall, Gator was still an imposing figure.

"Maybe," the boy replied. "Are you Adrien Krow?"

Now he really had my attention.

"Why?" Gator asked, suspicion obvious in his body language and narrowed gaze.

"Are you Adrien?"

"What do you want with him?" Gator asked with a narrowed gaze. My heart pumped adrenaline through my veins as I left my seat, my body twitched with anticipation, and my hawk was intently studying the young man. The brothers that stood between me and the interloper parted and cautiously measured the situation.

"I'm Adrien Krow," I announced with a daring lift of my brow. "Who are you and how the fuck did you get in here?"

The kid lifted his chin defiantly, though I caught the flash of uncertainty in his hazel eyes. Something about him seemed familiar, but I couldn't quite place him. He reached for his back pocket, but before he could finish the movement, there were no less than five pistols pointed his way. That's when the fear hit his gaze, and he stiffened.

He slowly lifted his free hand in the air in a show of surrender. Then he cautiously brought the other hand out that had a folded and wrinkled paper. His Adam's apple bobbed as he swallowed and raised that arm up too.

Everyone was on alert despite the boy's age. Sick, twisted people used kids in shitty ways. I wouldn't put it past any of our enemies to use a kid to do their dirty work. Since reopening the Dallas chapter, we'd acquired several. There were more than a handful of people that didn't like the fact that we were back on what they now considered their turf.

"Check him," I told Phoenix who was our SAA.

Tension filled the room as Phoenix patted the kid down to his ankles and back up, then plucked the paper out of his raised hand and passed it off to Gator. Satisfied, he stepped back and gave me a nod. "He's clean."

"Of course, I am," the kids grumbled. "Idiot."

The last word was softly muttered, but I still heard him, and obviously so did Phoenix. Phoenix postured threateningly, and I'd give the boy credit—he didn't so much as flinch. Gator was looking at the paper he'd taken from the boy's hand. A frown marred his brow.

"You didn't answer my question, kid."

"I'm not a damn kid," he muttered with a dark scowl.

"Really. Then do tell…. How old are you are?" I dared with a mocking cock of my head.

"Seventeen."

"Now, how about that name—unless you'd rather I just call you kid."

"Sam," he replied clearly with that defiant lift of his chin. Something in the movement sent tingles of awareness down my spine.

It wasn't long before disbelief hit me like a wrecking ball to the chest. I searched his features, looking for the little boy I remembered, but didn't find much that could definitively confirm my suspicions. It couldn't be—and if it was, then why? And why now? Yet another study of the young man standing defiantly before me discovered enough of the Krow characteristics that I could see how he easily could've thought he was my son.

Thanks to my momentary inability to breathe, I actually saw

black dots. Needing to collect myself, I spun on my heel and sucked in a ragged, stuttering breath.

"Give me a few, then bring him back," I instructed Phoenix before I stormed to my office and jerked the drawer open. After a rummaging through all the crap I needed to go through, I pulled out the silver flask, removed the stopper, and took a few hearty swallows. My brain was absolute mush. There was no way—was there?

Gator entered my office. "Bro—"

I held up a hand. "I need a minute."

He respectfully nodded and leaned back against the wall. The entire time, he watched and waited.

"P, are you okay?" Phoenix finally asked, drawing my attention to where he leaned on my doorframe. It was still weird to hear myself called that. Every time someone said P or Prez, I looked for Venom. Hell, maybe I actually wished for him because I sure as hell never wanted this. Except it was better this than not being able to be a Royal Bastard at all.

"Yeah," I replied before taking another swallow, then capped the flask and tossed it back in the drawer. "Bring him back."

Phoenix nodded, then his booted steps echoed down the short hall. The clubhouse here on the outskirts of Dallas wasn't as big as the one we'd had in Ankeny, but it still boasted quite a bit of land. At the moment it was overrun with fucking cedars, but we were slowly clearing them. On top of trying to find a few prospects. And get our reacquired businesses off the ground.

We were busy as fuck.

Now I had more shit to deal with.

"Raptor, I think you need to look at this before that boy comes back here." Gator was obviously tired of waiting. I nodded and held out my hand. He gave me the folded page, and I opened it. Memories assaulted me as the birth certificate in my hands became hard to read thanks to my shaking. Not that I needed to see the words—I recognized it. What I couldn't believe was what it still said.

"Prez, you ready?" Phoenix asked. I lifted my gaze and nodded. For a moment Phoenix tried to gauge the truth in my nonverbal reply. Then he reached out into the hall and dragged the boy—Sam—into the room.

"Sit down," I told Sam and the boy immediately complied, but he crossed his arms and stared up at me with anger and defiance.

"Not happy to see me, *Dad?*" Sam said with a sneer. The pain was akin to a knife being shoved through my ribs and twisted in my heart.

"Sam, I'm not your father," I finally told him, a chill skating through every cell of my body. The words were as much a dagger to the heart as they had been when Falina had said them almost twelve years ago.

He frowned and appeared confused, but he still tried to hang onto that attitude that he'd barged in with. "That's bullshit. So, you're telling me that's a lie?"

"Yes."

"You're the liar!" he shouted as he shot out of the chair. "It's not bad enough that you didn't want us, but now you have to lie? Your name is right there!"

I palmed my face, using my thumb and middle finger to massage my temples. This shit was giving me a headache. "I wanted you more than you'll ever know," I whispered behind my hand, then dropped it to my side. I debated how much to tell him. He was seventeen, but he was still a child. One who had obviously already been lied to and hurt more than was remotely fair.

Fucking Falina.

"Does your mom know you're here?" I asked him.

"My mom doesn't give a shit about what I'm doing. She's on

a vacation with her husband down in Brazil. Then they're going to wherever his new business venture is supposed to be. Supposedly they will be back sometime at the end of next week. But hell if I know when they're really coming back."

"Where's your brother?" I asked with a frown, wondering myself why it mattered to me.

He huffed. "At home with the nanny."

"Nanny? He's...." I had to do the math. "Almost fifteen."

"So?"

Exasperated at the level of hostility emanating from the lanky kid, I shook my head and heaved a sigh. "You believed I was your father, so you barged into my clubhouse. Did you come here to be belligerent, or did you have a purpose?"

"I didn't really have a plan," he reluctantly admitted.

I tried again. "Okay, how about why? After all these years, why did you choose now to seek me out?"

He swallowed hard and glanced away.

I patiently waited. One thing he didn't know about me was that I could wait him out. I could guarantee he'd crack before I would.

His jaw worked and the muscle jumped as he clenched his teeth. His arms remained crossed. Everything in his body language screamed closed off and stubborn. Good thing I was more stubborn than he could ever dream of being. As I figured it would, the silence stretched for about five minutes before he exhaled loudly, and his gaze found mine.

"We need your help. Except I thought you were our father. I thought...."

My senses were on high alert. They may not be my children, but I was protective of any kids. Still, I said nothing, but I cocked a brow to show I was listening. Sam's eyes flickered, and the gold seemed to be more prevalent than the green or brown. It was unnerving because I always thought he looked like me when he was little. I loved those boys so much that the day Falina told me they weren't mine, I practically drank myself into a coma.

He glanced around the room, nervously catching the steady gazes of Gator and Phoenix. He studied them carefully, then he brought his attention back to me. I searched that gaze for the signs I already knew I'd find. "Um, you might want your friends to leave."

"We have no secrets here, Sam." That was a big fat fucking lie. I hadn't told any of my brothers I was a shifter until we had come down here to help Voodoo. The situation we found ourselves in necessitated reaching out to my clan. Fuck, that first flight in years had been awkward at the start, but my inner hawk had quickly soared, reveling in the wind once again ruffling its feathers, rejoicing as he stretched his wings.

Sam inhaled deeply and let it out in a rough exhale before he stood up. That's when I saw his bare feet. I couldn't believe I'd missed that earlier. He paced for a minute as he tugged at his dark hair. My hawk was practically vibrating inside me.

"Sam," I quietly prompted as my heart seemed to quit beating. "Did you fly here?"

He stopped. With wide eyes, he turned to face me. Nervously, he chewed on his lip.

"This is a safe place," I promised.

The second he whipped his shirt over his head, my suspicions were confirmed, and my heart took off at a gallop. Though I should've known—he was of an age that he would've experienced his first molt. The glare he shot me when he grabbed the edge of his shorts might've been comical in any other circumstances.

"I'm not flashing my dick in front of everyone," he grumbled.

Phoenix snorted, and Gator chuckled before he asked, "Boy, you think you got somethin' we don't?"

145

Sam flipped him off, and it made me chuckle. He was more like me than... fuck. He wasn't mine at all, and the reminder hurt.

He dropped to a crouch and braced himself on his fingertips and a knee. A shudder shook his entire body before his back arched and his body seemed to contort. His skin went from a pale tan to brown before it rippled and twitched. The screech that filled the air was one I knew well. It was a blend of agony and primal power.

Credit to my brothers because they didn't bat an eye when a boy became a hawk before their eyes. Of course, my family had somewhat prepared them. I chuckled at the board shorts that hung off the tail and legs. He cocked his head and looked down before he shook his body and hopped until the shorts pooled under his feet.

He flapped his wings in irritation, and I spotted one generation of flight feathers, that told me he was in his first adult plumage. That, along with the lack of multiple tail bands, told me he was in the start of his second year—which was everything I would expect. What I *wasn't* prepared for were the markings on the juvenile bird in my office—the deep V of dark feathers were only present in the Krow bloodlines.

Heart hammering and head spinning, I swallowed down the bile of further betrayal. For Sam to have those markings, it meant that his father was one of my family members. It had to be Evan. His betrayal went deeper than I had imagined, and it made me sick to my stomach.

"Sam."

The sleek bird turned its feathered head, and its sharp gaze locked with mine. I was in a quandary. I wasn't sure he could make a smooth transition to human form. Nor did I want to put him through the agony of transition so soon after shifting. He'd already done it twice tonight.

As a new hawk, he wouldn't have had the time to develop a tolerance to the pain. Shifting back and forth was a bit tricky until you were in your third year. That was why a juvenile was always accompanied by a parent or an appointed elder to protect them when they were in the vulnerable transition period. Though the women of our clan didn't shift, they were raised to be strong and warrior-like to protect their young.

Finally, I stood. Mirroring Sam's actions, but not giving two shits if he saw my dick swinging, I quickly dropped my jeans and kicked off my boots. Anger fueled my movements, but it wasn't toward Sam. He was an innocent pawn in his mother's twisted game.

Adopting the same pose, I crouched and braced myself for the pain. It was as if the large raptor within shattered every bone as it burst free. My deeper shriek echoed off the walls despite my age—likely due to the length of time I'd gone without shifting into my inner hawk. It was almost like starting over.

Footsteps pounded down the hall, but Gator and Phoenix stepped out, and each lifted an arm to hold everyone back. Gator quickly closed the door. Rooster and Banshee didn't know everything about the chapters that had become a sanctuary for others like us. Thankfully, Phoenix and Gator were pros at maintaining our anonymity.

"Everything's fine. Raptor, uh, clicked on one of them YouTube videos and didn't realize he had it so loud." I heard Gator's excuse through the cheap hollow-core door, but I was too preoccupied to pay attention to what was said after that. I was focused on the wary eyes of the juvenile in front of me.

"*Your mother's husband—is he a shifter?*" I asked him through the telepathy we had when in hawk form. I already knew the answer—or I was pretty sure I did. I'd researched him when she married him because at the time, I believed the boys were mine. He was a rich guy with enough money for her to blow without making a dent in his bank account, but I hadn't seen evidence that he was a hawk. He sure as hell wasn't from my bloodlines or our clan, or I would've known. That didn't mean he wasn't one—it could simply mean he had the money to keep it from being found out.

"No." He practically spat his reply, which gave me some insight into what the problem might be.

"*Does he know your mom comes from a family of shifters?*"

"No."

Fucking hell.

"*Does your mother know you're shifting?*"

His head ducked and snaked before he fluffed his feathers. My chest seized for the boy who had no idea what he was doing and probably had no insight on how to process what was happening to him. He certainly couldn't teach his brother as he himself was muddling through the best he could. It was a frightening enough experience with preparation and support. Imagining him going through this alone made me want to throttle his mother. Did she think that if she didn't tell him what he was, he wouldn't go through his first molt?

"*Do you ever visit your mother's family?*"

"No."

Jesus fucking Christ.

"*So, no one prepared you for this. Christ, I bet that was terrifying for you.*"

"*Yeah, and I ruined a lot of clothes at first,*" he mumbled as his body rocked nervously, mouth open and panting. The boy was stressed.

"*Can you make a rapid transition to human yet?*" I asked, though I knew the answer.

"*Sort of.*" He dropped his head. "*Not really.*"

"*Shit, okay.... I want you to try, but when you do, I want you to visualize yourself as a human—imagine it in detail. Visualize yourself from head to toe, bone by bone. Breathe deep and slow. Concentrate.*"

With a bob of his head, he reversed the process, though the

transition back wasn't as smooth. The thought of him getting stuck as a hawk or making it halfway through a transition had anger brewing in me. He should've been warned and coached. As usual, Falina only thought of herself.

And Evan—I should've fucking killed him. Both for his betrayal and his neglect of his children.

I should've fought her for custody, despite what the paternity test results I received indicated. Except I was young, hurt, irrational, and angry. Then again, at the time, I never imagined it would be someone from my own family that she'd been having an affair with. Regret was a bitter pill to swallow, and should-haves could drown a man.

After I transitioned back, I dressed, then sat to pull my boots on.

"Have a seat," I muttered.

He did as he was told, and with much less hostility than he'd exhibited earlier.

"Your brother... does he remember me at all?" Sam was almost five the last time I saw him, and Seth was only three. How much could a three-year-old possibly remember? Surely, Sam didn't believe that Seth could possibly trust me or want to be near me long enough to learn—whether the boy believed I was his father or not.

"I found Mom's photo album when we moved the second time. I hid it from Mom because I was afraid she'd throw it out. He and I would look at it at when Mom wasn't around. I made up stories about you for him from the pictures. They were bullshit, but he didn't know that. Except he's old enough now that he has questions—and some understandable resentment." Sam shrugged like what he'd done was no big deal, but it showed that he loved his brother very much.

"Shit." I ran a hand through my hair in frustration. Like being on the ranch, thinking about the photo album brought back a lot of memories. Those were better times. Back when I still believed that they were my children and that the sanctity of marriage meant something. I was a fucking idiot. "What did your mother tell you about me?"

"That you didn't want to be bothered by us anymore."

"Jesus," I muttered as I closed my eyes to gain control of my anger. It wouldn't be right for me to make a seventeen-year-old boy deal with my rage. Especially not when he'd lived his life thinking I didn't want him. Nor would it be right to talk shit about his mother. It wasn't fair to put more on him.

"Then why do you think your brother would be willing to let me say two words to him?"

"I told him Mom lied. I told him you were actually in prison, and we couldn't visit you until we were eighteen," he mumbled, and I wasn't sure I'd heard him correctly at first.

"You what?" I asked once I decided that I had, and my jaw dropped. "What the hell were you going to tell him after he turned eighteen?"

"I hadn't decided. I figured I had another few years to figure that out." He shrugged.

I damn near fell out of my chair. What a fucked-up situation.

"Have you told your brother about this?" I motioned to where we'd perched on the floor in hawk form. "Does he have any idea?"

"No. I didn't know what to tell him. He's gonna flip the fuck out," Sam replied.

"Language," I warned. Then I wanted to laugh despite the situation because I sounded like Madame Laveaux.

He huffed. "You never answered me," he said sullenly as he stared at the wall.

No way was I going to be able to simply walk into the house and ask if I could teach a kid about the shit that would happen the first time he shifted. I'd have to fly in without his mom and stepdad finding out—and Sam would have to help me. Unless we could figure out a way to get them here. It had to be somewhere private without prying eyes.

"Yes, I'll help."

The relief in his gaze was damn near palpable.

Sam and I talked for a good two hours after that as we made plans. He was a surprisingly mature and intelligent boy despite who his parents were. Though I always thought Evan was a good person—until he had shacked up with my wife. It made me sad—no, it fucking devastated me that Sam wasn't mine.

When it was time, I flew with him to ensure he made it home to the elite neighborhood in Dallas.

Three days later another event rocked my world.

FOURTEEN

Sage ("Cookie")

"ANARCHY"—LILITH CZAR

Security was at an all-time high at the club. Word seemed to have gotten around to the underbelly of the city that girls were quitting or disappearing. Because of that, Blade took me everywhere I needed to go. The brothers were stretched thin ensuring the remaining employees were safe.

George obviously didn't like competition and dealt with it in the worst, most underhanded way. It seemed he wouldn't be happy until we were out of business. If we couldn't find any decent dancers, he might just succeed. The girls that were holdouts couldn't keep up the pace we were currently going. Everyone was getting tired and snippy.

We'd had to close early on several nights because we didn't have enough dancers. Customers were getting disgruntled.

All of that—combined with the stress of me dancing to cover

shortages and interviewing the few dancers who'd applied but didn't cut the mustard—had me wanting to pull my hair out. Telling myself I couldn't do anything about it by worrying, I blew out a heavy breath.

After logging off the computer, I double checked that I hadn't forgotten to do something. My brain was fried, and it was making me forgetful. Shutting off the lights, I sighed. I headed to the back door where Solomon waited.

"Ready?" I asked him. The girls had all been walked out to their vehicles by the rest of that night's security detail. Solomon and I were the last ones to leave as I had to count up the night's earnings and reconcile the books before I locked everything up in the safe.

"Whenever you are," he replied with a smile that crinkled the edges of his deep brown eyes. The man was almost too sweet to have been some kind of former Special Forces guy. He also looked like he should've been a GQ model, not some kind of badass military dude.

The prospect who was waiting outside by the back door stepped up behind us.

"Your daughter will be here for summer vacation soon, won't she?" I asked as we crossed the asphalt to my car and his truck, which were the last ones left in the lot. He scanned the surrounding area with a keen eye as we walked.

"She sure will. Three more weeks. I still can't believe she's gonna be eighteen soon. I'm not sure where the time's gone." He always spoke highly of his daughter, and his eyes lit up when he did. You could tell that even though the relationship between him and her mom didn't work out, he was a great dad.

"You enjoy your time. If you need more time off, remember, Venom said you could use some advanced vacation time," I reminded him.

He nodded. "Yes, I remember. We'll see how things go."

"Well, have a good night. Drive safe," I called out with a small wave and a tight smile that he returned.

Using my key fob, I unlocked my door, and he did the same. Once I was safely ensconced in my vehicle, I pulled up my favorite playlist for the journey home. The prospect got on his bike and patiently waited for me. Solomon also waited until I was safely in my car and for me to start it before he climbed into his. We both backed out and went our separate ways when we hit the street. The prospect stayed on my tail.

It usually took me about thirty to forty minutes to get back to the clubhouse. I had a small apartment that I'd had for years, but I rarely stayed there anymore. In the past, I liked the easy access of the clubhouse for fucking. Ever since Raptor, I preferred being there because I hated to be alone—I was more at ease surrounded by people I considered my friends. That thirty-minute drive was my time to unbox and get lost in my memories of Raptor.

I was about fifteen miles down the road with the windows down as I listened to the music, trying to clear my mind. I was making waving motions through the cool night air with my outstretched hand.

That's when I realized the glow behind me wasn't the single headlight of the prospect's bike. It was a vehicle with two of them that seemed to speed up and was closing in on to me. Glancing down, I checked to make sure I hadn't let my speed drop as I spaced off, but I was good there.

I tried to see if the prospect was behind the car, but they had their bright lights on, and I had to adjust my rearview mirror to prevent myself being blinded. "Dick," I muttered. "If you don't like my speed, go around me!"

Not like they could hear me, but they were pissing me off. I wasn't too concerned until I felt my car lurch as they hit my bumper. "Hey!"

They didn't back off, though. They pushed me from the back, causing my car to fishtail a bit before they let up. "What the fuck?" I shouted, starting to panic.

At first I thought maybe they'd fucked up and that maybe they had their cruise on and dozed off—it *was* after three in the morning. But then they hit me again, and harder this time. My heart hammered, and I became terrified when I realized their actions were intentional.

Trying to outrun them, I hit the gas as I blindly pressed the button on my console to call Blade. The phone rang several times before it went to voicemail. Trying not to lose my fucking mind, I called again.

And again.

"Please, please answer," I cried as I saw the lights closing the gap. Anxiety in full force, I was having a hard time breathing.

Right when I tried again, they rammed me from behind, and at the speed I was going, I didn't stand much of a chance. "Shit!"

My ears were filled with the sound of screeching tires as I lost control. My heart hammered and its beat pounded in my ears. Blade chose that moment to answer.

"What's up?"

He sounded out of breath, but I was unable to answer because my car had gone too far sideways, and it flipped. All I could do was cry, "Oh god, oh god, oh god," as I clutched the steering wheel for dear life. The side curtain airbags deployed, further scaring the shit out of me. When I came to a stop, I sat there unfocused and dazed. I fumbled for the release button on my seatbelt with one hand as the other found the door handle, but it took several tries and using my shoulder to get it to creak open. I'd used so much force that I fell out of the car.

"Oof!" I groaned.

Bright lights shone in my eyes, blinding me and causing me to wince.

Everything was blurry, and I tried to cover my eyes, but I couldn't make a move without being hit by savage stabs of pain from where my seatbelt had locked tight over my chest. My shoulder ached from trying to get the door open.

Silhouetted in the light was a dark figure approaching me. Ignoring the pain, survival instinct kicked in, and I scrambled backward in a crab walk, but I fell down when my hand hit an uneven spot in the ground. On my back, I prepared for what had been done to Fiona to now happen to me. I was so scared, I was frozen—unable to move and unable to scream.

When they got close enough that I could hear them, they stopped.

"Consider this a warning. You were supposed to be somewhere last Wednesday. Ring a bell? You should feel fortunate—I wanted to kill you for running your mouth to your fuck boys, but my boss is thinking with his dick. If I were you, I'd get on the phone and reschedule. Mr. Horacio's not a patient man, and you've already sorely tested what little he has. You involve those fucking Bastards again, and I don't care what he says—I'll slit your fucking throat and paint the wall with your blood." With that, he turned, went back to his SUV, reversed it, and went back the way he came.

Obviously, whoever Venom had sent to The Diamond Palace hadn't been as discreet or incognito as they'd thought.

I rolled onto my hands and knees, hanging my head. The roar of a motorcycle filled the night air. It screeched to a stop, and then I heard boots pounding on pavement. The same boots kicked up rocks and clumps of dirt as they skidded into the ditch I'd landed in.

"Jesus, Sage, are you okay?" Blade's concerned voice broke through my stupor, and I lifted my head. His worried face was half obscured by the tangled strands of hair that had escaped my hastily crafted bun.

"I don't know," I croaked.

"What the fuck happened?" he demanded.

Remembering the man's warning, I lifted my gaze and lied through my teeth. "Deer."

The look in his squinted eyes told me he didn't believe me. "Then where's the fucking prospect?"

A sob escaped me. "I don't know."

"Can you ride?" he asked.

Unsure, I still nodded. He got up and went to my car. I could hear him speaking rapidly but quietly on his phone as he went. After climbing in and rummaging around, he crawled back out, holding my wallet and my phone. Then he returned to the ditch and held out a hand. I took it as a lifeline and let him help me to my feet. I was proud that I only swayed slightly.

"I got the important stuff. The guys and I will come back later to get your car. It's not going anywhere anytime soon." He cast a glance over his shoulder, then looked back at me. "Not sure if it can be fixed, though."

"I don't care even a little bit," I choked out because I was more worried about where the prospect was. Blade gave me an assessing stare, then helped me up the slight incline to his bike. That's when I realized he was only wearing jeans and his untied boots. "You don't have a shirt on," I weakly scolded.

"Yeah, you're lucky I have pants on. I kicked Ruby out of my bed and hauled ass the second you screamed. I'm sorry I didn't answer." Though he appeared somber, I knew right away what he'd been doing. It made me feel so damn guilty for ruining his night. He had been my go-to for so many years that I didn't think before I called him.

In that moment, I worried that maybe I was completely alone.

Blade turned his bike around on the highway and we started down the road. We passed three of the RBMC members as he hit the throttle.

Riding back to the clubhouse, my arms tight around his waist, face pressed to his back, I cried. I'd been doing too much of that, and I hated it. It made me angry as hell. It was so unlike me, and I saw it as such a weakness.

He rested a hand on my forearm and lightly squeezed as if he could sense the jumble of emotions running through my mind.

Before I knew it, we were pulling through the gate.

When we arrived in front of the clubhouse, I breathed a sigh of relief. My knees gave out on me after I got off his bike and I nearly fell.

"I'm calling Angel to come in and look you over," he insisted.

"Hell no. I'm not having him leave his pregnant wife and their children in the middle of the night when I'm fine." I crossed my arms over my chest.

He grumbled under his breath, but he gave in when I glared and refused to back down. Frustrated with me, he ran his hands down his face with a groan. "At least swing by the clinic tomorrow to get checked out."

"Fine," I huffed. We went inside, and he walked me to my door.

"Sage, I'm not stupid. I saw the skid marks on the road. If I find whoever did that, I'm slicing them up so thoroughly, their own mother wouldn't recognize the pieces," he practically snarled before he stomped off down the hall to his room.

The second I went into my room, I collapsed onto my bed and stared blankly at the wall until I couldn't keep my eyes open any longer.

That night I dreamed of the way things used to be when I would fall asleep in Raptor's arms.

The next day, true to my word, I went to the clinic where Angel volunteered. Like I told Blade, I was just fine.

Mostly.

After what happened last week, Blade was crazy protective. I now had a reason to be just as protective. My phone had remained silent, which left me feeling like the other shoe was about to drop. Ever the rebel, I refused to let that hinder me from living my life as normal as I could. I also didn't use the number on the business card George Horacio had left with me. Fuck him.

"I'll give you a ride home tonight. You can leave the rental car there, and I'll have one of the prospects bring it home in the morning. I just have a job to do down in Des Moines, but it won't take long. I should be there long before you close."

"That's dumb, Blade. I have the rental, so I might as well use it."

"I don't care. Wait for me, and at least I can follow you home."

"That's just plain stupid. The prospect was run off the road following me. Solomon will be there, and he'll walk me out like he always does."

"You wait for me," he demanded as he pointed a finger at me. Of course, I stuck my tongue out at his back as he left. He was being a worry wart when there was no need. I'd been extremely cautious every time I left the compound. Besides, I hadn't heard a word from them since I'd been run off the road. I was keeping my mouth shut, and to my knowledge, the RBMC had stayed out of The Diamond Palace.

I hoped.

It had been a long night. After pulling two performances out of my ass, I was tired and ready to go home so I could climb into the shower. It wouldn't be long before I couldn't help out onstage. I glanced at the time once more and decided to call it a night.

Since Blade wasn't there yet, I rebelliously prepared to go home. I figured I would just send him a text to let him know I was leaving and that he should've been here. The girls all went out as I was standing by the back door, digging through my bag for my phone.

"You okay, Ms. Cookie?" Solomon asked as he waited for me at the door.

"Yeah, I'm good. I think I left my phone in my office. You can go ahead and leave. Blade should be here any minute." Pissed because now I'd have to wait after all, I gave him my brightest smile.

He searched my face to ensure I wasn't lying.

"Solomon. I'm good," I insisted. I wasn't. Because I was exhausted.

But I would wait.

Reluctantly, he looked over my head and down the hall. "Okay, but you shut this door. And you wait for Blade to walk you out to your car or drive you."

Solomon and the other guys didn't know all the details, but they knew I wrecked my car. Solomon also knew that another business was poaching our talent and harassing the dancers that refused to leave—me included—which was why I was afraid he suspected that what had happened was a far cry from a big buck jumping in front of me like I told him.

"I promise," I assured him.

Finally, he left. I watched his hulking form lumber out to the lot. He glanced back, and I closed the door with a quick wave. Heels clicking on the floor, I returned to my office. I hadn't lied to Solomon. Though it irritated me, I would wait for Blade.

I searched the desktop but came up empty. In case I'd shoved it somewhere in my rush to get onstage earlier, I checked the drawers—nothing. I got down on my hands and knees to look under the desk in case I knocked it off when I was finishing shit up for the night.

"There you are," I muttered when I spotted my phone up against the wall where it must've fallen.

A giggle came from the hall before I heard Blade murmur. Asshole must've had someone drop him off. I knew damn well his bike wasn't out back or out front because I could see both lots on the cameras as I closed up. Guess he got back sooner than he anticipated and was killing time. I rolled my eyes. On the other hand, now I really hadn't lied to Solomon—I'd waited. The whispered and continued laughter from both of them confirmed my suspicions. I stayed down because I didn't feel like being a part of their farewell. Gag.

By the shoes she was wearing, the woman with him was Ruby—the glittery red platform heels were her signature. I thought she had left after she finished her last set about an hour ago. Guess not.

"Here, I have the door, doll," I heard Blade say in his most charming voice. I rolled my eyes again. The man could pour on the charm when he wanted to—despite the darkness we both knew resided inside him.

Then I heard him open the back door, but it instantly banged against the wall. Ruby shrieked and I froze, phone in one hand, the other hovering over the panic button under my desk. I didn't want to push it and freak the guys out if it was nothing.

"Jesus—" was all Blade got out before a muffled shot rang out and I pushed the button. Ruby dropped to the ground like a rag doll, then two more silenced shots rang out, and I saw Blade fall back and whack his head on the floor. My hand over my mouth did little to muffle my cry. Ruby stared at me where I crouched under the desk, but her eyes didn't blink, and a dark red puddle formed slowly, the wavy strands of her golden hair appearing to float around her.

I cursed over the fact that my pistol was in my bag sitting on top of the desk.

Dress shoes covered in what looked like hospital booties appeared in my doorway. I screamed and dove for the corner as more shots rang out. The heavy wood from my desk splintered as papers flew around like we were in a mini hurricane. Trapped in the office, I covered my ears as I waited for bullets to fill my body.

"Tsk, tsk. It's a shame that you're so beautiful," the voice murmured. More shots rang out but suddenly stopped, and I heard the man curse before I saw him dart for the door. That's when I heard the approach of motorcycles.

Eyes squeezed shut, I violently shook as my teeth chattered.

A hand touched me, and I lost my shit. Swinging blindly and sobbing, I fought with everything I had. My foot struck and I heard a groaned, "Fuck!"

"Is she okay?" a familiar voice asked, and I paused, panting, my heart hammering. I cracked my eyes open to find a wincing Voodoo holding his junk while Venom stood by the door.

"I'm not sure. She has blood on her, but I can't tell where it's coming from because she booted me in the nuts." His voice was strained, and he spoke through gasped breaths.

"S-s-sorry," I stammered.

Voodoo got to his feet, but he left his hands on his knees as he tried to breathe through the damage I'd done.

Venom gently brushed my hair out of my face, and I cried out as he hissed and whispered, "Shit."

Tears welled in my eyes, not because of the pain, but because the thought of losing the one person who always had my back absolutely devastated me. I searched Venom's and Voodoo's gazes. Venom glanced over his shoulder.

"We need to get this shit cleaned up. The last thing we need is the cops sticking their nose in our business. Fuck. Ghost, Squirrel, go make sure there were no witnesses. Take the prospects with you."

The two men nodded with grim expressions.

"He used a silencer," I whispered.

Venom and Voodoo exchanged glances.

Thankfully the club was on the south edge of the city with very little surrounding it but a few other bars and warehouses that closed before we did.

"Did Ruby have family?" he asked me. It didn't escape my notice that he positioned himself to block the door from my view.

I inhaled a shaky breath. "I don't think so, but I'd have to check her file to be sure," I replied, my voice uneven. I blinked back the tears that were rapidly blinding me.

"It's okay, I'll have Facet check into it. I wasn't sure if you knew off the top of your head. We've got this," Venom assured me. "Now I know you've been through a lot, but did you get a look at who did this?"

I shook my head and winced at the sharp pain in the back of my neck. "But I think it might've been the man I saw across the street from Fiona's. If not, it was definitely someone working for George Horacio."

Venom cursed under his breath.

"I'm gonna need you in here, Angel," Venom said as he gently lifted my chin and turned my head side to side. I could feel the trickle of blood as it ran down my temple. He used a handkerchief to catch it.

"I'm fine," I insisted, trying to brush him away. "What about Finley?"

In my frazzled mental state, I said his given name. Venom cocked a brow at me in question.

"Blade," I clarified as I fisted my hands to stop the trembling.

"Oh, I knew exactly who you were talking about. I just hope you know what you're doing."

"What?" I asked with a frown that caused me to hiss in pain.

"Nothing we can't talk about later. Try not to frown. Or move your forehead." Venom winced comically.

"That bad?" I reached my hand up to assess the damage.

"Ah! I wouldn't do that," he advised as he grabbed my wrist in a light hold. Despite the insanity of the last hour, I inhaled a calming breath. My shoulders, previously knotted, felt loose and chill.

"You're an ass, but thank you," I sighed, giving him a lazy smile because I knew damn well what he'd done. He returned my grin. Over the years he'd been like a big brother to me—just maybe not on the same level as Finley, though, because he'd been my best friend since we were kids.

"Ohhh. Whoa!" Chains stopped short when he entered the room and gave me a wide-eyed stare.

"What the fuck is wrong with me?" I demanded, narrowing my gaze at them as I fought having a mental breakdown. I glanced down and saw the blood on my clothes. Panic bloomed and I tried to see where it was coming from. Though I hurt like a motherfucker, I was relieved to find it wasn't coming from where I thought.

"You, uh, got a little something, um," Chains hesitantly stammered as he made a nervous hand motion, pointing at his forehead. His lips were pursed, and his eyebrows were practically touching his hairline.

"Ugh, if that's all it is, I don't care about that. I'm not stupid—" I swallowed hard. "—I know Ruby is… didn't make it. But what about Blade? He got shot too."

Venom hadn't answered me earlier, and I was afraid of what that meant.

"He's gonna be okay," Angel replied as he passed between Voodoo and Chains to kneel next to me. His normally warm olive complexion appeared a bit pale. "Chains and Hawk loaded him up into the cage to get him back to the clubhouse. I'll get him fixed up, then he'll just need some rest. Let's see what we can do for you—"

I cut him off. "Angel, you don't have to. You look beat. I can clean up back in my room." Relief hit me at the confirmation that Blade would be okay.

"I'll be okay, I promise. You probably want me to take care of this before you go home." He gave me a comical look that screamed, "Yikes."

"I'd say you *definitely* want to take care of that," Voodoo agreed with a solemn nod.

"Fine." I rolled my eyes and ignored the pinch in my forehead.

Venom held my hand and my eyes suddenly went droopy. Angel held my hair back and reached for something on my head. His chocolate brown eyes were mesmerizing, and I started to feel like I was going to doze off. The sudden sharp pain made me gasp. Just as quickly as it came, it was gone, and a warm tingly sensation spread over the area. He repeated the process several times before he moved on to my cheek, then everywhere else.

By the time he was done, he was absolutely ashen and a little unsteady. It hurt my heart that helping me had done that to him.

"What's that?" I cautiously asked as I pointed at the small pile of bloody objects.

"Splinters of wood from the desk. You had them sticking out of your forehead and cheek like a freaking porcupine. Your neck and shoulder were grazed by bullets," Voodoo explained. "Damn, woman, you're lucky."

I sure as hell didn't feel lucky.

There was a good chance I'd have to leave the only place to ever feel like home—and the people I considered family.

And I'd be doing it alone.

FIFTEEN

Blade

"CRAZY TRAIN"—OZZY OSBOURNE

A groan ripped from me that originated in my chest. My eyes seemed to be full of sand as I blinked to get them to stay open. "How are you feeling?"

I turned my head slowly toward the form sitting next to me. I knew it was Voodoo, but hell if I could get my eyes to focus. A few more blinks and he came into view.

"What the fuck happened? I feel like I took a sledgehammer to the chest."

"Well, you did kind of get shot. Angel could only heal you to a degree so that he'd have enough left to take care of Cookie," he told me.

"What the hell?" I shot up in bed, my own injuries immediately

taking a backseat to concern for Sage. The foolishly quick movement made me wince, and the room spun.

"Easy, she's okay. I swear."

"I need to go see her," I insisted as I tried to get off the bed in
our infirmary. That was when I realized I had an IV and was naked
under the sheet. "Jesus, where the fuck are my clothes?"

"We had to cut them off you. You were shot in the chest and
the leg. But look, I need to talk to you for a minute. Then I'll get
Angel in here to unhook that shit. For Christ's sake, I tell you that
you were shot twice, and you don't ask what happened. Your first
instinct is to go to her." He sat in the chair next to me with his elbows resting on his thighs.

"Yeah, because her well-being means more to me than my own
fucking life. Back when we first got here? If it had been just me, I
could've cared less what happened to me. I was on a fast track to
hell, and she was the one bright and somewhat innocent spot in
my dark and ugly world. What makes me an unredeemable piece
of shit is that I didn't leave Luis's organization because I regretted
the things I had done—it was to save her. So, if you know something, tell me. Because I promise you, nothing is more important to
me than her—not you, not the club." I shot him a narrowed gaze.

He sighed and ran a hand through his dark hair. Ice-blue eyes
locked on mine. "Are you in love with her?"

"What? What are you talking about? Of course, I love her."

"No, I asked if you were *in love* with her."

"Not like that. Why?"

"She's been with you exclusively since Raptor left."

Fuck. I huffed a sigh and closed my eyes. Finally, I opened
them to stare him down. "We don't fuck."

He reared back as if I'd struck him. "Wait. You're telling me
you've never slept with her?"

Palming my face, I groaned. "Not exactly."

"What does 'not exactly' mean?"

"It's a long story. When we're together, she listens to me. She...." I couldn't reveal my weakness. "Look, why does that matter?"

"Because I think you need to get her out of here, and I know she won't like it, but for her safety...." He trailed off, and it wasn't helping my suspicions and worry.

"Spit it out. What the fuck do you know?" Voodoo had been my brother for years. If he or his grandmother said someone needed to do something, there was a reason.

"I had a vision of her being shot. That was all I saw. I might've thought it was the incident last night, but my granmè called me this morning. She said we needed to 'protect the girl' but when I explained what happened, she cut me off. She said there was someone who wanted her dead, and they wouldn't rest until they saw her bleeding out into the dirt. She said it's tied to Horacio, but it goes deeper than our friend George." His brow furrowed as he watched me.

"I will fucking cut off their balls and shove them down their throat until they choke on them. Then I'll gut them." I was dead serious, and I meant every word.

"Granmè recommended you take her to Texas. The thing is, I didn't want to send you down there if the two of you are together. That wouldn't be fair to Raptor."

A humorous laugh burst free and echoed off the walls of the sterile-looking room. "Oh, that's rich. He fucking left her without a backward glance. No calls, no messages, letters, or fucking carrier pigeons. Not a word to her. Not. One. And you're worried about what's fair to him? What if she *was* my girl? He left her. That makes her fair game, right? That's what the fucking bylaws say. *Right?*" I taunted, pissed to the core.

"I get it, bro. But Raptor is a brother. My loyalties will always lie with a brother, so despite what my grandmother suggested, I would've found a safe alternative location for her."

"And I'm not?"

"That's not what I meant," he argued. "And if you want to throw out bylaws, they say the former brother has to be okay with the new relationship."

I rolled my eyes.

"Well, since I'm not in a relationship with her, that's a moot point. What I am worried about is, have you told her she needs to leave? And have you told him she's coming?"

"I can't tell him. When I consulted Facet, he said he didn't advise sending the information out via phone or any other electronic means because we have no idea who is after Cookie or what they have at their disposal. You know Facet—anything electronic is fallible," he explained with a shrug. "As far as telling her, we figured it was better off coming from you."

"Great."

"There's one more thing." He covered his mouth as if he could physically hold the words back. What he told me next had me in a near panic state.

"Fucking hell."

SIXTEEN

Raptor

"NIGHT CRAWLING"—MILEY CYRUS (FEAT. BILLY IDOL)

Initially, I was supposed to go to the boys. Sam had messaged me to say he was pretty sure he could bring Seth to me. Their mom was supposed to be out of town for another week, and Sam told the nanny he and Seth were going to hang out with some friends for the night and would be back the next day.

I had no idea what kind of snacks two teenaged boys liked, but I was stopping by H-E-B to grab some shit. Tonight would be the first time Sam would bring his brother to see me. I hadn't seen Seth since he was a small child.

"Adrien?"

I froze. The voice slid like ice down my spine. Deciding to ignore her because that's what she deserved, I moved my cart forward, intent on paying for what I had and leaving.

"Adrien!" Rapid footsteps preceded the hand on my arm that I shook off. Full of fury, I spun to face the woman who had at one time brought my world crashing down after pulling everything out from under me.

"What do you want, Falina?" I practically spat her name out like a bitter pill. Fuck, she was supposed to be gone until next week.

I didn't want to tell her that I thought she was out of the country and her sons were coming to see me tonight. That would lead her to believe I'd sought her out or gave a fuck. I also couldn't believe she actually thought I had anything to say to her.

She had the nerve to pull back and look wounded.

"I didn't believe the talk that you were back. I…. You… you've changed," she whispered.

"No shit."

"Adrien, I have so many regrets—you just don't know."

"I don't give a flying fuck about your regrets."

She swallowed hard, and I wondered why I was still standing there, listening to anything she had to say.

"You used to be so different. All of that"—she waved at my ink—"is new. You never had any of that before."

"There are a lot of things that are different about me, Falina. I'm not that naive boy anymore. I'm so far gone from him that it would make your head spin. You don't know me. Nor do you know what I'm capable of anymore. So, leave me the fuck alone, and you won't have to worry about the dark, twisted, vengeful shit that goes on in my head when it comes to you." It was probably wrong of me to throw that at her considering I would be seeing her sons without her knowledge.

Both boys were legally minors, and if she found out, she would definitely make a stink and I wasn't sure if the restraining order she'd taken out on me was still valid. Speaking of….

"Aren't you nullifying the restraining order you had put in

place?" I glanced down at the four feet that now separated us. "Pretty sure that's not five hundred yards."

And there it was. The hateful little gleam that she quickly hid behind her bullshit sweet façade.

Without waiting for a reply that was likely to be a pack of lies or hateful vitriol, I walked away. Deciding what I had in my cart was good enough, I went straight to the checkout lines. Thankfully, there were no further interactions with my ex-wife before I got my ass through the checkout and out to my truck.

My phone rang as I was hauling ass back to the clubhouse. Seeing that it was Venom, I grinned and eased the death grip I had on my steering wheel. I pushed the button to answer. "Well, hello, stranger."

"Hello, yourself. I thought I'd check on you and see how you're settling in—Prez."

"Fuck, that sounds weird."

He chortled.

"I'm glad you find so much humor in this," I wryly commented.

"Sorry, bro. I do think it's funny. You hated filling in for me, but it didn't mean you were bad at it. You're a born leader, Raptor."

I sighed. He was more accurate than he knew, but I'd told my father that under no circumstances would I be taking over as our clan leader. "I don't know about all of that, but thank you for the vote of confidence. I'm glad one of us has faith in me. Truthfully, this position is a bit of a pain in the ass, but it's not too bad. Gator is one helluva VP, so that helps. Thanks to him, it's been okay so far—on the club front, at least."

"Meaning?" His tone took on a serious note, and I knew he'd zeroed in on my reckless admission.

"Shit, how much time do you have?" I gave a humorless laugh.

"For you? However much time you need." He was dead serious, and I appreciated that about him. I missed having him around to bounce ideas off of and talk to. Sure, I had Gator as my VP, and he really was badass, but I didn't really know him well enough to discuss the things that weighed heavy on me. At times, I felt very much alone down here.

I explained everything that had happened since I got to Texas. Everything from the task of getting a chapter re-established and the bullshit we'd encountered with the Demon Runners to Sam coming to see me.

He huffed out a pent-up breath. "Damn, brother. Have you talked to Evan since you've been there?"

Venom knew the backstory with me and my cousin better than anyone. He was the one who'd been there to keep me from completely drowning in a bottle after Falina hatefully informed me the boys weren't mine and she'd been having affairs since before we got married.

"Hell no. What could he possibly say to explain the fact that he was fucking my wife behind my back for years?"

There was silence.

"Holy shit."

"Yeah."

"Maybe she was lying. Maybe there's more to the story," he logically explained.

"I highly doubt it, but I hate your rationality." There was a part of me deep in my heart that had always had a hard time believing what had happened. "But the evidence that was shoved in my face, both then and now, makes it a little hard to deny. Sam's reveal was the final nail in the coffin built from my cousin's lies."

Evan and I had grown up as close as brothers, and it had damn near killed me when Falina left and went running into his arms. Crazy thing was, I think his betrayal hurt more than hers. The slim chance that I might've held a grudge for years based on information that might not be completely accurate didn't sit well. But I know what I saw.

"I'm not saying I'm right, but like I tried to tell you back then, you were basing everything off of something a woman said—a woman who'd obviously been lying to you for years. Something isn't sitting right with all this," Venom grumbled, and I sighed.

"Venom, how could he not wonder if those boys were his? How could he look me in the eye and ask me to talk to him, knowing he'd been sleeping with my wife ever since we got married?"

"Bro, I don't know, but my guts have never been wrong. Something isn't sitting right."

"How could he not want to be a part of his sons' lives? Not that I blame him for not being with Falina, because she was a pain in the ass, and fuck, you can't tell me he hadn't seen that over the years. Regardless, how could he leave the boys to navigate a shift unguided and uneducated? Hell, for that matter, how could she?" Frustrated, I rested my elbow on the top of the door and ran my fingertips back and forth over my jaw. After the trip down here for Voodoo, I'd had to come clean about the full extent of my abilities, so Venom now knew all of my secrets.

"I really don't know, bro," he replied. "Shit, I wish I had a better answer for you."

Silence ensued for a moment as I sat lost in my thoughts.

Finally, he cleared his throat. "Hey, I called for one other thing."

"Okay—what's up?" I hit my blinker to turn onto the clubhouse property. The gravel crunched under my tires as I came to a stop and rolled my window down. I entered the code and the heavy iron gate swung open.

"Are you gonna be around for a few days?"

I paused as I waited for the gate to close behind me. It sucked that we had to utilize an automated gate that moved slow, because we had to sit and wait to ensure it was secure before we drove off. "Yeah, as far as I know. Why? You coming for a visit?"

"Hell, I wish. Nah, just wanted to make sure you weren't gonna be on the road for club business. I'm sending you a, uh, package. It's time sensitive and something I can't discuss over the phone or Facet would have my ass." We both chuckled. Facet was always a stickler for privacy, and he was more than a little paranoid of doing anything that could be overheard or intercepted. He essentially trusted no one—well, except his brothers, but at times I questioned that.

"Yeah, I'll be here. I'll be working with Sam and Seth over the next few weeks, so I don't have any plans. Besides, we still don't have any jobs lined up. I'm not so sure the biological-cleaning business is going to be successful here." Satisfied that the entrance was shut and secure, I rumbled over the loose gravel to the clubhouse where I put the truck in park but sat with it running as we talked. It was hot as fuck out there, and I figured I might as well enjoy the AC as long as I could.

"Ahh, give it time. You just need to get your name out there. What about the other businesses? Have you gotten them situated?"

"Actually, part of that transition has gone well. The strip club pretty much runs itself, since the manager stayed on with us and so did most of the dancers. Not the same with the car washes. We had some trouble with the renter not wanting to give them up. He came back one night and trashed each location. Between that and getting goddamn cedar trees cut down, we've been busy. Those things spread like an STD in an orgy." We both chuckled.

"So uh, have you started seeing anyone?" he asked in a nonchalant way that I wasn't buying for a second.

My good humor evaporated. "I don't 'see' anyone, and you know it." Thanks to him bringing it up, I was thinking about Sage again. Motherfucker. For about two whole hours, I'd managed to keep her out of my fucking head. For the entire time since moving back to Texas, I'd been wondering if she already moved on. Was she back to fucking like a rabbit? Was she in a committed relationship? It drove me fucking crazy, and I wanted to ask him about her, but I knew it wouldn't serve any purpose other than to torture myself.

Fuck, I wanted *her*. That's what I wanted.

"You know what I meant," he amended.

"No. We don't have any club girls yet." That wasn't completely true. We had Lola, but I wasn't in the mood to discuss the fact that I had absolutely no interest in sticking my dick in anyone.

"Huh, okay. Well, maybe I should've sent you a few of those instead." He laughed, and I reciprocated, but it sounded hollow to my own ears.

"Did Facet ever find anything for Soap with the DSMC?"

"He has a few leads, but so far, each one has hit a dead end. Someone is very good at covering their tracks." He sighed. That had to be frustrating for everyone involved. I couldn't imagine.

"That fucking blows. Have you seen Soap at all lately?"

"No, but I think I'll check with Snow to see how he's holding up without any helpful news."

We bullshitted for a bit before I told him I needed to get my ass in gear.

"So, when do you think the package will arrive?" I asked.

"Oh, well… shit. Hopefully in the next couple of days. I'll check back with you to see if it gets there okay." Something about his tone seemed odd, but I had too much on my mind to worry about my old friend's idiosyncrasies.

After grabbing all the bags—because I wasn't making two trips—I went inside. The sight and sounds that hit me sent a pang through my chest. *They should be mine, and I should've been in their lives—then I would've heard that sound often.*

Sam and Seth were playing pool as Gator gave them pointers.

Their groans and laughter as they took their shots and missed most of them were music to my ears.

The second they saw me, Seth stopped and went quiet. Sam placed a reassuring hand on his shoulder. My breath caught in my throat because holy shit, Seth looked like me. Evan and I could've passed for brothers when we were younger, but it was a kick to the nuts to see it in one of the boys. Sam always looked a little more like his mother's family when he was younger, now I could pick out certain features of my family, but Seth…

Damn.

"You boys wanna help me unpack these bags?" I asked, trying my damnedest to keep my voice from cracking. Both boys scrambled after me when I headed for the kitchen. It was a lot smaller than the one in Iowa, but there was a big industrial fridge and plenty of cupboards to fill with stuff for the boys—if they continued to come around.

Jesus, I had to quit comparing everything to Iowa.

We're not in Iowa anymore, Toto.

"Daddy! I want a snack too," Torque's son, Rhaegar called out from the doorway. Torque's ex had not only been a hopeless drug addict, but she'd been a *Game of Thrones* fanatic. Personally, I felt like that boy and his cool name might've been the two single things she ever did right.

"Rhae, those aren't for you," he chided, and the little boy's face fell.

I turned and crouched down. "Tell your dad that I said they are for *all* the kids," I told him with a grin and a wink to let Torque know I was fucking with him.

Torque held up a middle finger, and his son turned to him right as he did it. Rhae's mouth dropped open. "Dad! You said that was a bad finger!"

"Yeah, Dad," I teased. Torque's gaze narrowed, and an evil

smirk twisted his lips. I knew he was going to get even later. Then it hit me. Slowly, they were becoming my family—each and every brother in my small chapter. My chest was a little lighter.

It didn't take long to see that Rhae had a bit of a hero crush on Sam and Seth. He followed them around and mimicked their actions. Everything was Sam this or Seth that—and they were great with him. It was... pretty awesome.

"Wanna watch *Cars* with me?" he asked the boys.

Seth looked down at him and ruffed his hair. "Sure, Sport." Then he looked at me. "Is that okay?"

"Absolutely. If you guys don't mind, I don't."

Rhae dragged the boys over to the new couches I bought for the common area. Yeah, I knew I was supposed to be preparing Seth and teaching the boys about the intricacies of shifting, but seeing them fit in seamlessly with my brothers and Torque's son was worth the wait.

Finally, the kid was crashed on the couch, and Sam approached me at the bar. "Did you want to start now?"

"Whenever you're both ready," I told him. He nodded and waved Seth over.

"Let's go for a walk," I suggested.

I grabbed a bottle of water for each of us and we went out the back door of the clubhouse. For a while, we all walked in silence. When we reached the lean-to that was toward the back of the property, I motioned for them to take a seat in the chairs I'd brought out there shortly after moving to Texas.

"I come out here to think," I explained as I settled into a chair. With the chairs positioned the way they were, we could watch the setting sun. I cracked open my bottle and took a long swallow. The boys did the same.

One might think the silence would feel awkward or

uncomfortable, but it didn't. In fact, things seemed more right than they had in a while.

"Sam said you weren't really in prison."

I took a deep breath and slowly released it. The sun slowly sank, and the soft sound of the wind rustled through the hated cedars.

"No, I wasn't."

"Then why didn't you want us?" His jaw worked and he didn't look at me, focusing instead on the arm of the lawn chair. His dark hair fell over his forehead, and he used the excuse of moving it out of the way to wipe his eye.

Fuck.

Sam glanced at me and nodded. "He's not a baby. He deserves to know the truth."

That got Seth's attention, and he lifted his gaze to mine. A confused frown marred his young face, and his eyes glistened with the tears he kept at bay. It was the face of a boy in the process of becoming a man—with eyes that looked like mine. My chest ached for him.

Resting my elbows on my thighs, I leaned forward. Then I set my bottle down to buy time. Finally, I looked him in the eye and told him the truth. "Seth, I wanted you and Sam more than you'll ever know. But your mom told me you weren't my children. I demanded paternity tests. When the results arrived in the mail, it was a knife to the chest. They said you weren't mine. The rest is a lot of legal bullshit that I'm not going to get into, but know that *I wanted you.*"

He looked as shocked as I'd been when that letter had arrived.

"I'm sorry, Seth. Trust me—I wish it weren't true."

"Then why are we here?" he asked, his voice almost hoarse.

That was Sam's cue to come into the conversation. "Because you know how you've been getting those bad headaches? And you suddenly started feeling restless? Like you're crawling out of your skin?"

Seth frowned, then reluctantly nodded. His knee bounced relentlessly as he nervously searched our faces.

"I went through the same thing. Should I show him?" Sam asked, turning to me for guidance.

"Sure, Sam." Talk about stress. A fifteen-year-old boy should've been prepared for this. Normally, he'd be educated from a fairly young age. This was so unfair. It was more unfair that Sam had gone through all of it completely alone.

"Dude!" Seth exclaimed and shot out of his seat when Sam started to undress.

"Be patient," I firmly instructed. Both boys looked at me, their inner hawks naturally ready to follow my guidance. Seth sat back down.

Sam crouched in the stance that had become natural to him. The coming shift was nothing new to me. But it was still a shock to watch the young man who I'd once loved as my son morph to the hawk he'd become. It was a feeling of both pride and regret—with a little bit of anger mixed in.

"Holy shit!" Seth scrambled up and back, his chair toppling over as he landed on his ass in the dirt. His wide eyes spoke of fear, confusion, and awe. It may have been years since it had first happened to me, but that had been my initial response too—and I'd been raised to know about it.

Seth's eyes darted wildly around as his chest heaved and his mouth hung open. "Is that gonna happen to me too?"

"Yes," I told him. "But unlike your brother, you won't be alone in this. We'll be here with you every step of the way."

SEVENTEEN

Sage ("Cookie")

"I DID SOMETHING BAD"—HALOCENE

I was stunned but ecstatic that Blade had survived. Ruby's death, on the other hand, had been heartbreaking. Before something more happened to the people I cared about, I knew I needed to get out of town. What I wasn't expecting was that Venom agreed and was sending me away.

"Cookie, this is what's best for everyone. Facet tracked down most of the other girls that quit showing up, and no one has messed with them or bothered them since. We'll work out a disguise so you look like one of the other girls when you leave. You'll be on Blade's bike with him with very little to give you away. Anyone that might be watching won't know it's you and will never suspect you're traveling cross-country. You'll look like you're simply going for a ride."

Venom explained everything very matter-of-factly, and I'd already known I would need to leave, but I was still reeling.

"Where are we going?" I asked, worry eating me from the inside out.

"Texas."

"You've got to be shitting me."

By the wee hours of the morning, we were ready. We packed only what we could shove into Blade's saddlebags and rode out of the compound. Dressed in Willow's clothes with my hair dyed back to its natural brunette and a tinted visor on my helmet, I could've passed for any number of the girls on the back of Blade's bike.

A sense of deja vu hit me as I wrapped my arms around Blade's waist. The only difference between now and when we'd first arrived, besides the years, was that we were no longer riding on a barely legal dirt bike, and we weren't looking for another bike to steal.

Blade rode hard once we cleared Des Moines and didn't slow down except to fuel up and for bathroom breaks. We stopped in Kansas City for breakfast and were back on the bike immediately.

Unfortunately, we had only been back on the road for about forty-five minutes before I was frantically tapping on Blade's shoulder. He pulled over, and I barely cleared the bike and got the helmet off before I was yakking in the ditch. Thankful my hair was braided for the ride, I hurled until I was dry heaving as Blade rubbed circles on my back.

"Do we need to stop for the day?" he asked with worry in his gaze.

"No. Not as long as you can pull over quickly." Though I tried to laugh, it came out more like a groan.

"Are you sure?" His sky-blue eyes were filled with concern.

"Yeah. Though I'm not looking forward to arriving, I'd like to put as many miles between us and that fucking nutjob as we can."

"Good—those were my thoughts exactly, but I was trying to be a sensitive fucker," he teased as he ruffled my hair.

"Stop! You'll mess my hair up!" I swatted at his hand, and he chuckled.

"You're on a motorcycle, or did that escape your notice? On a serious note, are you feeling okay? The back of the bike is the last place I want you right now, but I understand Venom's reasoning. It's a lot less suspicious with everyone coming and going on bikes all day long."

He tucked an escaped piece of hair behind my ear and pulled me in for a hug. "I'm going to do everything in my power to keep you safe," he promised. Clutching the back of his shirt, I hugged him back.

He helped me get my helmet back on and fastened because my hands were shaking. The look he shot me told me that he didn't believe I was okay.

"I promise, I'm fine," I assured him. "Let's get moving. We have a lot of miles to cover."

We got back on the road. According to Blade's GPS, it was an eleven-to-twelve-hour drive to Dallas. Though he'd offered to drive halfway and stay for the night, I declined. I wasn't kidding when I told him I wanted to get the hell out of Dodge.

Most of the time, I was a badass bitch. But seeing what they'd done to Fiona and the message left for me combined with the car accident and the shooting had me unraveling. My desperate hold on my sanity was slipping.

Thinking about where we were heading and what we could find when we got there wasn't helping either.

Unable to compartmentalize any longer, I cried silent tears as I relived our last escape on a bike.

Sage, almost sixteen years of age....

It's extremely hard to eat when someone is staring at you. Especially if said person is glaring and smoking like a chimney. Yet I did it, because if I pissed her off, the food would get taken away, and it was unlikely that I'd get anything else the rest of the day.

So I chewed what now tasted like wet cardboard as she had one arm crossed over herself, holding the crook of her smoking elbow. Her left hand was always her smoking hand. That way she could mete out punishment to me as needed without having to put her cigarette out. Because God knew dragging a child down the hall by the hair and kicking her as you went was hard fucking work. Not that I believed in God.

God was a fucking made up thing to give people a reason to look down their nose at others and to collect money from other people that couldn't afford it. Yet they were convinced that if they didn't slap that check in the collection plate every Sunday, they were going to hell. I had news for them—hell was right here, and I'd been in it my entire life.

Mama's cheeks hollowed as she took a deep drag. Then she blew it out over her head. The smoke filtered up to the stained and dingy ceiling, adding another layer of nicotine to the rest.

"You fucking that boy?"

A spoonful of cereal I hadn't had a chance to chew sucked into my throat and I started to choke. Tears filled my eyes as I fought to breathe. The smoke-filled air didn't help, and I fought gagging on top of choking. Finally an especially rigorous cough broke it free and sent it back into my mouth. Shaking my head so I didn't answer with my mouth full, I moved my jaw as fast as I could. Mama didn't like waiting for an answer.

"No, ma'am," I rasped out, my throat raw and burning.

She narrowed her yellowed eyes at me as she sucked on her cancer stick that hadn't in fifteen plus years given her cancer. Much to my disappointment.

"Good. Because it's time you earned your keep. Uncle Luis is coming to see you tomorrow night. We need to get you cleaned up so you're ready."

My heart slammed against my ribs. Uncle Luis wasn't my fucking uncle, and I was old enough to know that—I'd been old enough to know a lot of things I shouldn't for a long damn time.

Mama had a lot of my "uncles" come to visit over the years. We only had a two-bedroom trailer, so I had to share my room with them because she said they didn't like her smoking, or she had to get up early and didn't want to disturb them. When I was little, I didn't understand what it meant when they snuggled up to me and they had a long lump on their leg. All I knew was that Mama said not to be rude.

I fucking knew now.

The first time one of them touched my "kitty"—that's what Mama used to call my vagina—I was scared as fuck. People don't know what fucked up is unless they've lived inside of a five-year-old's head and seen the confusion there after they have their first orgasm. Even at that age, my mind knew it was wrong, but I couldn't understand how it felt good if it was wrong.

"Prematurely sexualized"—that's what my school counselor called it when I was ten and my teacher figured out what was going on because I slipped and said something I shouldn't have. She called "Seepyess," but I got scared and snuck out of her office before they got there.

I might've been young, but I wasn't stupid. What I knew was that the last time someone called CPS, Mama beat me so bad I couldn't go to school for two weeks. She told them I had the "flew," but again, I was young and thought I hadn't been around a stupid bird once. Later, I learned what the flu meant and what CPS was—it wasn't from flying and it wasn't a woman's name. It was an agency that failed kids like me every damn day.

The loyalty of a child and their parent can be a sick and twisted thing. Wanting to have the parent's love and approval, even though they don't deserve it. So I ran home and told Mama. I figured if I warned her about that lady, she would be happy and not get so mad at me. Before they could get to our house, Mama had us packed up and gone quicker than I could take off my shoes.

I never went back to school after that. Like I said, I was smart though, and I read everything I could get my hands on. The cereal box, the toilet paper wrappers, magazines I found in the neighbor's trash. If it had words, I read it—even if I didn't understand all of them.

"That boy" was Finley. He lived in the same trailer park as we did, way at the back. One day, he caught me going through their trash when he was out on his porch, smoking. He thought he was so cool because he was a year older than me and he smoked. I told him it was disgusting. How we became friends after that, I hadn't a clue, but I supposed it started when he took me under his wing and helped me sound out the big words I didn't understand and explained what they meant.

"He's just my friend, Mama," I promised. Maybe that was a teensy lie because he did kiss me once, but we separated with wrinkled noses and matching grimaces.

Finley worked for "Uncle" Luis. He made deliveries for him.

"You spend an awful lot of time with him, and I don't know if I like that," she grumbled as she eyed me and sucked on her cigarette.

"Mama, I promise you, he's just a friend. He's the only person that's close to my age. He's not interested in me. He's got lots of girlfriends." That wasn't a lie. Finley was good-looking and seemed way older than his seventeen years. He had a lot of girls that went to his house because his mama worked nights. Even the snotty rich girls who looked down their nose at me when they showed up and I was over there. Bitches weren't too snobby to slum it in our trailer park for a chance to be with Finley.

"That's exactly what I'm worried about," she muttered. "I know you ain't stupid, Sage. Your first time should be with someone who knows what they're doing—not some young punk-ass fucker. That's why Uncle Luis is gonna come over. He's gonna talk to you and make sure you know what to expect."

My cereal sat like lead in my stomach. Like I said, I might be uneducated, since Mama didn't let me go to school, but I wasn't dumb. "Uncle" Luis may not have had sex with me before, but he made me do a lot of other things that I was ashamed of.

Things that made me feel gross and wrong.

I hated him.

Not even Finley knew what I'd done to prevent having the shit beat out of me and for Mama to have money to feed us. Luis was a manipulative asshole. He threatened that if I didn't do what he wanted, Mama and I wouldn't have a place to live, and I'd get sent to foster care. He'd also warned me that once I was sixteen, I'd be a woman. He proceeded to tell me the things he was going to do to me—"for my birthday."

After he left that night, I puked up the food he'd brought from some fancy Italian restaurant.

Tomorrow was my birthday.

"Mama, I think I'll be able to figure it out when it's time." I tried to sound relaxed and nonchalant. Inside, I was screaming and losing my goddamn mind.

She harrumphed and stubbed out her smoke. The chair legs scraped across the old linoleum as she stood. "Hurry up and eat. We got shit to do."

Mama went to her room, and I could hear her drawers opening and closing. While she was busy, I shoveled the rest of my cereal into my mouth, barely chewing before I swallowed. I finished drinking the milk as I was standing at the table. Mama came out of her bedroom, and I hurried to wash the bowl and put it in the drain rack.

"Get your fuckin' shoes on, we ain't got all day."

"Yes, ma'am," I mumbled as I held my dark mop of hair back so I could see what I was doing.

We made several stops that day. If I hadn't known the reason behind it and whose cash Mama was using to pay for it all, I might've enjoyed it. Instead, the pedicure, haircut, brow—and oh my God—*down there* waxing seemed like preparations for my trip to the gallows.

As soon as we got home, Mama sat at the table and lit a cigarette from her new carton she bought today. Gee, wonder who paid for that? Then she pulled out her cell phone that Luis had also paid for, and I heard her talking to him. She took a drag, then looked up to see me standing there.

"What are you looking at? Get your ass in your room. I want it cleaned, and you need to go to bed early tonight."

I swallowed hard. "Yes, Mama."

Everything between my legs felt weird when I walked to my room at the other end of the trailer. It didn't take long to clean my room—I didn't have much. Then I sat on my bed, staring out of my window that was covered in dirt on the outside.

Hugging my knees, I rested my chin on them. For the thousandth, maybe the millionth time, I wished I could run away. I wished I had even the slightest bit of control over my life. If the stars hadn't started twinkling, I might not have had any idea how long I sat there. I made a foolish wish when one shot across the sky.

A light tapping on the glass made me jump. I glanced nervously at my closed door before I got on my knees and slowly slid the window up.

"What are you doing here?" I asked Finley who grinned as he held one hand behind his back.

"Come out. I have something for you," he whispered with that lopsided grin.

Nervous excitement raced through my veins and my heart pounded. It certainly wasn't the first time I'd snuck out, and it likely wouldn't be the last.

After casting one last glance at the door, I crawled under my bed and dragged out the tote my mom thought I had my clothes in. From underneath a few shirts and jeans, I carefully took the worn-out leggings that I'd stuffed full of old socks and crap Finley and I found in the trash. I arranged them on the bed in the position I normally slept in. Then I did the same thing with the hoodie. The three hanks of hair I'd cut from underneath and tied with thread were the finishing touches. Once the blanket was over the "body," I poked them under the stuffed hood and laid them out on my pillow to appear as if some of my hair was spread wildly around my head.

Cautiously, I lifted the window high enough that I could slip out. Grabbing my dirty pink Chucks that Finley had bought me at the Goodwill, I handed them to him. Then he helped me climb through. He was taller than me, so he quietly closed the window.

"Hurry," he urged as I held his arm for balance and I put my shoes on. As we ran silently through the tall grass, I kept listening for my mother's shout to ring out. Until we were out of sight, I worried that would be the night she finally caught me.

As we stomped up the uneven porch steps to Finley's back door, I giggled.

Hand on the doorknob, he turned to me with a twinkle in his pale blue eyes. "Ready?"

Biting my bottom lip, I rapidly nodded.

He opened the door, and we passed through the laundry room and down the short hall to his room. With a smirk, he flung the door open. "Surprise!" he announced.

My hands covered my gasp, and tears filled my eyes. Though I tried to blink them away, they rolled silently down my cheeks.

"Aww, don't cry. You're my favorite little spice, I had to do something special for you."

I couldn't help it, I laughed at our long-standing joke.

He had draped colored streamers from the ceiling and balloons were blown up and tossed all over the place. Candles lit the room, though I quickly realized they were little battery-powered ones, and a watery chuckle escaped from behind my fingers.

That wasn't all though. The quilt from his bed that his grandma had made him when he was little was spread out over the worn carpet. In the center was a small round birthday cake. A real honest-to-goodness store-bought cake. It had big pink frosting roses, and scrawled on the top in dark pink was *Happy Birthday Sage*. He had stuck one of the battery candles in the icing next to the flowers and above the writing.

"Fin… I don't know what to say. Thank you so much!" I threw my arms around him and hugged him as tight as I could.

He hugged me back, then separated us. "Sit down—you have to blow out the candle after I sing to you."

If his decorating lacked an artist's touch, his singing was DaVinci. His voice was so beautiful that if I was wrong and there was a heaven, then the angels gave it directly to him.

By the time he was done, I was clapping with a smile so big, my face hurt. He pulled the candle out, looked underneath it, then at me and said, "Make a wish and blow out the candle!"

I blew on the pretend candle, and he must've clicked its little switch, because the light went out of the fake flame. It was cheesy, but it was perfect.

He cut the cake with the biggest, scariest-looking knife I'd ever seen. But once we were eating the sweet confection, what he used to slice it was inconsequential. Between the two of us, we ate the entire thing. When we were done, we leaned against the foot of his bed, ready to pop.

"Happy Birthday a day early," he said with a groan and a hand on his still-flat belly. "Sorry, I have to work tomorrow."

"It's okay," I quietly assured him.

"What did you wish for?"

I shook my head.

"Come on, tell me what you wished for," he encouraged with a nudge of his elbow.

With my attention on my thumbnail that I'd started picking at, I chewed on my lip. Because crazily enough, the entire time I'd sat in my room looking at the sky, I'd been thinking about how I wished Finley could've looked at me like the girls that went to his house. Then my mom could've been right, and it could've been him instead. The problem was, I wasn't attracted to him like that.

I simply *trusted* him. And in my life, I could honestly say he was the only person I felt that way about.

"Sage?"

I felt those stupid tears forming again, but that time I sniffled and blinked them away. Unable to look at him, my gaze locked on my hands that he gently stilled. I mumbled, "Tomorrow, my mom is giving me to Luis."

"What?" The one-word question was flat and held a deadly chill that I'd never heard in his voice before.

"I wished it could be you. That's what I wished for."

"Sage," he choked out.

Brows pulled together, I looked at him with my best pleading face, trying to ignore the horror I saw reflected on his. "Trust me, I know we don't like each other like that, but I don't want him to have that part of me."

"Sage, I can't—" he started to argue but I placed my hand over his mouth.

"Finley, I know you won't hurt me. Please." The last was a barely audible whisper.

His usually dancing blue eyes went hard and cold until they resembled shards of ice. "He's hurt you?" Again, his words were flat and carried with them a blast of frost. I shivered.

"Finley, *please?*" I was almost desperate because all I could think of was the alternative. I knew he was sexually active. Not that we talked about it, but I wasn't a fool. The way the girls flocked to him, he couldn't be awful at it or mean. Besides, he was my best and only friend—the most important person in my life.

He covered his face with his hands and breathed deep and slow several times. Finally, he dropped them, looked me in the eye, and nodded.

The next several minutes were a blur until I found myself under his sheet without my clothes on. He turned his back to me, and I heard a rustling.

"What are you doing?"

He huffed. "I'm putting on a condom."

"What? Why?" I was confused.

"Cover your eyes."

I complied, and the bed dipped as his warm skin brushed against mine and I froze.

"Open them." This time there was no excitement in those words.

Propped up on his elbow, he looked down at me. His dark

blond hair falling over one eye. "Because you don't want to get pregnant, Sage."

My face flamed. My lower lip trembled. I felt so ignorant, I wanted to cry.

"Don't," he softly pleaded. He pulsed against my thigh, and I froze. "Jesus, this isn't going to work, Sage."

"I'm sorry. I just... I mean, how are you... like that?"

He snorted a humorless laugh. "Sage—" He looked up at the ceiling. "—it's a dick. It doesn't really take much."

"Oh."

"Sage, I'm probably gonna have to get you ready."

Oh shit. I truly hadn't thought this through. What the fuck were we doing?

"Can we turn out the lights?"

His sigh was heavy with relief.

And so, my first time was with my best friend. I didn't love him the way someone should when they did that with them, but in that dark room, I shed the last of my innocence—on my terms.

A week later, and we were racing away on his dirt bike with his blood-soaked shirt between us as I held on for my dear, bruised, and battered life.

EIGHTEEN

Raptor

"BED OF ROSES"—BON JOVI

The mysterious package that Venom was sending still hadn't arrived.

"Do you need another beer, Prez?" Lola asked as she leaned on the bar across from me. With the way she was positioned, her tits pushed up and practically spilled out of her low-cut tank top. She had come with Gator when we reopened, and she'd been very clear that she'd love to fuck me, but I simply couldn't. And that pissed me off because it was confusing as fuck.

Actually, that was a lie, and I'd lied to myself enough over the last several months. I'd stayed away from Sage for so many years because deep inside, where my hawk had lain dormant, the reason was also hidden. I'd known if I had one single taste of her, I wouldn't be able to let her go—that she would own me.

Heart.

And.

Soul.

And I'd walked away from her, thinking I was doing what was best for both of us. I was a fucking idiot. Another fuckup to add to my ever-growing list.

"Prez, there's a guy out at the gate with a Bastards cut. Says his name is Blade and that he wants to see you," Torque called out from behind the bar where the security monitors were currently placed.

Leaving my beer, I got up and went around to get a better look. Sure as shit, Blade sat there on his bike, visor lifted on his modular, flipping off the camera with a shit-eating grin. My gaze narrowed as I noticed the chick on the bike with him with her hands wrapped around his waist. For a second, I wondered. Hoped. Until I saw the dark strands that had escaped her braid, blowing in the breeze. Relief and disappointment warred within me, and I wanted to hit something.

"Let him in," I told Torque. He entered the remote code, and we watched as the lone bike entered the property. "Make sure the gate closes."

"Roger that," Torque replied.

I motioned for everyone to follow and turned to go outside. Lola moved back as I passed, and my hand brushed her ass. Her giggle told me it was on purpose, and I rolled my eyes as I shook my head but kept walking. Gator and I were going to have to have a very serious talk.

We pushed the door open and stepped out into the hot Texas afternoon.

A grin broke out on my face that matched the ones on both Blade's face and Phoenix's next to me. It was a bittersweet reunion of sorts. Blade plowed into me and squeezed my ribs until I thought they might crack.

"You crazy fucker," Phoenix shouted as he looped an arm around Blade's neck and shook him slightly. Blade released me to give a massive embrace to Phoenix.

"Goddamn, I missed you guys." He took a deep breathe, then exhaled, smile still in place. "It's so fucking good to see you—you just don't know."

"Are you just here for a visit, or are you here to stay?" Phoenix asked as he patted Blade's back patch and gave him another side hug. His smile faltered a bit, and I zeroed in on the change. Then his gaze darted back to his bike where his girl was taking off her gloves and unbuckling her helmet. She seemed to be moving in slow motion.

Several of the brothers appreciatively glanced around Blade at the perfectly curved chick in snug frayed jeans, knee-high black biker boots, and a tight red tank top. Someone let out a low whistle. The thick mahogany braid fell over one shoulder, and the end curled up around her peaked nipple. Deep inside, my hawk stirred.

I hated that I'd noticed anything about her because it felt like I was cheating.

And there was the crux of my problem.

Ripping my gaze from her, I glanced back at Blade who was looking at me strangely. That's when a set of tits pressed to my arm, and I looked down to see Lola watching the other chick with a narrow-eyed stare. The woman who arrived with Blade had tits that were enough to outshine Lola's any day of the week and twice on Sunday—and I only knew that because Lola occasionally entertained the boys by dancing on the pole.

"Jesus, Lola. Get back inside," I snapped at her with a glare. She fucking knew I didn't like to be touched, and I was getting tired of telling her. There was also no reason for her to come out here, but from her behavior, she must've been watching everything unfold through the window.

The brunette ripped off her helmet and threw it at me. I ducked and it hit the gravel behind me and rolled.

"This was a fucking mistake," she snapped and turned on her heel. Frozen in disbelief, I stood there and watched her upside-down-heart-shaped ass stalk away.

"You fucking asshole," Blade muttered and took off after her. I saw red.

It must not have been very subtle because I heard Rooster mutter, "Oh, shit."

Banshee quietly asked what the fuck was going on, but I didn't hear anyone's response. I'd taken off after Blade. The gravel crunched and settled, making it hard to run at top speed, but my legs were longer than Blade's. I grabbed his arm and spun him back. Surprise lit his face, but I ignored it as well.

Because when Blade started running after her, the little vixen took off, and I was gonna hunt her down. She stumbled when her ankle turned, and I tried to catch her, but she slammed into the chain-link fence next to the gate latch.

Momentum carried me into her, and I clutched the metal, my arms caging her in and preventing my body from smashing hers into the fence. She spun to face me, eyes spitting fire and teeth clenched. Instinctively, I lifted one hand and wrapped it around her neck. With light pressure, I squeezed, and her racing pulse pounded against my thumb and fingers. My body had a mind of its own and pressed flush against hers.

"Let me go," she demanded between bared teeth.

"Why? So you can go back to your new toy?" I was being intentionally hateful because I was furious and I was man enough to admit—jealous as a motherfucker.

"Fuck. You."

"You wish," I taunted against her ear and pressed the hard length of my cock up against her hip. I couldn't believe the bullshit that was rolling out of my mouth. None of it was what I meant, but my rage at the thought of her with Blade—my friend and brother—instead of me, was short-circuiting my brain. My mouth opened and stupid fell out.

"I hate you," she hissed.

The words stabbed through my chest like a jagged blade, and I gasped at the pain. My hand clutched her neck tighter. Not enough to hurt her, but enough that her face started to turn red. Of course, some of that was probably her fury that matched mine.

"You're mine, goddamn it," I rasped in a pained whisper.

A cold blade touch the vulnerable underside of my jaw and I went still.

"Do not make me choose," Blade ground out behind me. His voice carried both anger and pain.

Sage slowly wrapped her hands around my wrist. Holding me with a gentleness I didn't deserve at the moment, she slid her fingers up and loosened my hold.

Chest heaving, I staggered back a step into Blade, and my arms dropped to my sides. I'd fucked everything up, and now it was obviously too late.

"I'm pregnant, Adrien."

Shock ripped through me at her declaration. The hateful little voice in my head said history was repeating itself. No words would form as I fought to *breathe*. Doe eyes watched me as her lower lip beginning to tremble.

"Is it mine?" I asked, my voice sounding like I'd swallowed a thousand razors blades.

She slapped me across the face and my head snapped back because I didn't, for a single second, see that coming. But I grabbed her wrist before she dropped her hand and pulled her up against me. I ignored Blade simmering behind me. In a low and barely controlled warning, I told her, "Do that again and you won't sit for a week."

"You don't have that right anymore. You gave that up when you left."

"And *you* are in my *brother's* bed now, but you're pissed or surprised I asked if it's mine?" I lashed out as I lunged and shook the fence on either side of her in my fury.

The expression on her face was one of pained disbelief. And a look I'd never seen her wear around me.

Fear.

That gutted me.

Her chest heaved, which brought her tits against me with each breath. "Not that you deserve an answer with the way you up and left, but unlike you, I haven't fucked *anyone* since you walked out."

A stunned silence surrounded us.

"Maybe we should go inside where you can talk," Phoenix calmly suggested. "In private."

Gripping the metal in my hands so tightly I was afraid it would bend or cut my fingers off, I closed my eyes and took a deep breath. Swallowing the lump of acid in my throat, I let go and stepped back. Dazed and ashamed of my behavior, I glanced over my shoulder.

"Gator took everyone inside when you took off after her and I said this was a private matter," Phoenix explained.

Jaw clenching, I nodded, then swung my attention back to the woman who held my undeserving, tattered, and blackened heart in her soft and caring hands. My fury fizzled like a doused flame. "I—"

Her worried gaze searched mine.

Phoenix wrapped his hand around my arm and guided me back to the clubhouse. But I stopped. Ignoring my closest brothers who were there at the moment, I straightened my shoulders.

"This isn't me," I stoically began with a shake of my head. "I have no other excuse. I'll see you inside."

Her eyes were flat, and she was devoid of emotion. Her arms

were wrapped protectively around her middle. How did we come back from this? How did I make things right?

Or maybe the better question was—could I?

Phoenix and Blade exchanged a look that I ignored as I stormed back into the cool interior of the clubhouse. Without speaking to a soul, I went directly to my office. With a deprecating laugh, I poured myself more than three fingers of the Jameson 15-year-old Millennium Edition. It was a gift sent to me from Venom shortly after I'd arrived. Until now, I hadn't touched it except to place it in my bottom drawer—just like where he always kept his personal bottle in his desk.

Uncaring that it was a whiskey to be sipped, I tossed it back. Then I poured another.

"You in a better place?" Blade asked from the doorway. He stepped into the room and closed the door.

I folded my lips in and snorted.

"She didn't deserve that." His brows lifted as he waited for my reply.

His censure had my hackles up. Staring him in the eye, I dumped the second glass of the expensive whiskey down my throat.

"You think I don't know that?" I shook my head in disgust. "What the fuck is wrong with me?"

"Jealous?"

I cocked a brow at him.

"What? I'm just calling it like I see it. But look, bro, what she and I have is nothing but friendship. Always has been." He rubbed the palm of his hand over his close-cropped beard.

"You expect me to believe that? After all the times I saw you go to her room over the years?" The words were said without malice, merely an observation. In truth, I wasn't angry at him for what might've happened before I made Sage mine. That would be asinine of me—whether I liked it or not.

"What we did in her room is my business. But I can promise you, it was not sexual in any way."

I dropped into my chair and leaned back. Staring at the ceiling I went over everything in my head. Deciding it was irrelevant if nothing had happened after I left, I pushed that aside as something that wasn't top priority.

Fucking hell, she was pregnant. *Pregnant.*

"I was a supreme dick."

"Yep."

It was mine. And now that my head was clear, I felt that deep in my soul.

"Do you think she's ever going to forgive me?"

"Bro, I can't speak for her any more than she could speak for me."

"Ugh!" I brought the chair back up and buried my face in my hands as my elbows rested on my knees. I tried to imagine the rest of my life without her in it. It was impossible.

And she was *pregnant.* Crazy how that was just now sinking in. Fuck. And I'd practically attacked her like a goddamn lunatic. I needed my head read—but not until I won her back.

"Can I ask you a question?"

I let my hands fall. They dangled between my legs as I looked at one of the men I considered a brother, though we had no blood connection. Feeling defeated, I sighed. "Sure."

"That chick out there. Is it serious?"

"What?" I asked. I know my expression was telling him he was losing his fucking marbles.

"Tits McGee out there that was hanging on you outside," he explained.

Understanding dawned. "Lola? Fuck no. I haven't touched her. No interest, and that's a damn fact. She came with Gator, and he's gonna have a long talk with her."

"Good, because if Sage ever forgives you, and that club bunny out there tried that shit again, Sage will fuck her up—then you."

I snorted. "I don't doubt she could put Lola on her ass, but there's nothing there."

My resolve strengthened and I looked him straight in the eye. "I'm getting her back. Even if it means I have to grovel."

"Ohhh-ho! I'm definitely sticking around a while, cuz that's something I'd pay good money to see." He grinned. Fucker.

"Now that all of that is out of the way, do you wanna tell me what the fuck is going on that y'all came down here under the radar?"

He took one of the seats across from my desk. For the next hour and a half, he explained everything that had been going on since I left. To say I was furious would be the understatement of the century. If I—no, *when* I found them, I was going to take them apart piece by piece. Then I was going to have Phoenix torch the pieces back in our pit.

Looked like that pit just became dual duty.

I stood up. Now it was time to grovel like a motherfucker.

"Where is she?"

Blade got to his feet and lit a blunt. He held my gaze as he took a deep hit and put his lighter away. He held the smoke in, then blew it out. His voice came out a bit strained as he answered my question. "Your room."

Fuck. I poured another glass. Then I called Voodoo.

Knocking on my own fucking door was humbling. Especially when I was pretty sure she was going to ignore me. I didn't blame her one fucking bit.

Resting my head against the door, I pressed my flat hand to the wood like I could feel her on the other side if I did.

"Sage?" She wasn't Cookie to me anymore. Not because I was ashamed of what she'd been and done before now. Because fuck it, she was a grown, single woman and was entitled to whatever the fuck she wanted. But she was mine now—I just needed to make her see it.

There was silence.

"Baby, I don't even know where to start."

Nothing.

"I'm a fuckup. These last few months without you have been the worst of my life. And that's sayin' something. I should've asked you to come with me, and if you had said no, I shoulda begged."

I slid down to my knees but with my head still against the door and my hand splayed flat, hoping she was on the other side with her hand against mine. But on the other side.

Jesus, it's hot in here. Did the AC quit working?

Desperate, I turned my head, so my ear was to the door. If I could just hear her moving around, I would know she was okay. But she was still ignoring me. Maybe she was sitting there listening.

"Should we tell him that Sloane and Niara took her to their shop?" I heard someone whisper from somewhere behind me.

"Nah, I'm enjoying this," came the whispered reply.

"How much of that Jameson did you say he drank?"

"About half the bottle. Okay, maybe a bit more."

A low chuckle.

Huh? I opened one eye and peered down the hall toward the voices. All I could see were blurry blobs that seemed to be shaped like people. I thought that if I squinted, closed one eye, and tipped my head back, I could make them out better.

Wrong.

All that did was make me dizzy, and the next thing I knew, I was on my ass. Crawling back to the door, I banged my head re-peatedly. "Sage."

"What the heck is going on?" asked a third voice. But when I blinked, there seemed to be four blobs now.

"This, my fine young lads, is a prime example of how not to grovel," voice one explained. I glared.

"Says who?" I demanded.

"Oh dang. Adrien, dude...." That blob looked like Sam.

"Sam? Whachu doing here?"

He crouched by my outstretched legs. "We told you we were gonna come over tonight. Mom left again, and Seth's nanny dropped us off."

"Quit calling her my nanny," the Seth blob said, but then I wasn't sure because they both seemed to clear, then duplicate. "She's the housekeeper."

"Whatever helps you sleep at night," Sam blob ribbed Seth blob. This was whack as fuck. Sam blob got right up in my face, and he was suddenly clear.

"It's a miracle!" I rejoiced.

"Huh?"

I wasn't gonna lie, I had no idea who said that.

"Hey, bossman, let me help you out," Phoenix offered, and I realized he was standing there, holding out his hand. "Cookie's not in there. Let's get you to bed."

Frowning, I squinted to see him better. "Not Cookie. Sage."

"Yeah, okay. And you're fucking hammered."

Though I grumbled, I couldn't concentrate, so I reached for his hand and groaned as I got to my feet.

"Jesus, you're too goddamn big for this," I heard him mutter.

With a grunt, I glared at him. "Fuck off," I mumbled. Then I blinked a few times and saw Sam and Seth still standing there. Evidently, I hadn't imagined them. The incredibly minuscule sober part of my brain felt like a grade-A piece of shit. I was being a terrible example. "I'm sorry you're seeing me like this. Why do I feel like not a damn thing went right today?"

"It's okay, man, Seth and I can shoot some pool or just hang out. We're not little kids."

A heavy sigh fell from my lips. "Yeah. I know."

Phoenix ducked under my arm and helped me into my room.

"Fuckin' door wasn't even locked?"

"Apparently not."

With Phoenix's help, I shuffled to my bed where I proceeded to fall flat on my face, feet hanging off the edge. He pulled my boots off and I grunted but my eyelids weighed a ton.

That was the last I remembered until a familiar scent tickled my nose. "Mmm," I hummed appreciatively. Then I practically purred when gentle fingers sifted through my hair, lightly grazing my scalp.

"Hope you're prepared to grovel," a seductive voice whispered in my ear before the bed shifted and the intoxicating scent vanished.

Not only did I plan on groveling—I planned to kill whoever had tried to harm her.

NINETEEN

Sage ("Cookie")

"GANGSTA"—KEHLANI

Though we were halfway across the country, I was nervous going to Sloane's shop. It seemed like all I did was look over my shoulder these days. Yet the thought of staying at the clubhouse where Raptor was at the moment pissed me the fuck off.

"How dare he ask me if my baby was his? That motherfucker," I grumbled as I paced the back room of the metaphysical store Sloane and her mom owned. With the serene surroundings, my thoughts and emotions shouldn't be so chaotic. It made me really wish Venom or Hawk were here because I could use some of their calming juju.

"I mean, it's a legit question. You have been apart for some time, right?" Niara asked. I stopped in my tracks and shot her a "are you fucking kidding me?" look before I turned to Sloane.

"Is she always such a rant killer? That kind of rationality

isn't needed—at least not when I feel the need to be pissy." Arms akimbo, I shook my head.

Both women snickered. I threw up my hands.

Blade stuck his head in the room and asked, "You ready to head back?"

With a sigh, my shoulders dropped. "Yeah, I guess."

"If you decide you don't want to stay at the clubhouse, the offer still stands to stay at my house," Sloane reminded me as her nose crinkled.

"Thank you, I really appreciate that. I'm sorry I've been such a bitch. I know it's not a great first impression. I'm not really processing everything well. You girls have been amazing, and I appreciate that more than you'll know." They both stood up to give me a hug.

"That's what sisters are for," Sloane whispered as she held me tightly. That brought tears to my eyes because I wasn't an ol' lady, but she still considered me like one.

"You have my number saved, right?" she asked. She'd given it to me earlier, saying, "Just in case."

I nodded.

"Do you think it's safe for you guys to be riding around so much?" Niara asked with worry knitting her brow. "You kind of stick out a bit with Iowa plates." The fact that these women were still so kind after the bitchy way I'd behaved was endearing.

"We never saw anyone following us when we left, and Blade definitely took the scenic route. There were long stretches where we were alone on the roads, so I doubt it. We didn't make it obvious we were going anywhere for a long period of time, which is why I don't have much with me. Also, with my hair back to its normal color, I'm not really recognizable as Cookie." Those were all the things I kept telling myself to keep the panic at bay.

I finished saying goodbye, and then Blade brought me back to the compound.

"I can stay in another room," I argued when we stopped outside the clubhouse. "I don't feel right kicking Raptor out of his room."

"The problem is, the other rooms have bunk beds and share a bathroom. A few of the other brothers already stay in them."

I'd had no clue it was his room when I was taken there to shower the road grime off earlier. I'd simply been told it was the only room with a decent bathroom at the moment. When I'd seen some of the items I recognized as Raptor's on the bathroom counter, it had clicked. Sloane's offer to hang out had been perfect timing. I couldn't wait to get out of there before I did something I might regret.

Blade led the way inside. There was no sign of Raptor anywhere as I passed through the common area. Two of the brothers were sitting on the couches, watching a movie. Blade went over to them to talk while I made my way to the back.

"Please don't let him be with that little bitch from earlier," I muttered to myself. "I look terrible in orange."

Except I needn't have worried—he was passed out facedown on the bed and reeking of whiskey. Despite the muddy water under our bridge, I was unable to be that close and not touch him. It was probably the fact that Adrien Krow was the flame to my moth—I was drawn to him, and the fact that he had the power to destroy me didn't faze me.

The bed creaked when I sat next to his sprawled form. Trying to stop myself was a futile endeavor, because without thinking, I reached for him. Not to wake him—I was still pissed—but so I could run my fingers through his thick, dark hair.

"Hope you're prepared to grovel," I whispered in his ear. Then I feathered a light kiss over his cheek and got back to my feet. No way was I tempting myself by sleeping in the same bed. That was a recipe for disaster because the second he touched me, I'd likely combust.

I silently gathered my belongings and left the room.

Then I shot off a quick text to Sloane. She immediately responded with "HURRY!".

"Blade, do you mind taking me to Sloane's house?"

"Of course not. Are you okay?" He searched my gaze as I hugged my bag to my chest.

Blade was understanding and accepting of my melancholy mood. He helped me put my bag back on his bike, and then we were on the road.

The entire way, I was lost in my thoughts about Raptor.

Deep inside, where foolish dreams and hopeful desires danced, I prayed he believed I was worth humbling himself for. Because no matter how much he meant to me, he had deeply hurt me. There was no denying I loved him. Yet, no matter how deep my love was for him, I needed to be loved back—I *deserved* to be loved back.

It had taken me years, but even if I couldn't pinpoint the exact moment or event that made me realize it, I was worth more than I had ever given myself credit for.

Whether I ever went back to Iowa or not, Cookie was gone. She had come into existence in a time when I needed a strength that I never had at any point in my life before. But I wasn't that woman anymore.

For one, I was going to be a mother. Not for me, but for my baby, I decided to be a better version of myself. To maintain the same backbone and tenacity, but living for something other than finding pleasure in whoever I wanted in my bed for the night. My priorities had shifted.

Was I ashamed of Cookie? Hell no. I still loved sex, don't get me wrong. It was simply a matter of that chapter of my life being over—because I had no interest in being with anyone but one man.

A man that had made me so fucking mad, I wasn't sure how long it would take him to make up for his bullshit. A man that I hadn't been able to lock my heart against.

"So instead of talking to you, he went and got drunk?" Niara asked while tapping her fingers on the side of her glass.

"We could always mix up a little something for him," Sloane offered with a wicked smile.

I practically spit my water out at that.

"That won't be necessary," I choked out. "If he doesn't care enough to fight for me, then at the very least, he'll step up and be a father if it kills me to make him." I would harden my heart that at the moment seemed fragile and a breath away from shattering completely.

"There better at least be some diamonds involved in that groveling." Niara offered her opinion as she sipped her wine. Her long gauzy skirt pooled around her legs and drifted to the floor where she sat on the couch with her legs tucked beneath her. Though I had only met her that day, she seemed like a kindred spirit, and I'd already decided I liked her.

"And maybe a cherry-red Ferrari," Sloane added as she held her glass of flavored water up for me to tap mine against. The ringing of the crystal as they met echoed in the room.

"A Ferrari?" Phoenix drawled as he peeked his head around the refrigerator door and shot us a "you guys are nuts" look.

"Keep out of this, you. We're plotting," Sloane told him, though the love shining in her pale eyes made my chest ache.

Niara craned her neck to look over the back of the couch to glare into the kitchen. "Just because you finally pulled your head out of your ass doesn't mean your friend will."

"Brother," Phoenix corrected then returned to digging around in the fridge.

"Tomato, tomahto," Niara huffed as she waved her hand

dismissively in his direction. Bottoming up her glass, she leaned over to the coffee table for the bottle she alone was able to drink.

"It's not fair that you're the only non-pregnant one here," I grumbled. Both women went wide-eyed and stilled. "What?"

"Don't say things like that!" Niara told me with her big green eyes wide. That was when I caught the mesmerizing rings of gold around her pupils.

"What did I say?" I whispered to Sloane behind my hand.

"Do you know who you're in a room with?" Sloane blinked rapidly.

Glancing around before focusing my attention back on her, I whispered, "Who?"

"Phoenix!" Sloane shouted.

"Yeah, babe?" he responded from the kitchen where he was busy doing something I couldn't see. It was still very strange that he and Sloane opened their home to me. More so that Sloane already seemed like a friend. Especially after she told me that she knew he and I had slept together. Relief that she wasn't upset had hit hard, and I'd explained it was in the past and that it had never been serious.

To be honest, I had expected things to be awkward—they were far from it.

"She knows about the stuff all you guys can do, right?" she called out.

"Yes," he replied, intent on whatever task he was so diligently performing.

"Good." She returned her attention to me. "Niara and I— we're witches."

"Okaaaay?" I wasn't following her.

Sloane was slowly shaking her head as she stared at me. "You can't manifest things like that around us."

I laughed.

They didn't.

"You're serious, aren't you?" I sat there, mouth gaping.

"Girl—" Niara pointed at me. "—you should know better than to disbelieve."

Phoenix came into the living room, carrying a giant cutting board that he set on the coffee table in front of us. On it was an assortment of cheeses, crackers, grapes, and... "Is that beef jerky?"

"Yeah." He shrugged. "Sloane likes those charcoochie board things. We didn't have any pepperonis and shit. That was the best I could do."

I started crying. Phoenix pulled away with an expression of horror, looking at me like I had something contagious.

"Keagan!" Sloane admonished. "Be nice. She's still at that emotional stage."

"Stage?" Phoenix repeated in disbelief. "When does that go away? Because you're *still* emotional."

Sloane threw a grape at him that he caught in his mouth, then with a grin, he leaned down to kiss her waiting lips.

"Don't be an ass," she admonished.

Sniffling, I finally got myself under control. "I'm so sorry. That comes on without notice."

Sloane waved my apology away. "No need to apologize, I totally get it."

Niara leaned over to grab the biggest chunk of jerky and threw it at Phoenix. It bounced off his cheek, but he still managed to catch it. "Go hang out with your other brother in the family room. We're trying to have girl time out here. Unless, of course, you bore him, in which case, I could totally keep him occupied for you."

He narrowed his gaze at her. "Though he can handle himself, you stay away. Evil woman."

Her smile turned downright wicked. "You have no idea."

"I'm out. You girls have fun." He leaned over and whispered

something in Sloane's ear that made her cheeks turn a becoming pink. Then he kissed her in a way that was so hot, I was sure I saw sparks. It truly warmed my heart to see him so happy.

"Bro, you coming, or what?" Blade asked from the hall that led to the family room where the guys were supposed to be having some video game man time.

"Not even breathing hard yet," Phoenix shot back, and Sloane giggled. They were so damn cute, it made my lower lip tremble again.

"*You okay?*" I heard Blade ask. From the way no one else appeared to have heard, I knew the fucker was talking in my head.

After a glare for talking in my head, I nodded.

"*You sure?*"

My shoulders slumped and my eyes closed for a moment. Then I opened them and gave him a sad smile.

"*You okay out here with the girls?*"

I nodded. Then I noticed Niara raking her gaze over Blade like she wanted to eat him alive.

"*I so wanna fuck her,*" he said, causing me to laugh and almost spit out the water I'd just drank. With a chuckle, he followed Phoenix back to the den.

"Now, where were we? Pass me some of the cheddar," Niara instructed as she was filling her glass again. Sloane stacked some cheese on a cracker and handed it over, then did the same for me.

"Thanks." Not even trying to be ladylike, I shoved the whole thing in my mouth. Yes, I was totally eating my feelings.

"How will she know when he's groveled enough?" Sloane asked.

"Guys, I'm not even sure I really want him to grovel. I just want him to feel the same way about me as I do him. With maybe a little groveling," I admitted and held my thumb and finger a tiny ways apart.

The girls laughed.

"Well, until you feel he's back in your good graces, you're welcome to stay here. We have plenty of room, and Phoenix had a state-of-the-art security system installed. We'll give Raptor time to pull his head out of his ass, then we gotta do something about a house for y'all." Sloane arched one raven-black brow and smirked before she popped a grape into her mouth.

"Girl, you need to do something about a house for your damn self. When did you say your mom was coming back from Belize?" Niara asked as we all gorged ourselves on the makeshift charcuterie board.

"In a week," Sloane answered through a mouthful of grapes.

The rest of the night was spent laughing more than I had in months. My heart ached a bit because I hadn't heard a word from Raptor. Then again, he was probably still crashed out in his bed.

When we finally called it a night, I fell asleep—hoping and praying he didn't disappoint me.

The next morning, Niara and I helped Sloane make a massive amount of food.

"Holy crap, this is a lot of damn food. Are we expecting more people?" I joked as I piled the scrambled eggs I'd helped make onto a plate.

"Girl, you've seen these men eat." Sloane gave me a smirk. "Sometimes, I worry Phoenix will eat me out of house and home. Thankfully, he refills the fridge on a regular basis."

The doorbell chimed, and Phoenix checked the cameras on his phone.

"Delivery. You girls stay here. Blade, do you mind staying with them?" Phoenix asked.

"Of course not, but don't expect to have any bacon left when you get back," Blade replied as he reached for the plate that Sloane had set on the table.

Everyone chuckled and Phoenix pointed at him in warning. "I will torch everything you love," he threw out in jest and went to see who it was.

"Gluttony is one of the deadly sins," Niara told Blade over the rim of her coffee cup before she took a sip. Sloane snickered.

"So is lust, but I sure as hell don't shy away from that. If I'm going to hell, I'm making it worth it." Blade gave Niara a heated stare and I rolled my eyes. What I really wanted to tell him was "Down boy." He was lucky he was my best friend, and I loved his crazy ass.

We heard murmuring for a moment, then the door closed. Phoenix's footsteps preceded his return to the kitchen. I'd taken my first drink of orange juice and looked up to see a massive bouquet of roses obscuring his entire torso.

"Two guesses as to who these are for," Phoenix called out from behind the massive display of deep red. They were lush and fragrant—and must've cost a fortune.

"And so it begins," Sloane teased in a playfully ominous way before Niara added a dramatic "Dun, dun, dun" that had me laughing.

Phoenix set them on the counter, and I stood up to bury my face in the velvety blooms. There was a small pink card in the center. My heart fluttered and my fingers trembled as I pulled it out of its little envelope.

In a bold scrawl, it read:

I suck. Please forgive me.

Tears filled my eyes and Niara plucked the card from my hands. "No ma'am. Don't you dare let him get off that easy. But that is a good start."

"Oh, don't worry, I'm not letting him off the hook that easy, but I would never have guessed he would be the kind to send me flowers." I sniffled.

"Well, there was also this." Phoenix held out a small box wrapped with a bow.

"What the hell? How did he pull all this off so quickly?" It hadn't been that long since I'd arrived, yet, somehow, he had found the time to arrange this before ten-thirty in the morning.

Sloane laughed. "Well, the man does turn into a hawk. He probably flew his ass to where he needed to go. I'm a little jealous. Beats Dallas traffic in the morning hands down."

The corner of my mouth kicked up. Tugging on the end, I untied the satin ribbon that was wrapped a ridiculous number of times around the box. When I lifted the lid to peer inside, I quickly closed it again.

"Well, don't keep us waiting! What is it?" Niara asked as she strummed her fingers on the table.

"Ummm, nothing—just something silly that was a reminder of our days in Iowa," I replied in a falsely bright tone with the smile to match.

Phoenix and Blade both choked on their food. Of course, they would know what Raptor's tastes involved. I palmed my face.

"I'll just go put this in my bag. Be right back," I told everyone and rushed to the room I was staying in. Once there, I sat on the edge of the bed and tossed the ribbon to the side. If I thought my hands were shaking when I opened the card, they were worse as I removed the lid.

With the blood-red ribbon—long enough to wrap around my wrists and forearms—sitting on the comforter by my thigh, I stared into the matte-black box. Nestled in the black velvet was a set of magnetic nipple clamps and a magnetic clit clamp.

The second they registered, my nipples hardened to tight aching peaks and my core clenched.

The card in the box read:

I dreamed of you all night.

The rest of the week was much of the same. Flowers covered nearly every flat surface in Sloane and her mom's house. It smelled like a floral shop in there. Gifts were lined up on the dresser.

If I had to guess, Blade told him I'd left most of my things back in Iowa, because one gift was a long red La Perla nightgown and matching robe. Though pink had been my favorite color, thanks to Raptor, red was my second. I'm sure it was no coincidence that the gown was the exact color of the ribbon on the first gift.

He had tried to stop by several times, but I refused to see him. Mostly because where he was concerned, I was weak. For as long as I could remember, I had wanted him. For a brief moment in time, I'd had him. Then with a painful stab to the heart, he had gutted me—so while the young woman in me cried out for me to forgive him, the tough cookie in me dug her heels in.

His latest visit was heralded by the sound of his sleek black bike coming down the road. How I knew it was his when it could've been anyone's, I had no idea, but I sure as hell did. And my heart thumped double time when it pulled into the driveway. While I waited, my pulse increased to a rate that had to be unhealthy.

Excited and anxious, I peeked through the curtains at him standing outside on the porch. It was really kind of sweet, the way he paced and ran his hand over his beard before seeming to talk to himself. In over ten years, I'd never seen the man so nervous.

Finally, he knocked. I jumped to go get it, and Sloane shrieked behind me. Hand on her chest, she breathed heavy. "Girl, you scared me!"

"You! How the heck did I not hear you there?"

"Hmpf! Maybe because you were too wrapped up in staring

at that fine specimen of man-meat out there." She snickered and I gave her a playful swat.

"Stop it! You shouldn't objectify him like that," I teasingly admonished through my grin.

"Just callin' it like I see it." The comical brow waggle she added to her statement had me giggling.

"Am I making the right decision?" I asked, my smile falling and the worried wrinkle in my forehead turning the moment serious.

She sighed. "I wish I could answer that for you, but I can't. What I can say is that I believe he's sorry. Phoenix said he's been especially, um… surly this week. Now, do I think you need to keep that grovel train rolling? Hell yeah. Not for the gifts and sweet gestures, but because he needs to make sure his actions sink in, as the next time, he might lose you."

"What if the only reason he's doing this is because I'm pregnant?" I whispered.

She didn't say anything, but her worried gaze mirrored mine.

Once I stood before the door, I took a deep breath and fortified my defenses, then turned the knob.

TWENTY

Raptor

"FOR MY SAKE"—SHINEDOWN

When Sloane and Phoenix's front door opened, I needed to grab something to keep from falling over. My fingers gripped the doorframe. She was more beautiful than I remembered. So much so that she took my breath away.

"Sage," I whispered, unable to get anything else to pass my lips.

This was the first time she'd actually answered the door herself, and I was suddenly tongue-tied. Her sky-blue eyes seemed brighter with the dark hair that softly framed her face. My fingers twitched with the need to touch it.

"Raptor," she responded. And was her tone as needy as mine?

For several heartbeats, we simply stared at each other. Then I cleared my throat and reached in my pocket to withdraw the gift

I'd picked up yesterday. It seemed silly now that I was standing in front of her.

"Can we talk?" I asked.

For a minute, I thought she was going to say no and shut the door in my face. Her hesitation was a painful stab to my chest.

"Sure," she finally replied, causing my stomach to bottom out like a rollercoaster dropping from the peak. Quietly, she stepped outside, and I backed up to let her pass. When she sat down on the top step of the porch, I settled in beside her with my forearms resting on my knees.

"How are you feeling?"

"I'm okay."

"No morning sickness?"

"Not really."

"That's good." Jesus, I sounded lame as hell. This was the most stilted our conversations had been in years. Even before I'd given into my desire for her, things weren't this bad. I sighed. "What can I do to fix this, Sage?" Because at that point, I was willing to do almost anything. Crazy that it had taken me so long to realize what I'd had in front of me the whole time. As I stared at her profile, she wrapped her arms protectively around her legs and rested her chin on her knee.

Contemplative, she stared out in the direction of the house across the street. "Do you know how long I was in love with you?" she began.

It wasn't an answer to my question and her past tense use didn't escape me— it sent panic damn near racing through my veins. "No," I hesitantly responded.

"Since shortly after I met you the first time."

That was over ten years ago. Jesus, I'd wasted so much time being a close-hearted fucking idiot.

"And now?" I was terrified of the answer she'd give me.

She turned her head to look me in the eye. "I can't stop, no matter how hard I try."

Her revelation made my chest light, and my heart seemed to stutter to a stop before it took off racing. Needing to touch her, I reached out to catch the silky strands of hair that blew across her face. Gently, I tucked them behind her ear, then let the backs of my fingers trail down her cheek. Using my thumb, I traced her full lower lip.

"I don't want you to stop," I murmured, reveling in the softness of her skin, the blue of her eyes that matched the Texas summer skies. Having this woman's love was like winning the goddamn lottery.

"Why?"

I slipped my hand under her hair to cradle the back of her neck. Then I leaned over to softly press my lips to hers before I whispered against them. "Because you're mine."

A thrill coursed through me when she parted her lips to my tongue. Tenderly, I stroked into her mouth—tasting and teasing. Her whimper stoked my fire, but I held myself in check. The last thing I wanted to do was scare her away. Because of that, I forced myself to end the quickly heating kiss. Breathing heavily, I rested my forehead to hers.

I wanted to tell her I loved her. The problem with that was, it was only words. What I needed to do was *show* her.

An idea came to me, and I decided to hold onto my gift for the time being. "Go out to dinner with me," I urged as I stroked my nose along hers. Something about being close to her settled the disquiet within me. A softer side emerged, and if my hawk could purr, he would've in that moment.

"Tonight?" Her question was breathless, and goosebumps broke out along my neck from the soft puff of her breath.

No. Now. "Yes."

Her pause made my chest cave as I silently begged her to agree. "And we'll talk?"

After I fucked the living hell out of her. "Yes."

"Just talk," she clarified.

Fuck.

"Yes, just talk," I grudgingly agreed. My hawk seemed to ruffle his feathers and sulk.

The little smile that tipped up the corners of her lips sent my heart racing. The effect she had on me told me that she meant the world to me more than the words ever could. It made me want to say three other words to her—words that I hadn't said to a woman in years.

"So, like a date?" The slightly hopeful note in her question didn't go unnoticed.

"Yeah, baby, like a date," I rumbled, knowing that it would be our first official date. What we had before was something different. Sure, I gave her rides on the back of my bike, but I hadn't treated her like the queen she was. I had a lot to make up for.

I threaded my fingers through her chocolate brown hair and clutched tight. Rubbing my nose along hers because I simply liked to have contact with her, I breathed her in, then told her, "Like this look on you too."

Her airy little laugh made me want to kiss the fuck out of her.

"It's actually my natural color," she admitted.

"Hmm, so little junior will likely have dark hair, but do you think he or she will have your pretty baby blues?"

"No clue," she murmured back.

"Want me to pick you up on the bike, or do you wanna cage it?" It rubbed me the wrong way to have her on the bike when she was pregnant. Fuck, I wanted to cover her in bubblewrap and keep her locked away, but I remembered how pissed off the other ol' ladies had gotten when they weren't allowed to ride because they were expecting. The last thing I wanted to do was push her away, so I fought the part of me that wanted to demand her ass ride in the truck.

"While I really miss riding with you, I think I'd like to cage it. If that's okay, I mean," she replied. She pulled back to look me in the eye better.

"Whatever you want is what we'll do," I told her but neglected to mention how relieved I was about her decision. "How about I pick you up in a couple of hours? Will that give you enough time to get ready?"

"Yeah, that works."

I couldn't keep the grin off my face.

"Okay, then. See you soon." As I got to my feet, I paused. Then I leaned over and cradled her face in my hand before pressing a kiss to her lips. It was on the tip of my tongue to say the exact words to tell her how I felt, but I knew I needed to wait. There was too much riding on this—I needed to make it count.

The second I rode off on my bike, leaving her there for the time being, I wanted to go back. The time it took me to get back to the clubhouse, set up what I needed for later, and drive back to pick Sage up seemed to drag.

Finally, it was time, and as I stood outside Sloane's house, I hoped I was doing the right thing. Just because she said she loved me didn't mean she had forgiven me for making a piss-poor decision in how I walked away from her. Especially when leaving her behind put her in danger.

Nervous, I raised my hand to knock, but the door swung open.

"Cameras," Phoenix explained with a shit-eating grin. "She's coming down. But bro, I gotta say, this is insane. Who would've thought? You and Cookie."

"What the fuck is that supposed to mean?" I grumbled. "And it's Sage, not Cookie anymore."

"It means I never saw either of you settling down—and certainly not together. Hell, you avoided her like the plague for years. Then suddenly the two of you were fucking like rabbits, and she was exclusive with you. That's some crazy shit, bro." He shook his head, but his laughter told me he wasn't trying to be a dick. Sloane popped up under his arm that held the door, and she gave me a little wave.

"Yeah, well—" But that was all I got out before I caught sight of Sage coming down the stairs. My mouth went dry as I watched her descend.

The long dress she wore had a halter-type top that showed off her perfect tits—which had definitely gotten bigger. The silky fabric clung to her legs as she moved, showing off the still-amazing figure she rocked. I caught sight of bright pink polish on her toes that peeked out with each step. Her hair was up in a sexy tousled bun with wavy strands framing her smiling face.

"You kids behave. Don't do anything I wouldn't do!" Phoenix teased as Sloane dragged him into the kitchen.

"Ready?" I asked.

She took a deep breath that lifted her chest and made my mouth suddenly water. "As I'll ever be."

"You look stunning, babe." I might've pulled off acting cool, but inside I was a horny motherfucker. It should be illegal for a woman to look that good. Then I had to fight wanting to rip off that dress and worship her body and soul.

"Thank you," she murmured.

Dinner passed in a bit of a blur, though we talked about damn near everything under the sun—except for us. As I paid the bill, a strange feeling washed over me and my skin prickled. Casually, I glanced around as I wrapped a protective arm around Sage and pulled her to stand slightly in front of me.

When nothing seemed out of the ordinary, I took my receipt from the cashier, and I ushered her out of the building and into my truck.

"Can we get ice cream?" she asked. I didn't have it in me to refuse her, despite the odd sensation I'd had in the restaurant. Though nothing stood out as unusual and the feeling had passed, I remained alert.

"Anything you want," I told her. "But it might cost you."

With a playful waggle of my brows, I started the truck and left the parking lot. By the time we were a few blocks down the road, I was sure we were being followed. The last thing I wanted to do was ruin our night by freaking her out if I was wrong.

"What if we get the ice cream to go, and I take you somewhere that used to be special to me?" I was thinking fast, but when her beautiful smile lit up her face, I felt a little shitty that I had an ulterior motive. The clubhouse was too far away. The ranch was closer.

"Really?" Her expression screamed that her heart was melting because I was sharing a piece of my past with her. "That's… so awesome. Yes, thank you."

While we waited in the drive-thru line after placing our order, I shot off a text to Gator, Phoenix, and Blade. By then I was sure we had a tail. The dark-colored SUV that I suspected was behind us had pulled into the car wash across the road, but the driver didn't get out to do anything. Prepared to jump the curb to get out of the line if I needed to, I texted my brothers to tell them what I suspected and where we were heading.

They replied that they would head to the location ahead of us and wait until we got there to see if the tail kept after us. Blade had me share my location with him.

Then, though I hated to involve them, knowing it would get back to Evan, I messaged Drago to let him know we'd be out there.

"Everything okay?" Sage asked. The brief flicker of worry that I saw in her eyes pissed me off. She should never have to feel like she wasn't safe—especially when she was with me.

"Yeah, just letting the boys know where we're heading. Gator can be a bit like a mother hen." Though I wasn't feeling it, I laughed.

"So can Blade," she said as she too laughed. Fuck, I loved that sound. I prayed nothing happened tonight to take away that smile.

I made it to the window without the suspicious vehicle or the person inside it moving. As quickly as I could make it happen, we had ice cream in hand and were heading out to the ranch I used to call home. Appetite lost, I ate about a third of mine, then tossed the rest out the window.

She gasped and I almost shit my pants. "That's ice cream abuse!"

"Fuck, you scared me for a second," I muttered, heart slamming against my rib cage. I tried to make light of my reaction with a shake of my head and a smile.

"Sorry." She laughed. "Where are we going?" she asked while watching the miles pass by as the sun sank lower and the sky darkened. Horses grazed in some pastures, longhorn in others. The occasional ranch home dotted the landscape in between.

The other vehicle had backed off quite a bit since we left the lights of town behind, but despite the other cars on the road, I knew it was still there.

"You'll see," I replied with a wink. It wasn't long before the two live oaks that flanked the driveway came into view. I turned in, entered the gate code, and we drove through. I waited until the gate closed to continue. It wasn't my imagination that the SUV slowed down to a crawl as it went by, but I breathed a sigh of relief when I watched a hawk swoop around it, then follow us.

"Adrien?" she asked as we went around a curve in the gravel drive.

"Patience," I teased.

Finally, we pulled up in front of the house. My mom was already out on the porch. It didn't surprise me, but I knew Sage was wondering where we were. At least until a hawk landed on the railing. I cursed under my breath because I'd forgotten she knew my family's secret.

"Oh my God. You didn't. Adrien!" she harshly whispered. "Please tell me you didn't bring me to meet your mother!"

"I didn't take you here to meet my mother." It was essentially the truth, as I hadn't planned on it—yet. But when I didn't know who was following us, I wanted to get to the closest place where I knew we'd be safe.

She angrily flipped the visor down to look in the mirror. "Holy shit, I look like doggy doo!"

When my dad came outside, she silently raged. If she could spit fire, my truck would be up in flames—and me along with it.

"Sage," I began as I reached for her hand. She jerked it away.

"Don't you *Sage* me! I'm not the kind of girl you take to meet your parents!"

I froze. "What did you say?"

"You heard me," she mumbled as she frantically searched through her small purse. I placed my hand over the one she had inside her bag.

"Sage," I began again, but more gently that time.

She hung her head, but I gently took her chin in my hand and turned her to face me. The sheen that glistened over her eyes gutted me. "Don't you dare," I ground out.

Shock had her jerking in my hold. Eyes wide, she recognized the tone I used with her before I left Iowa. She swallowed hard and blinked.

"You are perfect. They will love you because you're mine. But even without me, you are worth more than you give yourself credit for. Why do you think I've been doing everything in my power to show you that you mean the world to me? To show you that I may not be worthy of you, but with you, I'm a better man. Because I'm the one who isn't good enough for *you*—but together, we're perfect."

"Adrien—" she whispered.

"Are you my good girl?" I interrupted.

Her lips parted, and I watched as her nipples peaked under the silky knit fabric.

The corner of my mouth quirked wickedly in a satisfied grin. "That's what I thought."

I leaned over to brush the lightest of kisses to her lips. After I reluctantly pulled back, I brushed my thumb over her full lower lip. "I want them to meet you and you to meet them. Because I don't plan to let you go. If you want to wait to tell them about the baby, I'm okay with keeping it to ourselves for a little bit."

Her throat bobbed with her hard swallow. "Okay."

I felt a little trepidation within because I hadn't told my parents about her. Yet a little part of me was elated. Because nothing had ever felt so right in all my life.

I got out of the truck and rounded to her side that was out of sight of my waiting family. When I helped her down, I caged her against the vehicle. She clutched the sides of my shirt and looked up into my eyes. Her chest rose and fell as she scraped her teeth over her bottom lip.

"Fuck, baby, I missed you," I whispered, knowing my parents were waiting and Drago was sitting on the porch railing.

Her lips parted, and I ducked my head to steal a kiss. Heart hammering, I had to force myself to keep it light. With the taste of her lip gloss in my mouth, I pressed my forehead to hers. It wouldn't do to introduce her to my parents with my dick hard. "Ready?" I asked.

She nodded, and I stepped back but held her hand. Together, we left the privacy of the truck and approached the house.

"Adrien," my mother greeted, but I didn't miss the hopeful look in her eyes as she studied Sage. My father quietly observed.

"Mom, Dad, this is Sage. Sage, my mom, Priscilla, and my dad, Allen," I introduced.

"It's so nice to meet you, Sage. Why don't you two come in? I made Adrien's favorite today," my mom offered. My dad was quiet.

As we followed them inside, I chuckled. "Do you have ESP, Mom?"

She looked over her shoulder with a soft smile. "No, but a mother can be hopeful."

Sage's hold on my hand squeezed tighter. In a show of reassurance, I pressed a kiss to the top of her head. Then we followed my mom into the kitchen where I pulled out a chair for Sage.

When I tried to help my mom with her preparations, she pointed at the table. "Sit!"

"Yes, ma'am," I replied with a shake of my head and a smile.

We all took a seat at the table as Mom bustled around, getting plates and slicing the apple-cinnamon bread. She filled a pitcher with ice water and set it on the table. "If you want something other than water, you just let me know."

"Water is fine. Thank you," Sage softly murmured when my mother placed the plate in front of her.

"So how did you two meet?" my father asked, and Sage froze, hand halfway to her glass.

"We've actually known each other for about, what, over ten years?" I asked as I turned to her for confirmation.

She gave me a nervous smile. "Yes, I think it's been at least that," she agreed.

My father let the half-assed answer fly, and I sent him a glance of thanks. He knew more than anyone about my secrets, and after helping us out at the clubhouse after Sloane's situation, he knew some of my club's, too.

Before we could say anything else, my phone vibrated. When I glanced at the screen, I stood up. "I'll be right outside. I need to take this."

Sage shot me a panicked gaze, but my mom quickly stepped in and started telling stories about me when I was little. As I stepped out onto the front porch, I heard her musical laughter and I smiled. All the embarrassing childhood stories were worth that sound.

"Wondered if you were ever coming back out," Drago said from the swing where he was wearing a pair of board shorts with nothing else.

"Any word?"

"Yeah. Malachi and Anton followed the SUV. He pulled off into the driveway to the Miller's pasture. They are watching to see if he leaves or gets out. What do you want us to do?"

Drago's immediate deference to my orders was an ingrained one that was misplaced, as I wouldn't be taking over the clan. Evan would be the next in line, but after what I'd learned, I wasn't so certain he was what the clan needed. How could the clan look up to someone who had betrayed his family the way he had?

"Is there a problem?" Dad asked from the doorway. I hadn't wanted to pull my family into my club's issues again, but regardless of my rationale for why I'd come here, I'd still brought them into it by coming here instead of going back to the clubhouse. Which was why I now opened up and told my father what was going on.

"We'll watch over Sage," he promised me after I finished telling him everything. "Your mom is already half in love with her, you know." Dad gave me a half smile.

"Me too," I replied.

Dad nodded and went back inside.

I prayed Sage would be able to handle my parents.

"Show me where he is." I demanded, then I went around the wraparound porch to the side of the house. I stripped down and shifted. Drago did the same, and we took flight. In no time we reached the location to which they had followed the vehicle and landed in a nearby cedar to watch and listen.

"*I don't recognize him.*" Drago's hawk said.

"*Me either,*" I replied without looking away from the man in the SUV.

For a moment I hated that I'd led him to my clan's safe haven. But when I saw him open a laptop and click through images of Sage, a fury burned in my chest. The images were all taken without her knowing. Then he clicked again, and there were images of me.

Both in Iowa and here.

What the fuck?

His phone rang and he answered it, but with the windows up, I couldn't really tell what he was saying. I flew to the ground and walked closer to his door.

"I told you, I have it covered. This is what I do, so why don't you trust that I know my job. Just make sure you have the rest of my money because you won't like what happens to people who stiff me. They'll have to leave eventually, and then she won't be a problem." He ended the call, so I silently returned to my perch.

"*I think he's after Sage.*"

"*What do you want to do?*"

"*Can you guys watch him?*"

"*Of course. You know we will.*"

"*Thank you.*"

Unsettled, I flew back to the house. Ignoring the pain of shifting to my human form, I dressed and went back inside. I ran my hand through my hair to try to straighten it a bit as I walked through the entry and back into the kitchen.

"Everything okay?" Dad asked.

"Yeah, I think so. There was a problem with the well." That was always the clan's code for trouble.

"Pump go out?" *Is it imminent and a danger to the clan?*

"Don't think so. They've got a temporary fix for now."

"Well, if you need help with it, you let me know. I have a guy that helps us with things like that."

After the way I'd turned my back on my family, the unconditional support my father offered me made my chest tight. "Thanks, Dad."

TWENTY-ONE

Sage ("Cookie")

"NEVER SAY GOODBYE"—BON JOVI

When we left Raptor's family's ranch, it was with a profuse welcome back from his mom. In a way I felt guilty that she thought I was a dance instructor, but I didn't have the heart to tell her I'd been a stripper. I actually really liked his parents, but I was a little pissed that he'd left me alone with them right after first meeting them.

"I can't believe you did that," I grumbled as we parked outside the clubhouse. "And why didn't you take me back to Sloane and Phoenix's place?"

He sat there with both hands on the steering wheel, staring out the windshield. The tension in his body was evident, and I wondered why I hadn't noticed sooner. Probably because I was too much in my head on the way back.

Finally, he took a deep breath and roughly exhaled. "There was someone following us."

"What?" I jerked around to look behind us down the gravel drive. Panic chewed at my insides. Fear that they had found me started to choke me. Nausea roiled in my guts and my hands trembled.

"Not here. We're safe, but I was afraid to leave you at Phoenix's, knowing someone had been following us."

"Did you tell them?" God, I'd never forgive myself if something happened to them because someone was after me.

"I called him before we left the ranch. They know, and they have taken the necessary precautions."

"Wait. You knew this before we left there? So whoever it was followed us there? To your *family*?" I stared at him with my jaw unhinged.

"Trust me when I tell you that place is a fortress."

Then my heart seized. "So that's the only reason you took me to meet your parents?"

"Fuck, no. Did I plan on doing it tonight? No. Was I taking you there soon? Damn straight I was." His intense hazel eyes were heavily gold and locked on mine.

"So if someone was following us, where are they now?"

"They are being followed too."

"Are you sure we didn't lead them here?"

"Positive."

My gaze narrowed on him, but I had to believe him because I was afraid not to. After everything I'd seen before Blade snuck me out of Iowa, I needed to know I was safe. I was teetering on insanity at the thought of that person finding me here.

Suddenly, I was completely overwhelmed. I started to question everything. With a probing gaze, I turned to him. "Why do you care if I forgive you? You left me without looking back. How can I mean anything to you at all?"

"Do not for a moment think I didn't look back. Even if I had wanted to, I couldn't get you out of my head. No one has had a chance of replacing you. It took walking away from you to realize something."

"What?"

"That you? You're everything. Understand?"

"Am I?" No matter how much I wanted to believe him, I wasn't sure if I did.

"Yes. Tonight didn't go quite as planned, but your safety is important to me, and I don't regret taking you to meet my parents. But I do have something for you. Come inside, and I'll show you," he begged as he leaned over the console to thread his fingers through my hair and gently tug.

I pouted for a bit, but he ran his thumb over my protruding bottom lip.

"Please?" he prodded.

I don't know why I pretended I wasn't going to go with him, because I had every intention of giving in. Honestly, I was surprised I'd lasted this long. The man was an addiction of the first order. No matter how angry and hurt I'd been that he'd walked away from me, I still wanted him.

Craved him.

Loved him.

"Okay. Fine." But I still had to keep up the pretense that he had to prove himself—because goddamn it, he really did.

Relief loosened his shoulders, and he got out. Though I wanted to wait to have him open the door for me, I was afraid that I'd jump into his arms if he did.

And he needed to sweat it a little.

But damn. The man was larger than life. When he cornered

me against the side of his big ol' freaking truck, my self-restraint evaporated, and I was a goner. I grabbed the front of his shirt and jerked him down to kiss me. What started as him laughing against my lips quickly turned to a groan.

His hands and mine were everywhere. My need to explore his body bordered on desperation.

Thoughts of danger and death were the furthest things from my mind.

In my defense, it had been months since I'd been with him, and I wasn't just falling off the wagon, I was jumping off headfirst. Before I knew it, my maxi dress was bunched around my hips, and he held my ass in his hands. Both breathless and eager, we fought to be closer—to lose the barriers between us. With little effort, he had me hoisted up, and used his teeth to pull the fabric down to expose my tits to his hungry mouth.

"Adrien," I sighed when he closed his lips over my nipple, whimpered when he sucked hard. The feel of his teeth scraping my skin and sinking into my flesh had me writhing as my inhibitions were cast by the wayside. My head fell back against the truck as everything around us disappeared.

The sound of a throat clearing sifted through my consciousness. When I realized what I was hearing, I tugged at his dark hair. "Adrien!" I whisper-yelled as my heart raced for another reason.

With a theatrical growl, he released me with a wet pop. "What the fuck do you want, Gator?"

"Well, I came out to have a smoke before I crashed and wasn't planning on a porno for entertainment when I did so. But hey, I'm always up to watch some fucking if that's what y'all are into," he replied, and though I could hear the teasing in his tone, I wanted to crawl into a hole. In my past, I wouldn't have given two shits about someone seeing me fucking. The problem was, I didn't know these guys, and the last thing I wanted was to be looked at or treated like

I was a pass-around. After all, I'd arrived with one brother, and here I was, practically fucking their president in front of the clubhouse.

"Fuck. Off." Adrien snapped as he stepped away from the vehicle with me still held aloft in his muscular arms.

Cheeks burning, I buried my face in his neck as I tried not to giggle.

Grumbling under his breath, he stormed in through the door Gator held open and then stomped to his room. Once inside, he kicked the door shut and braced me against it. He nibbled on my earlobe, then my neck, sending shivers of pleasure skating across my skin. Needy, I speared my fingers into his hair and held him in place.

"Mmm, you smell good," he mumbled as he nuzzled behind my ear.

Ever accommodating, I tilted my head to grant him better access. Instead of continuing on, he gently set me on my feet, causing me to huff and pout as I went weak in the knees. He grinned mischievously.

"Remember I said I had something for you?" He interspersed his words with lightly feathered kisses along my heated flesh.

"It's not your cock?"

He practically sputtered with laughter before the smile fell from his face and he searched my gaze. "I mean, yeah, sure, but there's something I need to do for you first."

"Okay?" I decided to play along as I gave him a coy tip of my lips. Besides, this was definitely better than the bullshit events of my life over the last few months.

"Go in the bathroom and get ready. Don't come out until I call for you."

"Um, sure. But what exactly am I getting ready for?" I asked in a hesitant and distrustful drawl.

"You'll see."

With pursed lips and a narrowed gaze, I studied him. "Trying to win me over with mystery?"

"Is that all it takes?"

"Hell no. You'll need to work harder than that." I shot him a smirk.

A rumble started in his chest, and he swatted my ass, making my mouth fall open.

Using two fingers, he lifted my chin and stared in my eyes. Then with a no-nonsense demand, he uttered a single word. "Go."

Heart fluttering and body tingling, I nodded and hurried to the bathroom. When I closed the door, it was to find a pale pink nightie made from the richest satin with a matching sheer robe hanging on the back of the door. Unable to stop myself, I traced the embroidered cream roses that ran along the top of the bodice and dipped low in the center where the satin was open to the hem. This was not a gown for sleeping—this was pure seduction.

Letting my dress fall to the floor, I set the robe on the sink. Then I slipped the nightie over my head, reveling in the way the luxurious fabric caressed my breasts as it fell over them. My hot pink panties didn't exactly match. Thankful I'd had time to do a little maintenance before he picked me up, I pushed them off. Then I slipped my arms through the robe and gazed in the mirror to assess. The supple, clingy material did nothing to hide that my nipples were hard and aching. Removing the clip, I let my dark hair drift down to lay in waves around my shoulders. It set off the blue of my eyes, but the rosy hue of my cheeks wasn't from makeup.

"You ready?" I heard him call from the bedroom.

"As I'll ever be," I whispered to my reflection.

I was wrong. Nothing could've prepared me for what I found when I opened that door.

Adrien was spread-eagled on the bed, not a stitch of clothing on. That wasn't the part that took my breath away, though. It was the fact that both ankles were tied to the corners of the footboard and his wrists were cuffed to the headboard. On the battered bedside table was a small key with a red ribbon tied to it in a bow.

All I could do was blink as my lips parted and my jaw dropped.

"You said I'd never tie you up," I gasped as I tried to process what was going on.

His fingers flexed and I could see his pulse racing on his throat. The rapid rise and fall of his chest drew my attention to all of his glorious ink on display. The designs wrapped around and caressed muscles that tensed as if my gaze was a physical touch.

"I know." His hazel gaze was locked on mine, and in that moment, I understood what he was saying by making himself vulnerable to me. It was a statement far louder than if he had shouted the words. No amount of gifts or groveling could express his feelings to this degree.

Initially unsure of what I should do, I approached with caution. My fingers tingled with the need to touch him. Slowly, I reached out and trailed my fingertips over the top of his foot. Reverently, I dragged them up his lower leg, teasing over the dark hair. When I went higher, I splayed my hand over his thick muscular thigh. Lightly, I dipped to the sensitive area of his groin and teased along his rapidly lengthening erection, making him hiss.

I followed the thin, dark trail of hair upward to his belly button where I dipped a fingertip in then ran my palm over the hard ridges of his abdomen.

"Beautiful," I whispered as I traced the tattoos there, then moved on to the ones that spanned his chest. As I circled his flat nipples, I leaned over to rub my lips along them, then licked them with the tip of my tongue.

He groaned and tensed.

The rest of my exploration continued with my mouth and both hands as I reintroduced myself to each and every inch I could reach. I allowed myself to revel in the power he'd handed me as I scraped my teeth along his shoulder and up to his neck. By the time I licked along the thumping pulse in his neck, his breathing was ragged, and he strained against the bonds that he'd secured himself with.

Pulling back to look him in the eye, I noted his heavy-lidded expression and the way his teeth gripped his lower lip. My gaze swept over his firm body once more, and I paused to appreciate the clear puddle his thick cock had leaked onto his stomach.

"Sage," he groaned, causing my lips to tip up in satisfaction.

My mouth watered as I braced one hand on the bed beside him and leaned down to lick up his length. I loved the way it jumped as if begging me for more. I swirled my tongue around the tip, gathering the clear liquid and sucking lightly.

"Fuuuuuccck," he moaned, and I watched his eyes slam shut as he pushed his head back into the pillow. His hips lifted, and he pushed himself further into my mouth. Taking my time, I went forward until he hit the back of my throat. When I swallowed, he whispered the word yes in a repetitive litany.

Though I could've played like that for hours, I realized that wasn't what I truly wanted.

So, I pushed myself up, then glanced at the red bow and the key. Taking it in my hand, I held the cool metal as it warmed. Finally, mind made up, I unlocked each cuff from his wrists. I untied the soft rope from his feet when I came back around, then dropped the key back in its original place on the scarred wood.

Hungrily watching my every move, he quietly sat up. As his eyes devoured me, I went down onto the floor to sit with my ass resting on my heels and gently laid my hands on my thighs. Holding his gaze, I lowered my head until I was forced to look down.

My heart hammered, and the blood rushed in my head with a loud whooshing in my ears. A slight tremble shook my body as

I waited. The mattress shifted, and the rustle of his movements on the linens signified that he was on the move.

"So perfect," he murmured. He crouched in front of me, and with one finger, he lifted my head as I closed my eyes. "Look at me."

Obediently, I did as he instructed. He gently wrapped his large hand around my throat, feeling my racing pulse before he moved his thumb up to caress my jaw.

"I love you." The words spilled from his lips and my breath caught in my chest. My own lips parted, and he nodded.

"I love you too" was my whispered reply.

In the blink of an eye, he gathered me up as if I weighed nothing at all. He sat on the edge of the bed, and I straddled his thighs. Similar to what I'd done to him earlier, he slid his hands under the pale pink silk and traced my curves. He cupped my breasts that were heavy with need and dropped his head to kiss me as he pinched my nipples through the fabric.

"I love you," he said again as he pushed the robe off my shoulders, causing me to shiver as the gauzy material slipped over my shoulders. His rough fingers gathered the narrow straps, and he slowly drew them down my arms. The expensive gown pooled at my waist.

"Fuck, you're prettier than ever," he murmured, his voice gravelly with desire. He gripped my hips in his broad hands and guided me up to my knees. Then he teased my clit with his thumb before swiping it down to stroke through my wet slit. He grunted in approval when he found me ready and waiting. After he lined his tip up with my eager pussy, he drove his hips up as he pulled mine down, filling me with his thick cock.

My nails dug into his shoulders as I cried out at the blissful invasion that bordered a bit on pain as he stretched me to accommodate him. Slowly, I rose up and worked my way back down. My walls tightened and pulsed around him, and he groaned.

"Fuck, yes. Squeeze my cock in that tight little cunt. I want to feel you riding me and taking everything I give you. I want to fuck you until neither of us knows where one ends and the other begins." He thrust up again, burying himself as I gripped him and welcomed him into my body.

He held me tight to his chest with one hand buried in my hair, pulling my head back. He worshipped my throat with kisses and his tongue. All the while I fucked him exactly as he instructed.

By the time sweat slicked us and shimmered in the low light, we had lost all finesse. He roughly scooted us back on the bed, then flipped us over so he blanketed my body with his.

I wrapped my legs around his hips, and he grabbed my thigh. As he held most of his weight on one arm, he pushed my leg up to give him a better angle. Then he slammed into me so hard, I saw stars and couldn't breathe. Over and over, he drove deep, and I fought for something to hold onto. I clawed at the bedding, ripping it loose and bunching it around us.

"What do you want?" he breathlessly demanded as sweat rolled down his neck.

"Fuck me! Fuck me hard! Please," I begged—and he delivered.

In an animalistic frenzy, his hips snapped harder—faster. Until the room was filled with moans, grunts, and the slapping of sweaty flesh on flesh. With each stroke, he hit that perfect spot.

My nails scored his back and dug into his tight ass. With each pounding thrust, the pressure continued to build. Finally, with my breath ragged and coordination nonexistent, I shattered. Pulsing euphoria washed over and through me as my pussy throbbed, squeezing around his frantic strokes until he drove deep, and joined me in the explosion. His cock spasmed within, filling me with every drop he had to give until he shuddered and collapsed, still buried deep inside me.

Ragged breaths accompanied the fading aftershocks. He

buried his face in my neck, and I wrapped my arms around his trembling shoulders.

"I love you so fucking much," he hoarsely whispered.

"Not as much as I love you," I murmured between heaving breaths. He hummed before nipping my neck.

Sex with this man had always been amazing, but this… this was indescribable.

We fell asleep, still connected, limbs tangled and locked as if we were both afraid the other would disappear in the night. Though we needn't have worried. If we somehow drifted apart in the dark, we would instinctively find the other.

Because we were two halves of a whole.

TWENTY-TWO

Raptor

"CRIMSON AND CLOVER"—JOAN JETT & THE BLACKHEARTS

Reluctantly, I disentangled myself from Sage's warm body. She mumbled in her sleep and reached for me, but then she immediately settled with a sigh. Grabbing my jeans from the floor, I quickly put them on without fastening them and went to answer the door.

"Boss man, I'm sorry to bother you, but this is important," Gator softly explained when I scowled through the crack of the door.

"I'll be right out."

Pissed that I wouldn't be climbing back into bed with my woman, I quickly dressed. When I stepped into the hall, Gator was still there.

"What the fuck couldn't wait?" I grumbled.

"You'll see," he evasively replied and walked off. I followed him as he went directly to the front door and then outside.

A man lay bound and gagged on the ground. His face was bloody, and it didn't take long to see that it was because he was missing both eyes and the deep gashes around them were still bleeding.

"Motherfucker," I muttered. "What the fuck is this?"

"I brought you a present, Adrien," my cousin Evan announced as he came from behind my truck, carrying a laptop that he handed me. It didn't take long to figure out who the guy was when I saw the SUV parked on the other side of mine. When I opened the laptop, I was surprised to see it wasn't locked and password protected.

"I took care of that for you," Evan explained, his jawline distinctive and hard. "You might want to take a look at what he has on there."

It didn't take me long to see what Evan was talking about.

"Get Blade," I instructed, and Torque hurried to make the phone call. "We need to get him out of sight."

"What about the old shack toward the back of the property?" Gator asked. "It's not much to look at, but it will get him out of the way."

"Make it happen," I directed, my blood boiling. Gator, Torque, and Tigger loaded him up in the back of the UTV we'd picked up. He fought and thrashed the entire time to no avail.

"You're welcome," Evan snapped as if he had any right to come onto our chapter's property uninvited. Drago stood off to the side, silently watching everything unfold.

Though it soured my stomach to owe him a goddamn thing, I gritted my teeth and replied, "Thank you."

Everyone including Drago went inside, leaving me alone with my cousin.

Body tense, heartbeat hammering, I stood there watching him.

Neither of us said a word. Chin held high, he glared back at me.

"I brought him as a peace offering. This is the second time I've tried to help you. We need to talk," Evan finally ground out.

There was a sharp edge to my laugh as I imagined wrapping my hands around his lying throat. "What the fuck do we have to talk about?"

"Falina."

Her name on his lips set me off. It didn't matter that I could no longer stand the bitch—it was like a crackling flame reaching a pile of dynamite. Without further processing, I lost my shit and rocked his jaw with everything I had. The satisfaction I thought I'd feel as he hit the ground was hollow.

"You fucked my *wife*? The entire time I was married? We were like brothers, Evan. Especially after my own brother died. *I. Loved. You. Like. My. Brother.* Yet you repeatedly betrayed me. The crazy thing is, that I had no idea how deep your backstabbing went until I saw Sam transition. To be cut open again by that knife you buried in my back was like it happening all over again." My chest heaved, and the agony of his disloyalty nearly brought me to my knees.

"Goddamn it, Adrien!" he cursed as he wiped the blood from the corner of his mouth with the back of his hand. "They aren't mine!"

"Bullshit! They have our mark! She ran to *you*! I found her in *your* bed!" I thundered.

He didn't even try to get up. Instead, he laid on the gravel, staring at the sky. Then he palmed his face before he rose onto his elbows to glare at me. "I know what you saw. But I swear to you, what she told you was a lie. Did I sleep with her once after she ran to me? Yes. But I didn't mean to."

"You didn't *mean* to? What the fuck are you talking about? Did you slip and fall and your dick just went right in? I'm sorry, Evan, but I don't know how you can *not mean* to fuck someone but do it anyway." My lip curled as disgust filled me at his pathetic excuses.

He pushed himself up to a sitting position with his arms resting on his spread knees.

"Because I didn't know what she was capable of. I can promise you that I didn't plan to sleep with her, nor did I realize I had slept with her. I've tried to tell you what happened, but you were so pissed off that you had blinders on! Think about what you said. They have our mark. Those boys aren't mine, Adrien. I never slept with her before the night you found her in my bed—that I swear to you. So, whose boys are they?"

His gaze locked on mine as confusion swirled inside me and a cold chill skated over my skin. If what he was saying was true, then who *was* Sam and Seth's father? Had I been wrong all these years?

Turning my back, I speared both hands through my hair and tugged.

My phone rang, and I almost didn't answer it. Except something told me I needed to. I pulled it out of my pocket and caught the caller ID. When I saw Voodoo's name on the screen, I knew I was right. Shooting one last glare at Evan where he still sat on the ground, I answered it as I restlessly paced.

"Brother, this isn't a good time. Evan's here. He just told me some unsettling news, and I don't know what the fuck to believe." That was probably the understatement of the century.

"Well, that's kind of what I called for," he began.

I frowned. Though I'm not sure why I was surprised. The dude had a freaky way of knowing things that never ceased to amaze me. The thing is, he hadn't ever really seen anything that had to do with me personally, so this was odd.

"Christ, lay it on me. What's one more thing?" My head dropped and I rubbed the back of my neck.

"You need to do a paternity test on your dime."

Complete silence—because my mind immediately went to my current situation with Sage.

"What?" I asked with deadly calm. My world was on the verge of imploding if he said anything that undermined the faith and belief I had in Sage.

"Sam and Seth."

"Wait, what?" That wasn't what I expected, and I was at a loss. After the conversation that had transpired between me and Evan, I was a little taken aback. Chest tightening, I waited for whatever he was going to drop on me because now he was talking craziness.

He sighed. "I had a dream last night. I wasn't sure if I'd interpreted it correctly until I went to my altar. I tried casting bones, I read the cards—it was all the same. When I questioned what I'd seen, I called my grandmother. She backed what I saw. Raptor… those are your boys."

"Who fucking hired you?" I demanded of the man who was hanging by his arms from the rafter. Blade had already worked him over, and he was covered in dried blood—and he had pissed himself.

"This motherfucker isn't talking. If you would let me really have at him, I might be able to get more out of him." Blade stood with his arms crossed and his jaw ticking.

I sighed.

"This motherfucker *shot* me! He fucking killed Ruby, then went after Sage! He's lucky I haven't peeled his skin off in one-inch sections. Fucking piece of shit," he muttered before he punched the guy in the side with a roar, eliciting a pained cry from the man slumped and dangling from the rafter. It was behavior unlike what

I was used to from Blade. The man simply didn't lose his cool like that.

"Jesus Christ," I muttered. Then I really looked at him, taking note of his corded neck and hands that clenched and unclenched. Considering how badly I wanted to simply slit the man's throat for coming after Sage, I understood. "You know what? Do it."

The guy sputtered and groaned. Blade stilled before he gave me a wicked grin. Though calling it that was being generous. His lips pulled back, baring his teeth, and I could've sworn the fires of hell flickered in his eyes.

"Let me know when you have something. I need to get back to the clubhouse." The boys would be here soon. The problem was, did I tell them what we suspected? Or did I secretly attempt to gather their DNA without their knowledge?

The ride back to the clubhouse was quiet. Though I was fully aware of the sidelong glances Gator gave me, I remained silent. He parked the UTV behind the building and sat in the seat, leaning on the steering wheel with one arm as he studied me.

"What?" I muttered, finally turning to look at him.

"Do you want my advice?" He tilted his head and cocked a brow.

"Do I have a choice?" I held his gaze until he dropped his for a moment, then lifted it to lock with mine.

"Always."

"Then, yes."

He huffed a laugh. "Those boys aren't stupid. It seems as if they've been through enough shit in their lives that honesty would be appreciated. They may be young, but they are wise beyond their years."

Foot propped on the dash, I slouched slightly in the seat and rested my arm on my upraised knee. My chest seemed to squeeze, and my stomach clenched as I thought about telling them.

"What if it comes back that I'm actually not their father?"

"Then they're right where they are now."

"And if I'm their father, they learn that their mother lied and kept them from me out of pure spite and hatred."

"Either way they lose something, I suppose, but if Voodoo is right… they win a father that loves them and will teach them what they need to know to be men—men with an amazing gift."

The sound of an approaching vehicle signaled the arrival of the boys. I climbed out of the cart in time to see the car round the cedar trees that flanked either side of the road. My heart raced as I watched them climb out. Sweat trickled down my back.

Their smiles and laughter faded when they saw my expression, and I regretted that I was the reason for their somber faces.

"Boys, we need to talk," I announced.

They shot nervous glances to each other before they looked back at me.

They followed me to my office, and once they were seated, I closed the door and rounded my desk. Seth fidgeted in his chair and picked at his thumbnail, but Sam boldly made eye contact with me the entire time.

"I don't know where to begin." I took a deep breath and slowly exhaled. "I have reason to believe that I was wrong."

"About?" Sam asked with a lift of his chin.

Swallowing hard, I reached into the lowest drawer and withdrew a folder which I set in front of them. They both looked at it as if it was a snake that would strike if they moved.

"Go ahead. Open it." Then I had second thoughts and slapped my hand over in. "Wait. I'm sorry, I fucking suck at this shit. There's some amount of resentment that I'm dealing with—and not well. I wasn't sure how to explain this, so I was going to try showing you… Jesus, I'm fucking this up again." I palmed my face and dragged it down with a groan.

"Adrien, we're not babies. We've also seen some things that would send a lot of kids to the looney bin. I mean, how many teenagers can say they morphed and sprouted feathers, then flew? My guess is not that many in the general population could lay claim to that," Sam boldly explained. "So let me see whatever it is you have, then we can discuss it. Fair?"

A puffed laugh blew through my nose at my underestimation of the boy's maturity.

Sam narrowed his eyes but bravely flipped the nondescript manilla folder open. He frowned. Then looked at me with a pinch between his brows and a slow blink. As if he might've missed what I wanted him to see, he looked it over again.

"Why are you showing us the paternity test results?" Sam finally asked as he studied the page, repeatedly straightening it with the other papers in front of him. Considering they confirmed what we'd all been told—that they weren't mine—it probably was confusing.

"Because I think they may have been falsified or forged."

"What?" Sam gasped. Both of their jaws dropped.

"I'm not going to mince words with you. As you pointed out, you're not children—despite your ages. An extremely close friend of mine had a vision. He conferred with his grandmother who also has a similar gift. Both of them told me—" I took a fortifying breath and exhaled roughly. "—you are my sons. Initially, I was going to find a way to run the tests without telling you, but I believe you have a right to know."

Sam and Seth fell back in their seats as they stared at me, slack-jawed.

"Another thing to think about is that Sage is going to be sticking around. So, if you're actually my sons, I'd like you to get to know her. I know you haven't had a lot of interaction with her since your time here has been limited, but I'd like that to change, if you're willing. If she'll agree to it, I want to marry her. Not that I expect you to be over the moon about that since you don't really know either of us, but like I said—full disclosure. Fuck, I'm rambling, aren't I?" I winced as I pinched the bridge of my nose in an attempt to stave off the headache that was creeping up on me. Then I gave them an apologetic smile that was probably closer to a grimace.

"Damn, you sure know how to get even, don't you?" Sam asked with wide eyes.

"Huh?" I uttered, dumbfounded.

"Well, I flew in here and dropped a bombshell on you, so it was your turn," he explained in what I realized was a weak attempt at humor. Seth elbowed him and shot him a glare that made him look so much like some of my old pictures, it drove home the possibility that what I'd taken for Evan's traits could actually be mine. Christ, what a mindfuck of a situation.

"If you don't want to know and would rather stick with what we believe, I will respect your feelings and wishes. You tell me how you want to proceed. If you need time to think about it, that's okay too." My knee bounced rapidly as I waited to hear what they would decide.

Seth's side-eyed glance at his brother told me that he would defer to whatever Sam decided. Sam's jaw ticked, but he lifted his chin. "What would we need to do?"

TWENTY-THREE

Sage ("Cookie")

"YOU'RE SO VAIN"—MARILYN MANSON

After everything I'd been through—the threats, the attacks, the flight from the only place that had felt like home in my life, I was feeling cooped up. Though I moved into the clubhouse with Raptor of my own free will, I was restless. He meant well, but he didn't want me to leave the property until he had answers regarding all the shit that had me fleeing Iowa.

Except he was gone—off with Phoenix to meet up with someone in town. And I was sitting here with my little private guard and a fortified eight-foot-high fence surrounding the entire property.

I needed a break.

Blade told me he would be off working in the back of the property where they were trying to clear trees and shit.

"Hey, Torque, can you take me back to see Blade?" I asked the tawny-haired man behind the bar as I leaned on the surface and propped my chin on my hand. He was a probationary patch, but seemed like he was a solid guy. I was glad Raptor had him in his chapter. In fact, I liked all of the men in the small group so far.

"I'm sorry, but Prez was explicit that you weren't to go anywhere until he got back." While he did look apologetic, it did nothing to sooth my building irritation.

"I wouldn't be leaving the property," I argued, trying to smile to make light of it.

"I get it, but orders are orders," he replied as he cringed a bit.

"Dad! I have a problem!" Torque's son, Rhae, shouted from the hallway. His wide-eyed gaze paired with his rapidly waving hand gestures had Torque hauling ass after him.

Not sticking around to see what Rhae's emergency was, I ducked out the door, closing it as slowly and silently as I could. For crying out loud, it couldn't hurt to go for a walk to stretch my legs. Since arriving in Texas, I hadn't been able to work out once. Unless you counted the workouts I got with Raptor. At that thought, I snickered.

The week that had passed since we made up had been, um... active.

I didn't make it ten feet from the clubhouse before the sound of a couple of Harleys grew closer. The faint rattle of the front gate followed, and I debated running back inside or running around back. One of those bikes was Raptor, for sure. He'd probably have my ass for being outside alone, but I crossed my arms and stood my ground.

Sure as shit, he parked in front of me, killed the motor, and tugged off his helmet. Without a word, he hung his helmet from the handlebar. The cocked brow he sported as he observed me might've been sexy as hell, but he certainly didn't look happy. A thickness in my throat damn near choked me.

"Caught me," I weakly admitted as I made goofy-as-hell jazz

hands, then wanted to smack myself for being such a dumbass. Why didn't I just say I heard them pulling up and came out to greet them? Ugh!

He made quick work of dismounting, then stalked my way. Once he was practically toe to toe with me, he grinned evilly. "Going somewhere, are you?"

His big hands gripping my sides sent a shiver of longing through me.

With a bright smile and an exaggerated flutter of my lashes, I looped my arms over his shoulders. "Only into your arms."

Raptor's bark of laughter accompanied a shake of his sweat-soaked head.

Phoenix was shaking his own head with a grin as he climbed off his bike. I'd been so focused on Raptor, I'd neglected to notice the third rider who had arrived with them. Previous boredom alleviated, I peeked around Raptor's muscley tatted up arms.

"Who's that?" I whispered as the third biker who had messy dark hair that hung in wet waves over his forehead, pushed his shades up to the top of his head. The movement brought attention to the tattoos that wrapped one arm and peeked out of the collar of his T-shirt. His blue eyes might've been stunning if they didn't appear so hollow.

"His name is Memphis. Used to go by the road name of Soap with the Demented Sons up in Iowa. Been through some serious shit, and his President reached out to Venom. I'll explain more later. Thinking about taking him on as a probationary, since they allotted us up to four," he quietly explained as he glanced over his shoulder to look at the newcomer. With both of us looking at him, Memphis's attention was drawn to us.

"You sure that's a good idea? A man with eyes as haunted as that has nothing to lose. With you recently re-establishing the chapter here, you don't need liabilities," I observed. No, the club wasn't my business, and their choices weren't mine, but I'd been around their club long enough to know certain things.

He sighed. "No, but Snow was worried about him. He sent him down to visit their central Texas chapter, but he struck a deal with me when he found out I was down here. Venom and I both thought a change of scenery and a new purpose might be good for him."

"Like I said...."

"You let me worry about Memphis. You get that sexy ass into the bedroom. I have some things to discuss with you in private, and I need to be inside you. Not in that order."

His words had my immediate attention. Phoenix walking off with Memphis barely registered. My panties were instantly wet as my pussy clenched and I wet my lips. Heat burned my insides, and it had nothing to do with the temperature outside. A startled yelp escaped my throat when he swatted my ass—hard.

"Move." His demand was quiet and controlled. "Unless you want me to bend you over my bike right here. You have to the count of three."

A shuddering breath shook my chest, leaving my painfully peaked nipples in its wake. I took a sidelong glance at his bike.

"One... Two...." The countdown quietly rumbled, but I stood my ground because I'd never shied away from a little exhibition-ism. At least until I thought about Sam and Seth popping in—or someone else from his family.

Before he got to three, I broke loose and darted for the club-house. Raptor didn't run after me.

He didn't need to.

Because he knew I'd be there waiting.

Like a good girl.

EPILOGUE

Raptor

After over three weeks of Blade's special brand of torture, the asshole in the shed finally spilled. Well, what he knew, that is. I had to hand it to the guy—he lasted a helluva a lot longer than I thought he would.

What he had to say left me stunned—and that took a lot. Granted, we still didn't know exactly who had hired him, but we knew whoever paid him to kill Sage had required him to send a picture of her dead body to the phone number that hired him and then to me.

Which was why I had no qualms about the bullet I sent between his nonexistent eyes.

It didn't make sense that it would be George Horacio, the guy Sage and the other girls were having issues with—I hadn't been up there when he moved in and started his shit. Not to mention, I had no specific beef with the asshole. Or so I thought.

"Raptor, I hate to tell you this, but the phone is a burner—like we expected. Purchased in Denver, Colorado at a small chain store. The trail pretty much ends there. Wish I had more for you, but I have some other ideas I'm going to try to see if I get anything more. No promises," Facet explained.

"Brother, I appreciate your help more than you know," I assured him. "Thanks."

"Anytime." He ended the call, and I sighed in relief. I hated the fucking things.

"Raptor, I have no problem staying down here until you figure out who's trying to fuck with you. It would be for you and Sage both—and I already cleared it with Venom," Blade told me as he washed the blood from his hands with the old-fashioned water pump back by the rundown cabin.

"I'd actually really appreciate that," I admitted. It was tough dealing with a shitstorm when it was a new group of brothers that I did know, but not like I knew my brothers in Iowa.

Once his hands were mostly clean, he dried them on the disposable coveralls he wore when he was "working." He peeled the soiled garment off and wadded it up before shoving it and the shoe covers in the trash bag that he'd brought out when he finished.

"Fucking hell," I grumbled at the putrid smell that rolled out of the bag in the short period of time he'd had it open.

"Hey, getting answers can be messy business. Now don't you have an ol' lady to tend to?" He chuckled as he double bagged his trash, then tossed it in the back of the UTV Phoenix was waiting in.

"Already wore her ass out. She's zonked at the moment," I replied with a smirk. "Probably wear her out again later tonight too."

Blade's face scrunched up, and he shook his head like he was the one who'd smelled something vile. "No. Just no."

Phoenix laughed. "Hurry up, fucker. Let's get that crap torched so I can get the hell out of here. Sloane should be home from her shop, and I have my own work to do when I get there."

"Fuck you both," Blade muttered.

They took off in the UTV, headed for the pit we'd dug, and I hopped on the utility quad and made my way back to the clubhouse. When I parked under the carport we'd erected in back, I saw Memphis sitting on the ground with his back against the building, smoking. He faced the setting sun.

Not asking if he cared, I sat next to him and held out my hand for the blunt he was presently taking an insanely large hit from. Without fuss, he handed it over and blew smoke out to the side, away from me.

"You decide if you're staying?" I asked him before I took a drag and handed it back.

"Possibly," was his vague reply.

"Well, I have something I want to discuss with you," I began. His gaze flickered in my direction, then returned to the sinking sun that lit the Texas sky up with a warm kaleidoscope of color. Finally, the darkness settled in. Crickets began to chirp and still, I waited.

"Okay?" He hit the blunt one more time and held it in until he stubbed the end on the metal of the building. The cough that briefly shook him was what he had coming for hitting that shit so hard.

"What would you think of joining my chapter?"

The quick movement of his head from my peripheral was the only sign he heard me. "How can I simply 'join' your chapter? I'm not a member of your club, Raptor."

"Understood. But right now, I've been given special privileges to ensure the chapter gets a fair start."

"You mean, like a patch for a patch deal?" Now a frown furrowed his brow, and I had his full attention.

"Sort of. I've been granted permission for probationary members. Essentially, you'd wear the same three-piece patch as we do, but you'd be on a one-year probationary period instead of prospecting. Lets me build my numbers without having to go through all the red tape and bullshit if you don't work out." I shrugged.

He sat there in silence with his mouth hanging open. Finally, he huffed out the breath he'd been holding. "You're serious." It was a statement, not a question.

"No shit. I don't make offers I don't mean. I've always liked you. Snow always speaks highly of you. You have a job you want done… we can do it," I explained as I rested my forearms on my bent knees. Then I turned my head to lock my gaze with his, and I dropped my voice. "Snow also said you had an interesting… talent… that might come in handy for us."

At that, his eyes widened. It was the first real emotion I'd seen from him in months.

"He told you that?" The question was softly spoken. And though he tried to pass it off as nonchalant, the rapid way his chest rose and fell, along with how his fingers tightly curled into his palms, told me he was anything but.

I stood up and brushed off the seat of my jeans.

"You think about it, but I do need an answer by Friday night. We have church."

"Sure. Thanks. I'm honored by the offer, but I think I will take advantage of that thinking time you offered." He swallowed hard, then cast his gaze up at me.

"Wouldn't have offered if I had a problem with that. I'm a fair man, Memphis. I don't like drama and bullshit. I cut to the chase, and I hate talking on the goddamn phone. Right now, all I can offer you for accommodations are three hots and a cot in one of the bunk rooms. Will this be an easy gig? No. It sure as hell won't be. But I can promise you that if we find the people responsible for what happened to your girl—and we will—you'll be included on the mission. The only stipulation is, you show us you can do so without going berserk and risking yourself or my chapter."

"Roger that," he murmured.

I gave him a head nod, then grabbed the door handle. Checking that the folded sheets of paper were still in the inner pocket of my cut, I swung it open. There was something I needed to address, then I had some making up for lost time with Sage to do.

The door banged as it closed, and the two dark-haired boys at the bar turned to look in my direction. Seth was still chewing as he held the giant burger in his hand. Gator pushed off the bar he'd been leaning over while talking with them. The easy smile he had on his face fell when I met his gaze. He knew what was coming. I took a deep breath, slowly let it out, and pasted a grin on my face.

"Got someone to feed you, did ya?" I teased them as I pulled up a stool next to them.

"Yes, they did," Sage replied as she came out of the kitchen with two slices of pie that she set in front of the boys with a sweet tilt of those beautiful lips. "We were just getting to know each other better."

The adoring glances they gave her had me snorting.

Well, shit.

"While I'm glad y'all are getting along, she agreed to be *my* girl—so don't get any crazy ideas," I joked with them. "I'd say I'm pretty lucky. Wouldn't you?" My chest fluttered as I stared into her bright blue eyes.

"Well, if she always cooks like this, you're on the road to getting fat," Sam quipped. He hid his twitching lips with a big bite of his half-eaten burger.

"Keep it up and you'll be in the gym doing my workout with

me," I shot back with a middle finger raised in his direction as I fought my laughter. Little smartass.

Then I sobered.

"Maybe it's best I have you all here at once." I scrubbed my hands over my face before I rested my elbows on the bar. Sage placed a soft hand over my nervously tapping fingers and gave me a curious tilt of her head.

"Boys, remember we sent the tests in?"

"Yes, sir," they both replied. Sage stepped back, and I could tell she was going to leave. I'd briefly told her about what Voodoo had told me and the tests I'd sent in to the guy Facet knew. She hadn't met the boys yet then, and I figured I'd find out the test results before I introduced them, but here we were. I quickly grasped her retreating hand and held her in place.

"I have the results."

Sam set his food down and swallowed hard. Seth gave his brother a worried glance, then looked at me.

Sam spoke up. "And?"

Another deep breath didn't help like I thought it would, because I still felt a little lightheaded. I huffed it out. Reaching into my cut, I grabbed the papers and set them in front of the boys.

I didn't miss the slight tremble of Sam's hands when he reached for them. Seth read over his shoulder. The sharp inhale told me they'd reached the line that stated the final results. Sam quickly went to the next page. Seth gripped the edge of the bar so hard, his knuckles turned white.

"But why?" Seth whispered. I knew what he was referring to, but I didn't have a good answer that wouldn't be talking absolute shit about their mother.

Sam's nostrils flared, and two bright spots appeared on his cheeks beneath the jump of his jaw muscle.

"Because Mom wanted to hurt Adrien—um," he stammered,

and I knew it was because he now wasn't sure how to address me. Seth's eyes glistened with unshed tears.

"Sam, I don't want either of you to feel pressured to call me something in particular. You can still call me Adrien if that's what makes you comfortable. I'm just happy to know the truth, despite being pissed about the years we lost. I don't want any of us to miss another day, and I'm going to do everything in my power to make sure you know that you mean the world to me and we're a family now, for life. Which is why I'm hitting you with everything at once. You're about to be big brothers too." I'd debated withholding that last bit, but I hated the thought of keeping any more secrets from my boys. I held my breath as I waited to see if I'd fucked up and put too much on them.

Sage shot me a side-eyed glance filled with concern.

Seth and Sam wore matching open-mouthed expressions of surprise that quickly morphed to laughter. Seth sniffled as his laughter died down, and he turned away to hide the quick swipe under his nose.

"Do you know if it's a boy or a girl?" Seth finally asked as he turned back to us.

"I find out next week," Sage softly told them as she rested her free hand over her belly that had developed a slightly rounded curve overnight.

"Can we go with?" Seth blurted out. Sam cuffed him in on the back of the head.

"We'll be in school. And Mom will be home," Sam muttered with a frown.

"Oh. Yeah."

Seth looked so dejected, my chest caved. My head was reeling at how well they were taking the news, but anger at all the lost years simmered in the back of my mind. "How do you guys feel about all of this?" I finally asked.

Sam dropped his attention to his plate in front of him. He absently picked at the rest of his food. "I'm mad."

"Me too," Seth quietly agreed.

Sam lifted his gaze to lock with mine. "But I'm happy. I don't think I could've asked for a better person to be our dad."

That three-letter word hit me like a fastball to the gut, and if I hadn't been sitting down, I might've dropped to my knees.

"What do we tell Mom?" Seth asked as his brow drew down and he picked up a potato chip and crumbled it onto his plate.

Releasing the hold I had on Sage, I stood up, placed a hand on his shoulder, and gently spun him to face me. Then I crouched so I could look him square in the eye. "I'll handle that. You two just worry about school and our training. We'll work the rest of it out as we go. Together."

Seth scrambled out of his chair and threw himself into my arms. Taken aback, I stiffened, but it didn't take me long to wrap his slender frame in my arms. Sage caught my eye from behind the bar. A fat tear tracked down her cheek as she held her lower lip between her teeth.

Sam slammed into us, and his arms wrapped around us both.

I freed one arm to put it around him. I palmed the back of his head and pulled him until our foreheads touched. Staring him in the eye, I made a promise.

"Nothing will ever come between us again."

EPILOGUE TWO

Memphis (Soap, DSMC, IA)

As a member of the Demented Sons MC in Northern Iowa, they called me Soap. Not many people knew it was because as a prospect, my dumbass didn't know you couldn't put regular old dish soap in a dishwasher. Hell, I'd never had one. How was I supposed to know?

The hours I spent cleaning suds up off the kitchen floor earned me my road name, and I'd worn it proudly.

Until the day my world crashed at my feet.

Tasha was always too good for me, yet I couldn't stay away from her. It didn't matter that she was a stripper at the club we owned—I was fucking drawn to that girl. No matter how bad I wished things could be different, I wasn't worthy of her and never would be. Too bad I never got the courage to try before I lost the chance.

They might've called me Soap, but I was a soulless husk. I was going to find out who had done this to us, and I would rip them apart limb from limb.

Because I was a demon bent on revenge hiding in a man's body.

For months, I was on Hacker. Each day asking if he'd found anything. When Snow mentioned talking to the RBMC down in Ankeny, I was the first one on my bike.

I'd been saving nearly every penny I'd made since I joined the DSMC. Other than my bike and my dues, I didn't have much to spend it on. I was prepared to pay out of my own pocket to find the fuckers responsible for Tash's death.

But I had a catch—I wanted to be the one to take them out. They refused. Said that wasn't how they worked. With each day that went past with no viable leads, I lost a little more of my soul. Finally, when I'd been ready to throw in my colors, Snow shipped me off to Texas. Told me to take some time to figure shit out.

Fuck that.

What I didn't expect was Raptor's offer or that it was approved by Snow.

I told Raptor I'd think about it, but it really was a no-brainer. Was I demented as fuck inside? Fuck yeah, I was. But more than that…

I was a heartless bastard through and through.

Read Memphis's story in *Sparking Ares!*
Raptor and Sage's story continues in *Raptor's Revenge!*

ACKNOWLEDGEMENTS

Curious—do any of you actually take the time to read this part of the book? If so, I thank you from the bottom of my pea-pickin' little heart. BIG KISSES! Again, I apologize if you're getting the sense of déjà vu. The thing is, there are things in life that deserve repeating—even if I feel like I'm giving you a grammy speech. Hahahaha!

My first *thank you* goes out to my family who brag about me being an author (despite the genre in which I write!) and for always believing in me. I do kind of wonder if you know exactly what I write or if your friends then read it and are traumatized.

Thank you to every single one of you who keep reading everything I write. I'm blown away by your loyalty (and your constant encouragement when I fall behind on my deadlines. LOL), and the depth of your love for my words. If someone had told me five years ago that I'd have the followers I have now, I would've laughed at them. I would've said it was a dream and we'd see. Well, here we are! Holy hell!

If this is my first book you've read, you may not know who he is, but a huge thank you goes out to **PSH**, my very own "Porn Star Hubby" (if you ever meet me, or friend me on social media, ask me to tell you the story). You're the best book schlepper, one man cheerleading squad, and pimp-er of my books that ever walked the earth. Love you bunches.

To my squad: **Pam, Kristin, Brenda, Lisa** for being my betas and letting me bounce ideas off you at all hours of the night (it's good to know there are other kindred spirits in my night owl world). I seriously couldn't do this without you. YOU ARE AMAZING!

Thank you to **Kristine's Street Team**! Y'all are the best! I cannot thank you enough for your time and your efforts in sharing my book babies with the masses! Hugs and kisses!

Christie, this book is also for you. You're the one who named Cookie because before you mentioned the name "Sage," it wasn't on my radar. But besides all that, a long time ago when I worried about one of my books being different, or a change from what my readers were used to, you said something that almost made me cry. You said… "I would read anything you wrote. I would read your grocery list." It touched me in a way that I've never forgotten it.

Penny. Once upon a time there was a girl who didn't believe in herself. Then came a red-headed girl that smacked the first girl upside the head and said, "You can do this!" Thank you for believing in me enough for both of us in the beginning and always. You are never surprised at my success and *that* is humbling. Now I'm smacking you back and telling you that you are going to be a rock star of a nurse. Chin up!

Lisa and **Brenda**, all those years ago, we met through our love of books and look where we are now! You invited me to join you at a book signing when I had no idea what they were (crazy, huh?). I had two books out and still didn't really know what I was doing. Your support, advice, and friendship have been priceless. I love you guys! Thank you for loving the fact that my mind is always moving and my characters take over at times.

Glenna, I cannot thank you enough! Raptor's cover is perfect. I look forward to working with you again on the rest of my RBMC boys! MUAH! (PSST! If y'all haven't read Glenna Maynard's books, you're missing out!)

Wander, thank you for this image of Jonny! I still remember the day it posted during the pandemic. His long hair was so out of character for what we were used to from him, but it was PERFECT for this character. You're a genius behind the lens!

Jonny, thank you for a fantastic image to make my cover

over-the-top. Fist-bump, my friend. Also, please don't judge the fact that Raptor is a naughty boy. It was very difficult having you on the cover of this book once I started writing him and figured that out. I have a confession—I pictured someone else during the schmexy-time scenes. Bahahaha!

Stacey of **Champagne Book Design**, you are and forever will be a goddess! I hope to see you at Shameless this year! Thank you for making my pages a work of art and for being so understanding of my "don't kill me" messages and emails. LMAO.

The ladies of **Kristine's Krazy Fangirls,** y'all are the best. You're the lovers of my books, the ones that I share my funny stories with, the ones who cheer me on when I'm struggling with a book I promised you, and I love you all to pieces! (((BIG HUGS)))! I can't thank you enough for your comments, your support, and your love of all things books. Come join us if you're not part of the group www.facebook.com/groups/kristineskrazyfangirls

Often, I try to spin the military into my books. This is for many reasons. Because of those reasons, my last, but never least, is a massive thank you to America's servicemen and women who protect our freedom on a daily basis. They do their duty, leaving their families for weeks, months, and years at a time, without asking for praise or thanks. I would also like to remind the readers that not all combat injuries are visible, nor do they heal easily. These silent, wicked injuries wreak havoc on their minds and hearts while we go about our days completely oblivious. Thank you all for your service.

OTHER BOOKS BY
KRISTINE ALLEN

Demented Sons MC Series - Iowa

Colton's Salvation

Mason's Resolution

Erik's Absolution

Kayde's Temptation

Snow's Addiction

Straight Wicked Series

Make Music With Me

Snare My Heart

No Treble Allowed

String Me Up

Demented Sons MC Series - Texas

Lock and Load

Styx and Stones

Smoke and Mirrors

Jax and Jokers

Got Your Six (Formerly in Remember Ryan Anthology)

Pinched and Cuffed Duet with M. Merin
The Weight of Honor
The Weight of Blood (by M. Merin)

La Famiglia De Luca
Part of the MMM Mayhem Makers Collaboration
Blood Lust
Blood Money (Coming April 7, 2023!)
Blood Ties (Coming in May 2023!)

ABOUT THE AUTHOR

Kristine Allen lives in beautiful Central Texas with her adoring husband. They have four brilliant, wacky, and wonderful children. She is surrounded by twenty-six acres, where her five horses, four dogs, and six cats run the place. She's a hockey addict and feeds that addiction with season tickets to the Texas Stars. Kristine realized her dream of becoming a contemporary romance author after years of reading books like they were going out of style and having her own stories running rampant through her head. She works as a night shift nurse, but in stolen moments, taps out ideas and storylines until they culminate in characters and plots that pull her readers in and keep them entranced for hours.

Reviews are the life blood of an indie author. If you enjoyed this story, please consider leaving a review on the sales channel of your choice, bookbub.com, goodreads.com, allauthor.com, or your favorite review platform, to share your experience with other interested readers. Thank you! <3

Follow Kristine on:

Facebook www.facebook.com/kristineallenauthor

Instagram www.instagram.com/_kristine_allen_

Twitter @KAllenAuthor

TikTok: www.tiktok.com/@kristineallenauthor

All Author www.kristineallen.allauthor.com

BookBub www.bookbub.com/authors/kristine-allen

Goodreads www.goodreads.com/kristineallenauthor

Webpage www.kristineallenauthor.com

Made in the USA
Monee, IL
06 May 2023